SWIPE RIGHT FOR MONSTERS

MONSTER MATCH

R. O'LEARY

Copyright © 2024 by R. O'Leary

All rights reserved.

No part of this book may be reproduced in any form or by any electronic or mechanical means, including information storage and retrieval systems, without written permission from the author, except for the use of brief quotations in a book review.

Cover Design - R. O'Leary

Editing - The Fiction Fix

For all the goblin girlies who just want to wear sweatpants, drink iced coffee, and get dicked down by hot monsters with fat bank accounts.
Same, girl. Same.

1

NICOLE

Whoever invented tequila shots was a dick. No, not just a dick—a giant, ugly dick who deserved to be pointed and laughed at.

"To Nicole and her shiny, new PhD!"

"To Nicole and defending her thesis like a bad bitch!"

She raised her shot glass and clinked it against her two cackling best friends'. At the rate Ashley and Miri were going, they were going to drink the bar dry. She'd lost count of the number of toasts they had raised in the last hour and of the number of shots they had downed.

Still, it wasn't every day a girl achieved a decades-long dream.

"To me!" Nicole laughed.

"How does it feel to finally be an adult?" Ashley asked, slamming down her shot glass.

"I *am* an adult." The frown lines and circles under her eyes in the bathroom mirror every morning were proof enough of that.

"Yeah, but now you're like an adultier adult, with—"

"Adultier isn't a word," Miri interrupted.

Ashley shot her a look, eyes narrowing. "How many shots does it take to turn off teacher mode?"

"At least one more." Miri smirked and grabbed another shot. "To proper grammar!"

"As I was saying before the grammar lesson—" she rolled her eyes at the drunk redhead—"is that now, you're a grown-up adult. No more homework, or studying for exams, or throwing out your back hauling around a metric ton of textbooks. You're going to have a job in your actual field now."

"Don't remind me," Nicole sighed.

A real job… and real bills. It wouldn't be long before her student loans would come due. Plus, her monthly credit card statement. And utilities. And groceries.

Suddenly, it wasn't the tequila threatening her with a room-tilting headache.

"At least you don't have to pay rent," Miri added gently. Patting her hand, she smiled. "The mortgage on your aunt's house is paid off already."

"You're forgetting about property taxes… and the fact the house hasn't been updated since before the internet was invented," Nicole sighed.

"It's not that bad!"

No, it really was. Even calling the old wreck a "house" felt generous when the hot water didn't work, the roof leaked, and a family of squirrels had turned the attic into their own private bungalow.

Why her great aunt had thought it was a good idea to leave the old property to a niece with tens of thousands of dollars in student loans was beyond her. Nicole was an apartment dweller. She'd never mowed a lawn in her life, let alone fixed a dripping faucet.

She hadn't even known how to use a wrench until last week, when the third straight hour of listening to her bathroom sink drip had driven her out of bed. Staring bleary-eyed at instructional videos on the internet wasn't her idea of a good night's sleep.

"You know those fixer upper shows I used to love?" Nicole grimaced and grabbed another shot of tequila from the tray. "Shiplap? No, it's more like ship-lies."

"That doesn't even make sense," Ashley muttered under her breath.

Probably not. Nicole ignored her and embraced the tequila fueling her anxious rant. If they didn't want to hear about the cost of light fixtures and power saws, they shouldn't have insisted on celebrating with so many toasts.

"Do you have any idea how much a new water heater costs? Or a new roof? New kitchen backsplash? Subway tile, my assssss," she drunkenly hissed. "At this point, my fingers are crossed that the whole thing will just collapse in on itself while I'm out running errands! At least then, I'd get the insurance money!"

What she wouldn't give for a small, localized natural disaster. Maybe a cute little tornado that only landed on her house. A lucky bolt of lightning. She'd take anything at this point.

As long as the squirrels got out okay, of course. She wasn't a complete monster.

"To Nicole's upcoming mental breakdown!" Ashley toasted cheerfully.

"To Nicole's house turning into a sinkhole!" Miri raised her glass.

"To Nicole finding new friends!"

They clinked their shot glasses and laughed. At this point, what choice did she have but to laugh? Her life was a mess, but it was *her* mess.

"Let's talk about something less depressing." Nicole

turned her attention to Miri. "How's it going with that guy you started seeing? The history teacher, right?"

"I thought you wanted to talk about something less depressing," she deadpanned. "That crashed and burned last weekend."

"Oh shit. What happened?"

"He said that I was 'wife material' but he wasn't ready for that, and hopefully, I would still be waiting for him when he was."

"And you said?"

"I told him he could shove that 'wife material' straight up his ass and go fuck a—"

A passing waitress raised her eyebrows, and Nicole choked on her laughter as Miri's cheeks burned as red as her hair. Short and curvy, with a wardrobe of rainbow cardigans and polka dots, she was the last person anyone expected to curse like a sailor.

Naturally, it was Nicole's favorite thing about her.

"You know the best way to get over an ex-boyfriend..." Ashley wiggled her eyebrows. "Get under a new one!"

"Preferably one with a bigger dic—" Miri snapped her mouth shut as a hush fell over the bar.

Heads craned toward the door as two newcomers stepped inside. Bright red eyes flashed from the face of a tall man leading his date to the bar, and Nicole forced herself to ignore the tiny prickle at the back of her neck.

Conversation picked up as everyone's manners kicked back in and overpowered their human instinct to run. It wasn't everyday a vampire casually strolled in on the arm of a human. It was becoming more and more common, but the first glance always drew a couple double takes.

Monsters always did.

"Now there's an idea." Ashley pointed with her empty

glass. "Get yourself a vampire sugar daddy. You'll have that house fixed up in no time!"

"Haha. You're so funny."

It wasn't bad enough she was in crippling debt? What was a little blood loss thrown into the mix? Anemia and ripping up old carpet, the perfect weekend combo for a stressed-out single woman.

"I wasn't joking!" her friend insisted. "There are dating apps for this kind of thing now. All you need is a vampire who has been collecting interest on his savings account since World War II, and boom, no more student loans."

"Genius," Miri agreed. "Plus, those fangs are kinda hot."

"Crazy hot."

"No more tequila for you two." Leaning over the table, Nicole dragged the last shots over to her side of the table. Clearly, they had all had too much to drink if becoming a naughty juice box for loan repayment was on the table.

Hell, she'd never even met a vampire.

Monsters had come out of the shadows and smoothly integrated into human society when her grandmother was still in pigtails. According to all those history classes she had napped through in undergrad, the monster population wasn't particularly large.

In fact, Nicole could count the number of monsters she had knowingly met on one hand. There was that golden-eyed demon in her finance classes, and the sweet barista at her favorite coffee shop who was some kind of wood nymph. Besides a werewolf who had ended up wearing her drink after grabbing her ass at a party, that was pretty much it.

"I don't think dating a vamp—"

"Oi! Blondie!" Ashley loudly called across the bar, cutting off her argument. "You two meet on a dating app?"

"Ashley!" Miri and Nicole shushed her.

"What? I want to know!"

"You don't need to yell at them across the bar!" Nicole hissed.

Ashley shook her head, her long blonde hair swishing over her shoulders. She smoothed her hands over her mini skirt and fixed the two of them with the no-nonsense, ice queen stare she used at work every day.

"Your house is a dump, and you won't take money from me," she said shortly. "I am offering you a lovely solution that will not only pay off your loans, but get you laid—something you also desperately need."

"Rude—"

"Don't interrupt," Miri hushed. "She might be on to something."

The last time they had let her pitch an idea after this much tequila, they had ended up blackout drunk trying to go whale watching in a rowboat... and they didn't even live near an ocean.

"No—"

"Would you prefer PowerPoint slides about the pros and cons of dating outside your species?" Ashley asked innocently. "I have some free time tomorrow afternoon to prepare a presentation."

Damn it. If Nicole let her have time to actually prepare, she would end up sitting through a twenty-page dissertation and a professionally produced commercial for the top-rated supernatural dating apps on the market. Her friend was nothing if not thorough.

"You have thirty seconds."

"One—" Ashley started ticking off on her fingers. "You need companionship outside of Miri and I. Preferably someone who provides orgasms, because we're definitely not going to take on that responsibility."

"Hating this conversation already," Nicole grumbled under her breath.

"Shhh. Two, you don't have a job lined up yet and I know for a fact that you can barely afford spaghetti right now."

That wasn't true at all. She could absolutely afford the noodles... just maybe not the sauce.

"Three, you're a catch. You're gorgeous, smart, and you have a great ass. There's no reason you can't find a demon or something who would want to pay your electric bill just to get a look at it."

Right... but... actually, that didn't sound too terrible. Maybe it was the tequila talking, but it wasn't the worst idea Ashley had ever had.

"Excuse me," their judgmental waitress interrupted. "This is from the blonde at the bar."

She dropped a napkin onto the table and gathered up their teetering tower of empty shot glasses. Ashley snatched up the napkin as soon as she walked away.

"What does it say?" Miri asked eagerly.

She slid them the napkin and grabbed Nicole's phone off the table. Nicole leaned over and read the scribbled message with Miri.

"The app is called MONSTR. Good luck!"

"Holy crap," Nicole muttered under her breath. "She really did use an app."

"An app you just downloaded." Ashley grinned, her nails tapping away on the phone screen. "Are you a 'long walks on the beach' type of girl, or more of an 'afternoon hike' girl?"

"Neither," Miri answered. "She doesn't like the outdoors or bugs."

"Right. More of a 'coffee shop and bookstore date' kind of babe."

Wait... was Ashley really filling out a dating profile for her?

Nicole leaned over the table and snagged the phone from her hand. Her stomach dropped as she read the annoyingly accurate bio her friends were typing up. They were actually doing it.

"Oh my God!" she groaned. "That's the profile picture you're using?"

Miri grabbed the phone and glanced at the screen. "What? Your boobs look great in that one."

Looking back and forth between the grinning faces of her two best friends, Nicole sighed. She had never been able to say 'no' to them. Besides, she could always delete the app tomorrow.

What was the harm in letting them make a profile for her?

"I'm going to need more tequila," Nicole grumbled. Flagging down the waitress, she silently apologized to sober-Nicole for what was going to be the world's worst hangover.

Miri passed out the remaining shots at their table and raised hers high.

"To Nicole finally having time to get laid!"

"To Nicole putting the D in PhD!" cheered Ashley.

Nicole raised her own shot glass. "To getting plastered and finding some monster dick!"

The trio knocked back their drinks to the sound of laughter from surrounding tables.

Sitting back in her chair, Nicole listened as her two favorite people in the world set off on a mission to get her a boyfriend with horns and a hefty bank account.

It was going to be a long night.

A SUNRISE AND TWO BOTTLES OF TEQUILA LATER...

. . .

A LOUD CHIME pierced the silent morning. Doing her best to ignore the hammering in her head and the nausea turning her stomach into a paint shaker, Nicole blindly patted the blanket for her cellphone.

If she could just turn it to silent, maybe she could get another couple hours to sleep off her tequila regrets. They had been drinking tequila, right? Last night had become a blur of toasts and laughter, followed by a whole lot of nothingness.

There had been something about fangs... and Nicole distinctly remembered Miri telling the waitress to shove her attitude up her ass. Had they gotten thrown out of the bar?

Or—based on the pounding in her head—maybe straight into a brick wall?

The phone chimed again, driving a spike through her headache. She raised the cellphone to her face and squinted at the screen.

DAVE

Hey, gorgeous. You look good enough to eat!

CEDAR

Have you ever dated a dryad? I've got some wood you'll love :)

ETHAN

Sup, girl? Wanna get a drink? Maybe a djinn and tonic? Haha get it?

Nicole blinked at the fanged heart icon on her screen. What the hell did they do last night?

2

NICOLE

"Oh, no," Nicole groaned. "No, no, no, no!"

A monstrous groan rumbled from beneath a mountain of blankets. She ignored it. She had monster problems of a different kind, and they were pinging obnoxiously from the traitorous cellphone in her hand.

Why did she have a monster dating app downloaded on her phone? No, better question; why the hell had she marked that she was looking for *multiple partners*?

One monster boyfriend wasn't enough? Drunk-Nicole was desperate enough for dick to request her own harem? Drunk-Nicole was clearly delusional.

"What the hell was I thinking?"

Keeping up with one man was hard enough, and she'd just announced to the world that she was down for her own parade of paranormal paramours like it was nothing. Never in her vast experience of making colossally stupid mistakes had she come close to a fuck up of this magnitude.

Well, no. That wasn't entirely true.

There was that time she'd knocked back one too many tequila shots and ended up falling off the bar onto an elderly gentleman celebrating his eightieth birthday. If he hadn't needed his walker before that night, he certainly did after.

"Fuck tequila," she muttered. "Never again."

The blanket bundle beside her stirred. "Wha—?"

"I'm never drinking again."

Ashley bolted upright, the blankets falling away as she batted her arms free. A wild blonde tangle floated around her blinking face. "Blasphemy."

"Never. Again."

Nicole scrolled through the matches, wincing as each flirty message popped up. Fangs, claws, something alarmingly furry. Did that one have two-foot-long horns? How did he even walk through doorways?

> HOGAN
>
> I'll show you my magic wand any day of the week.
>
> RANDY
>
> If you think I'm a monster, you should see what's in my pants!
>
> ASH
>
> You look like a girl who likes to howl at the moon. Saturday??

"Are you dying?" Ashley asked seriously.

"Of mortification."

Leaning over her shoulder, she peered at the phone in Nicole's white-knuckled grip.

"Holy shit, look at that tongue!" Ashley ripped the phone out of her hand and stared. "Girl, you have got to go on a date with him."

"He's part lizard!"

"He can be part gecko and try to sell me car insurance

for all I care. Imagine what that tongue could be doing to your bits right now!"

Nicole gaped at her. She was still drunk. She had to be.

"With a tongue like that, he'd be licking the inside of my ribcage. And he has *scales!*"

Shaking her head, Ashley flipped through the matches. "Stop always trying to play it safe. It's a *monster* dating app."

Nicole blinked. Was she playing it safe? She hadn't thought she was... then again, she had just balked at a lizard man whose interests were traveling and baking sourdough bread. In her defense, he had been holding a fish and shooting a peace sign in his profile picture.

Her standards were low, but they weren't that low.

"You are being incredibly loud," Miri yawned from a pile of pillows on the floor.

Nicole jumped. In her early morning panic, she had completely forgotten that the quiet redhead was there too. Great, another person to witness this clusterfuck.

"Miri, you gotta check this out." Ashley nudged her with her foot. "Some of Nic's matches are super fine. This one is a werewolf with abs for days!"

Shifting a throw pillow, Miri buried her head further from the noise interrupting her hangover. Good. One down, one to go.

"We should just delete the app and forget about it. This was a bad idea drunk and it's an even worse idea sober," Nicole tried desperately. "And multiple boyfriends? That's crazy. I can barely manage one."

Ashley balanced the phone on her knee and focused her full attention in her direction, her face a stony mask. The same sharp, ruthless face she used in meetings when colleagues tried to talk over her and underestimated her skills because of her cutesy appearance.

"Why are you being so negative about this? Is it really the fangs or is it something else?"

"Maybe?" Or maybe she was just being a little chicken who was afraid of change. "I don't know!"

The only reason her friend had talked her into this scheme the night before was because of the copious amounts of tequila in her system. Now, Ashley wanted her to find not just one, but *multiple* supernatural monsters? It was insane.

What the hell kind of monster would want to date her anyway? She wasn't gorgeous and confident like Ashley. She wasn't creative and sweet like Miri. Nicole was just... Nicole. She was boring. Her idea of a good time was iced coffee, trashy television, and a nap.

"I just... this isn't *me*!" she finally snapped.

"You're being a coward."

"Okay, well, you're being a meddling—"

Faint mumbling echoed from the mound of pillows on the floor, interrupting her sharp words. Nicole glanced at Ashley, who shook her head and nudged the talking pile.

"What was that?"

A hand blindly fumbled for a throw pillow. Raising it off her face, Miri lifted her head and glared at the two of them. "Either delete the app or shut up... please."

Her head thumped back on the floor.

The hard lines of Ashley's face softened, and when she looked at Nicole, the boss attitude had leeched from her expression, leaving only concern.

"Why are you pushing this so hard?" she asked her friend.

"I worry about you, Nic," Ashley admitted. "You have so much going for you, but it's like you want to hide yourself away. I don't want Miri and I to be the only ones who see how amazing you are."

Nicole bit her lip. Great, now she was going to make her cry.

"I know you hate change, but you need to step outside your comfort zone once in a while." Ashley pointed at the phone. "Even if this doesn't work out, at least you'll have tried something new... like a demon threesome."

Nicole opened and closed her mouth. Damn it.

"Okay," she sighed. "I'll try... but I reserve the right to say 'I told you so' if I get eaten by a yeti after dinner and a movie."

"Noted." Ashley turned back to the waiting monsters. "Now, how do you feel about minotaurs?"

"He's seven feet tall, Ash. If things get heated and he's... proportional... my cervix is going to end up in my lungs."

"Weenie."

"I don't want my first date in over a year to land me in the emergency room!"

"They don't call it having your guts rearranged for nothing."

"Ew." Nicole cringed. "I'm tiptoeing out of my comfort zone here, so cut me a little slack. Let's keep it human-ish for now."

Besides, the whole fur thing seemed like a disaster with her house's ancient plumbing. One oversized furball, and the pipes were a goner. At least a shifter was human most of the time. A minotaur? She'd be lint-rolling her clothes twice a day.

"How about a werewolf? This one is hunky, and he's a mechanic."

Presenting his profile picture with a flourish, Ashley wiggled her eyebrows. Nicole eyed his cheeky smile and golden eyes. He *was* good looking—if you were into that roguish, devil-may-care kind of thing.

"He looks like the type of guy who would give you the

best sex of your life and then vanish before you wake up in the morning."

"Your vagina has needs too, Nicole." Ashley zoomed in on his abs. "I'm swiping right on him no matter what you say. Even if he isn't your monster daddy soulmate, your car is a deathtrap, and you need an oil change."

Nicole snorted. She wasn't wrong, though. Had she checked her oil recently... or ever?

"Oooh! That one's a contractor!" she pointed over Ashley's shoulder. "And a were-cougar!"

Goodbye orange countertops and hello discount marble.

Maybe this wasn't a terrible idea after all. "Do you think he'd wear that tool belt in bed?"

Ashley raised her eyebrows.

"What?" Nicole shrugged, but the heat rising in her cheeks gave her away. "I like cats, and I've got a thing for guys who work with their hands."

"You little freak," her friend laughed. "I love it. I bet he'd wear a hard hat for you if you fluttered your lashes and showed some leg. In fact, that should be your opening line."

She stared at her. "What should be my—Oh my God! Don't write that!"

"And send." Ashley grinned. "You're going to be drowning in monster dick if it's the last thing I do... *he already answered*!"

NICOLE

I love cats and men who work with their hands ;)

DRAKE

Meet for coffee? Tomorrow?

CHEEKS PRESSED TOGETHER, they leaned over the phone screen. Ashley's excited screech stabbed at her ears. Had she really just made a date with a guy who regularly turned into a giant cat?

"Girl, he is *so* fine," Ashley gushed. "He's got that whole frowny, stoic thing going on."

"Do you think he coughs up hairballs?" Nicole asked hesitantly. She really needed to read up on monsters if she was going to be going on dates with them.

What did she even know about shifters? Werewolves were the most common, and they howled at the moon and... actually, that was pretty much it.

"Hairballs?" Ashley grimaced. "I have no idea. We'd better get a couple more conversations going just in case. You don't want to find that out two months down the road and have to start all over again."

Fair enough.

They went back to flipping through profiles, oohing and awing over every new kind of monster as Miri snored on the floor. Nicole's head felt like it was overflowing with monsters by the time she finally wrestled the phone from Ashley.

It had taken an hour, but they'd eventually settled on the cougar contractor, a fae gardener with kind eyes, a pair of vampire lawyers—because, according to Ashley, every woman should have a threesome at least once in her lives— and the werewolf mechanic.

Between the five of them, hopefully at least one would fall madly in love with her and fix her life... or, at the very least, pay for the occasional dinner.

"We need donuts and coffee," Nicole announced abruptly.

Enough carbs and caffeine, and maybe she could stave off the panic threatening to overtake her. She needed an hour or two to stare into space and come to terms with the path Drunk-Nicole had placed her on.

Not that she was going to admit that out loud. That would come after Miri and Ashley had finished shaking off their hangovers and stumbled their way out.

"Yes! Donuts sound amaaaazing!" Jumping off the couch, Ashley poked at Miri's pillow fort with her foot. "Get up, Miri, or else we'll eat all the chocolate and sprinkles without you."

"Hngf," the sleepy lump grunted.

"Get. Up. Now." The bossy blonde punctuated each word with a toe poke. "You need to hear all about Nicole's monster beaus."

"Beaus? Go make coffee," Miri grumbled. Shoving herself upright, she glared sleepily at them. "What did I miss?"

Nicole laughed. Nothing much—only her life jumping on a speeding train to who knows where.

Her phone buzzed for the thousandth time that morning. Glancing down at the screen, she swallowed her groan.

> GRAYSON
>
> Sup, beautiful? How do you feel about feathers?

It was going to be a long day.

IGNORING the headache pounding through her head, Nicole scrubbed at her kitchen counter. She had too much to do to nurse a hangover. Unfortunately.

Miri and Ashley had left later than she had anticipated —they had all been having too much fun scrolling through the profiles on MONSTR and eating their body weight in glazed pastries.

Throwing the sponge aside, she stumbled into the laundry room and started to sort through her whites and darks before she paused and eyed her holey socks. Honestly, did she even care? More importantly—did her hangover care?

So, what if her whites ended up a little dingy? It's not like she was going to win any fashion awards anytime soon.

Nicole jammed the entire load of laundry into the washer and set it to run. Her headache stabbed at her skull, and she scrubbed her knuckles over her aching forehead. Cleaning sucked enough without adding in a tequila hangover.

Not even the cheery afternoon sun could drag her out of her daze. Nicole glared out the window. Didn't the universe understand it should be dark, and gloomy, and quiet right now?

Her phone buzzed on the counter, and she sighed. Probably another unsolicited dick pic. The amount of poorly angled dick selfies in her inbox was truly astounding—though she had to admit, she had spent way too long studying a couple of the demonic appendages.

Who knew demon cock had special features? She would have paid a lot more attention in Sex Ed if that had been part of the lesson plans.

Her phone buzzed and buzzed and buzzed, every notification chime spiking her painful headache. Why was the universe punishing her?

Trudging outside, Nicole steadfastly moved on to the next item on her to-do list; tending to the overflowing garden boxes. She eyed the drooping weeds. Nope. Not yet.

She turned and walked back into her kitchen. Dragging her favorite mug out of the cupboard, she splashed a couple inches of wine into the bottom. If Tylenol wasn't going to do its job, she might as well throw some more alcohol at the problem.

Nicole fished through the leftover box of doughnuts and jammed a raspberry-filled confection into her mouth. Stumbling outside with a mouth full of sugar, she ignored the dry grass crunching under her bare feet. She ripped a bite of her doughnut off, her wine clutched in her other hand, and moved to the weeds choking her flower bed.

She rested her mug on the edge of the flower bed and stuffed the rest of the doughnut into her mouth. The grass stabbed through her leggings and poked her knees as she knelt on the ground. Beads of sweat formed on the back of her neck with each handful of weeds she ripped out.

Stupid manual labor. She really should hire someone to take care of this... right after she went on a treasure hunt and found a chest full of pirate gold to pay for it.

Her phone buzzed in her pocket, vibrating her entire leg.

"For fuck's sake!" Nicole shouted into her backyard.

How long could this go on before her phone shut down entirely? The pile of weeds grew beside her, and the phone just kept on buzzing. The monsters in her town were ridiculously horny.

Seriously. Some kind of group therapy might need to be mandated by the City Council.

Pausing for a break, she picked up her mug and drained half the waiting moscato. Fishing her phone out of her pocket with dirt-caked hands, Nicole swiped through the matches and the messages.

"No, no, no," she mumbled under her breath. There was no way in hell she was going on a date with something with that many teeth.

She flipped open her messages. All the monsters that were already "Ashley and Miri approved" wanted to set up dates right away.

Coffee on Saturday? Dinner on Friday? Hiking?

Sitting back on her butt in the grass, Nicole stared off into the woods. She could devote her entire weekend—and possibly next week—into crossing off some of these dates. Or...

Flopping back onto the ground, Nicole raised her phone and copied and pasted the same message into every chat.

NICOLE

How would you feel about a group date?

There was no reason she couldn't bang some of these out in one go... figuratively... or not.

Lying in the grass under the hot sun, she waited with bated breath. The first reply chimed.

NICOLE

How would you feel about a group date?

WES

Saturday?

Nicole laughed. Maybe this didn't have to be so difficult after all.

3

NICOLE

Nicole pulled up outside the Italian restaurant, parking her car on the far side of the parking lot to give herself time to calm down. Her stomach churned in dizzying circles. She had thought it was a brilliant idea to get all the dates done in one go, but facing the reality of walking into a restaurant filled with monsters was terrifying.

Nicole took a deep breath, forcing herself to breathe out slowly. It was going to be okay. There was no reason to panic. Even if everything went sideways, at least she would still have garlic bread.

Climbing out of the car, she ignored her heaving stomach and smoothed down the breezy skirt of her sundress. She had worn one of her favorites to give herself a confidence boost—pale green with little white flowers and tiny pearl buttons up the front. Every time she breathed, it dipped low over her cleavage.

Even if the date was a disaster, at least her boobs would look great.

Hurrying inside the restaurant, her eyes were scanning

the tables before the door had swung closed. Oh God, they were already seated. Every single one of them.

Was she late, or were they just early? Nicole was too afraid to glance down at her phone and check the time. Well, there was nothing she could do about it now.

Nicole ran over to the table, apologizing as she drew closer. Several monsters were already glaring at each other, looking like they wanted to throw punches over the garlic bread in the middle of the table. She cringed; that did *not* bode well for the coming evening.

"Hi. I'm sorry if I'm late... am I late?" She smiled nervously, her hands twisting in her dress. "I didn't think I was— I'm rambling, aren't I?"

Smiling, one of the vampires rose from his chair and leaned over to pull hers out. She quickly moved forward and sat down, deciding it was better not to waste any more of their time.

She glanced up to thank him and blinked at the entranced look on his face as he pushed in her chair. Did he just sniff her hair? That wasn't super fucking weird or anything. Then again, she had set up a group date with a bunch of monsters. What did she know about normal?

"I'm Nicole... obviously... otherwise it would be weird if I were sitting here..." Her cheeks burned, fire blooming and turning her face red as the five monsters at the table turned to stare at her. They all stiffened in their seats, except for the fae; he was too busy sneezing. "Thank you for agreeing to do this all together. I know it's not exactly normal for a first date, but this is the first date I've been on in a while, and I figured it might be easier to bang it all out at once."

Silence. Five monsters stared at her, some with mouths gaping open. The were-cougar looked like he was trying not to laugh.

"Oh God, I didn't mean bang like... you know—"

The werewolf raised his hands to cover his face, quietly laughing.

"Can someone else please talk now?" Nicole begged.

She was off to a great start. Two minutes in, and Nicole was ready to sink into the floor and die. Preferably before she could open her mouth and nervously ramble some more.

"It's okay, sweetheart. Everyone gets nervous on a first date." The werewolf reached over and patted her hand, still looking absolutely delighted with every word coming out of her mouth. "I'm Wes."

"I'm Hawthorne." The silver-haired man waved and sneezed again. Turning to look at Wes, he eyed him suspiciously. "Not to be rude, but are you some kind of dog?"

His dark head whipped around. "Excuse me? I am not a *dog*. I'm a werewolf."

The fae flushed, his pointy ears glowing bright red. Nicole tried not to smile, but it was so damned cute. At least she wasn't the only one at the table with all the blood rushing to her face. She had an ally—a pointy-eared, elven ally.

"I'm allergic to dogs, and you're starting to make my eyes water," he said apologetically.

The big guy on the other side of the table shook his head and rose from his chair. Nicole studied him—short, sandy beard, gray eyes, and muscles that looked like he could bench-press a car.

A were-cougar, if she remembered correctly. What was his name again? Duke? No, Drake.

He started walking around the table, and her heart leapt into her throat. Oh, no. Was he leaving already? That was completely fair... and disappointing. Nicole wasn't making a good first impression, and the rest of the monsters at the table certainly weren't helping.

Drake waved for the fae to switch places with him and sat down in Hawthorne's empty seat. Wes sniffed him, his smile dropping incrementally.

"I'm Drake." The were-cat leaned forward to shake her hand. "It's nice to meet you, Nicole."

Her blush lit up again. She noticed he didn't say it was nice to meet anyone else at the table; she wasn't sure if that was good for her or bad for them, but at least he was being kind.

Nicole turned to look at the red-eyed vampires who had yet to introduce themselves. Both sat primly in their seats, dressed in immaculate suits. Her eyes lingered on fabric that no doubt cost more than her car. The blond vampire leaned forward, propping his chin on his elbow as he winked. A sparkle lit up his red eyes, promising dirty deeds in dark corners.

"Call me Jasper."

The dark-haired vampire who had sniffed her nodded and raised his wine glass. "Atticus."

"Great!" Nicole said brightly. "Now that we all know each other... what's everyone ordering?"

She quickly snatched up her menu to hide her flushed face. They were not off to the greatest start, but at least everyone knew each other's names now.

The waiter chose that moment to sweep by and start asking for orders, thank God. She made a mental note to leave him one hell of a tip for rescuing her from this catastrophe.

"Can I get the spaghetti?" Nicole ordered.

She immediately regretted it. There was no way she was going to be able to eat that gracefully, but it had been one of the cheapest things on the menu... and it came with more garlic bread. She needed something to fortify her for the rest of the evening. It may as well be garlic butter slathered baguettes.

Her eyes widened as the waiter turned to the shifters and they started ordering insane amounts of food. Soup, salad, pasta, *and* two entrees each. They hadn't even seen the dessert menu yet.

How could they possibly fit all that into their bodies? That was more food than she ate in a week. More importantly—how did they eat that much and still have abs? Nicole had seen Wes' cheeky ab selfie on his profile, and the man had nothing to be ashamed of.

"Is the eggplant parmesan vegetarian?" Hawthorne asked hesitantly.

"Yes, sir."

"Perfect." He snapped his menu closed and passed it to the waiter. "I will have that, please."

The waiter vanished as Wes snorted into his drink.

The elf turned to look at him, his eyes narrowing. "What?"

"Nothing." He shrugged. "Nothing at all."

The werewolf had ordered a steak with his pasta, so Nicole was pretty sure he was judging the vegetarian elf. Her eyes narrowed along with the Hawthorne's. Wes was choosing a hell of a time to be judgmental and rude.

"Do you have a problem with vegetarians?" Hawthorne's ears had turned bright red again, but he didn't back down.

"Nope. I'm just wondering if you feel bad when you eat salad... You know, the whole plant connection thing." Wes looked at him, a smirk on his face.

How Hawthorne had not stabbed him with his fork yet was beyond Nicole. She had dumped her drinks on men for less. Though—and she would never say it aloud—the wolf did kind of have a point.

The were-cougar rolled his eyes at the werewolf. "Stop being an asshole," Drake snapped.

"I am not—"

One of the vampires sighed, shifting in his seat. "You can't take them anywhere."

Drake and Wes stopped and glared at the vampires across the table.

"What's that supposed to mean?" Wes growled.

"You're being rude," Atticus answered succinctly. "Leave the elf alone."

"I was just asking him a question! I was genuinely curious!"

Nicole sat there, her mouth gaping as they volleyed arguments back and forth. Someone insulted someone else's mother, and she started counting down from one hundred in her head. When she reached zero and they were still arguing, she glanced around for a quick exit.

Exactly how long was she supposed to sit there before it was socially acceptable to get up and walk out? Hopefully, the answer was two minutes, because she wasn't waiting much longer.

The waiter returned quickly—most likely sensing his evening tips were in danger from their table's caterwauling—and started to pass out food. The monsters at the table didn't even notice, too busy arguing with one another. Someone bumped the waiter's arm, and a bowl of pasta fagioli stained the white tablecloth orange.

Nicole pinched the bridge of her nose. This was a terrible idea. The next time she saw Ashley, she was going to smack her right into her next life. Monster boyfriends sounded great and all, but they had forgotten one very important part of the equation.

They were still men. Argumentative, competitive men, and she had put them all at one table.

Nicole looked up at the wide-eyed waiter. "Can I get a to-go box, please?"

He quickly stepped away to grab her one. Nicole scooped her spaghetti and bread into the box and sealed it shut. She passed him a crumpled twenty-dollar bill and rose from her seat. If she had more, she would have gladly put it in his hands and told any debt collectors that came knocking to go to hell.

"Well, I think it's safe to say this was a giant mistake." She raised her to-go box in a mock salute as the monsters at the table fell silent. "Goodnight, gentlemen."

Nicole stormed out to the parking lot, her cheeks burning with fury and embarrassment. What the hell had she been thinking? She was deleting that cursed app as soon as she got home.

Nicole threw open the driver-side door and climbed into the car. She jammed the keys in the ignition, the engine clicking when she turned the key. Nothing. She turned the key again and listened to her engine click hopelessly.

Groaning, Nicole stared out of the windshield before her head rocked back against the headrest and tears welled in her eyes.

Could this night get any worse?

4

JASPER

"Well, that was a disaster."

Jasper laughed at his friend's groaning. Two hundred years old, and Atticus' petulant frown could rival that of the most spoiled child. For such a serious man, the vampire was such a brat when he didn't get what he wanted.

"It definitely did not go as we'd hoped."

"Those damn shifters," Atticus glowered at the hulking shifter brushing him past them, a stack of to-go boxes in his arms. Some kind of cat, if Jasper's nose didn't deceive him. "If they could have shut up for ten minutes, we would have a had a chance to seduce her."

He ignored the pouting vampire beside him. It would have taken a lot more than silencing the other monsters at the table to get sweet Nicole into their bed. She'd been squirrelly and ready to bolt from the moment she had entered the restaurant.

Not that he blamed her. The smell of garlic coming off the risotto had been overpowering.

Jasper clapped a hand on his old friend's shoulder.

"Stop whining. It was one date, and there are other luscious little fish in the sea."

Stopping in his tracks, Atticus shot him a glare. "I am *not* whining."

Jasper rolled his eyes at the imperious look in his red eyes and shoved him out the door. It was going to be a long drive home. Maybe he could put some of that awful violin music that Atticus loved on the radio. That usually worked to lure him out of his cantankerous moods.

A soft, floral scent caught his nose. Jasper inhaled deeply, savoring each delectable note. It really was too bad Nicole hadn't been willing to continue the evening. Her scent was absolutely delicious.

The scent grew stronger in the evening air as they made their way across the parking lot, and Jasper's fangs pricked at his lower lip.

"I think we might have another chance at wooing the lovely creature," Atticus interrupted his musings.

"First off, don't say 'wooing.' We might be old, but it's just weird," he said grumpily. Nicole's lingering scent was making his mouth water. "Secondly, she already left. Unless you're willing to message her for a second date, it's time to move on."

"Not quite."

Jasper's eyes followed the arm pointing down the line of cars. The woman in question stood in front of her car, the hood open as she stared into the depths of the engine and pinched her delicate nose.

"I believe the damsel is in need of rescue." Atticus shot him a satisfied grin and veered in her direction.

Jasper sighed. "You're a two-hundred-year-old vampire who can barely figure out how to use a corkscrew, but sure, we're going to know exactly how to fix an engine."

Atticus could barely work his smartphone on a good day.

Downloading MONSTR had been a herculean labor on its own—learning how to actually set up a profile nearly had his old friend tearing out his perfect hair.

Not that Jasper wouldn't have loved to see it. The amount of time the prissy old fool spent preening in front of the mirror every evening was exhausting. There were only so many hours in the night, after all.

He hurried to catch up. There was no way Atticus could pull this off on his own. Not that Jasper was much better, but at least he knew wiper fluid from motor oil.

"Is there something wrong, love?" Atticus asked.

Nicole's head whipped up, and the tension in her shoulders eased as she recognized the two men approaching her.

Jasper choked back a laugh. Relaxing in a dark parking lot filled with monsters? She might be a tasty morsel, but there had to be a screw loose in her pretty head.

"My car won't start. I popped the hood, but—" she waved a hand at the complex twist of metal and wires that made up her engine and swiped at her teary eyes— "I have no idea what I'm looking at."

That made three of them.

"We would be happy to assist," Atticus said smoothly.

He turned to stare down into the engine. His thoughtful expression never wavered, but Jasper had been his best friend for over two centuries. Atticus may as well have been staring at an alien artifact for all he understood. The old git could pretend all he wanted, but he had no idea what he was doing.

"Hmm... yes... the, uh, gasoline is... stable."

Rolling his eyes, Jasper elbowed him gently. He pulled out the oil dipstick and gave it a quick glance.

"Plenty of oil," he muttered as he poked at the few things that looked familiar. "Battery is connected."

"Maybe it just needs a jump?" Nicole asked hopefully.

The two vampires exchanged a quick look. What the fuck was a "jump"?

"Uh... maybe," Jasper mumbled.

"Problem?" a deep voice cut in.

They turned to find the were-cougar and the quiet fae melting out of the shadows. Oh good, more people to witness this shitshow.

"My car won't start." Nicole waved at the two vampires. "They offered to take a look and hopefully get it running again."

Two sets of eyebrows soared. Jasper didn't have to be a mind reader to know they were trying their hardest not to laugh. The balled-up receipt in his pocket would have better luck getting the stubborn engine to turn over than the combined efforts of two ancient vampires.

He shook his head infinitesimally and willed them to be cool.

"Right, four heads are better than two!" The fae smiled brightly. Elbowing the stoic shifter before he could mutter anything sarcastic, Hawthorne peered down into the engine. "Maybe between all of us, we can get an idea of what's wrong."

Jasper could have kissed the pointy-eared bastard on the spot. Clearly, he was an ally in the making. Once he and Atticus had successfully wooed Nicole, maybe the elf would be a welcome addition to the group.

Definitely not the shifter, though. Atticus had never cared much for cats... plus, Jasper really didn't want to listen to him whine about the shedding for the next century.

The were-cougar poked at a couple mysterious parts in the engine and muttered under his breath as the three monsters beside him made noncommittal noises in agreement.

Atticus shot him a satisfied smirk. They might pull this off after all.

"A second date? And no one invited me?"

All four of their heads shot up as the final attendee of the world's worst group date strolled up to the car. The brash werewolf glanced between the open hood and the group of confused monsters huddled around it.

"Please tell me none of you touched anything." The werewolf sighed and pushed past them. "For future reference, babe, vampires and fae are useless with machines—"

"I am not—"

"How dare you—"

"Rude—"

Ignoring their sputters and glares, the wolf crossed his arms over his chest and leaned back against the front bumper.

"If even one of you can tell me what a spark plug is, I'll take it back," he said, smirking. "Anyone?"

Nicole pushed to the front of the group, her sweet scent curling around Jasper as she stepped past him. Jamming his hands into his pockets, it took every ounce of his control not to reach out and pull her back against him.

"Can someone just fix my car already?" she growled. "I didn't walk out of that tragedy of a dinner just to continue it in the parking lot!"

Jasper bit his lip. The angry flush coloring her cheeks only made her scent that much stronger. If she was trying to tempt the horde of monsters around her, she was on the right path... and dangerously close to finding a certain vampire's face buried in her throat.

"Yes, ma'am."

They all rolled their eyes as Wes fired off a snappy salute and turned to study the engine.

"Ten bucks says he doesn't know what he's doing," the were-cat whispered in his ear.

"Make it twenty."

The wolf might be a loud pain in the ass, but he was confident. Jasper was willing to put some cash on that swagger.

"I can hear you, you know," Wes said as messed with a mysterious part of the engine. "You'd better be ready to pay up, pussy cat. I'm a mechanic."

Straightening up, he wiped his dirty hands on his jeans. He ignored the rest of them and faced Nicole. "Sorry, gorgeous. You need a new alternator."

Drake cursed under his breath. Fishing in his pocket, he slapped some cash into Jasper's waiting hand.

"Are you sure?" the pretty human asked desperately. Her pale face was only growing paler as they stood there.

"Definitely. It looks like some liquid got inside the alternator and short-circuited it." The werewolf pulled a wrinkled business card from his pocket and pressed it into her hands. "I'll have the car towed to my garage. If I can get it fixed tonight, you should be able to pick it up tomorrow."

Dismay sloped her shoulders. One more inconvenience, and Jasper had a feeling they would be staring at tears.

"We'll give you a ride home," Atticus said gently.

The other monsters moved to argue, but Jasper shot them a look. If Atticus wanted to give her a ride home, they were putting her into a car and taking her home.

The were-cat looked him up and down—no doubt wondering which one of them would win in a fight—and glanced at Nicole.

"Are you okay with that?"

"It's fine," the sweet human sighed. "I just want to go home."

"Let us know when you get there," Hawthorne said softly. "So we know you're safe."

Atticus glowered at the fae as a frown twisted Jasper's own lips. Did the elf think they wouldn't get her home in one piece? That she wasn't safe with them?

What kind of scoundrels did he think they were? If it wouldn't absolutely scare the shit out of Nicole, he would drain the fae on the spot for the audacity.

"Come on, pet." He gallantly offered Nicole his arm. "Let's get you home."

Turning their backs on the silent monsters, the two vampires led her to their car and tucked her into the back seat. His blood was still boiling as three sets of eyes watched the car turn out of the parking lot.

"I don't live too far from here. Just two miles up the road and then left at Pine Street," she said nervously. "I probably could have walked—"

"No," Atticus interrupted. "A lady should never have to walk home in the dark."

A light hint of her floral scent teased them as they drove in silence. The fire that was burning in his belly slowly died with each street they passed. It wasn't her fault the fae had been rude.

Jasper glanced at her in the back of the car. Flipping the business card absently in her hands, she stared at her lap. A pink flush spread across her cheeks before Nicole looked up and met his curious eyes.

He refused to look away. The pink in her cheeks darkened, turning her whole face red in the shadows of the backseat. Her soft brown eyes gleamed under his scrutiny.

The delicate human wasn't the most beautiful woman Jasper had seen in his long lifetime, but there was something about her that captivated him. Maybe it was the soft curve of her lips, or the warmth of her eyes, or the way she'd steeled her spine before breezing into a restaurant full of monsters.

The vampire had no idea what was drawing him to Nicole, making him want to climb over his seat and pull her into his lap... but he was dying to find out.

Her eyes widened as she caught the heat in his gaze. Maybe the enticing human wasn't as opposed as she'd seemed at dinner.

"Ouch!"

The business card landed in her lap. Nicole frowned at her fingertip as red beaded on her skin, dripping slowly down the length of her finger.

A fresh wave of her scent crashed through the car. Atticus's head whipped around, the red of his eyes gleaming under the light of the passing street lamps.

"Are you all right, pet?" Jasper asked, the tiniest moan escaping with his words.

"Just a paper cut," she muttered. Popping her finger into her mouth, Nicole sucked on the tiny wound.

It was too late. The scent of wine and candied flowers had flooded every corner of the vehicle, and for a brief second, Jasper considered opening his door and throwing himself out of the moving car. Just for a moment of clarity, one minute of letting the logic return to his brain—but it would be futile. He couldn't have escaped the heady scent even if he wanted to. It was burned into his brain as surely as the curves of Nicole's pink lips.

Jasper gritted his teeth to hold back the groan climbing up his throat. One little paper cut, and suddenly, his pants felt like they were strangling his cock. He didn't have to look at Atticus to know his old friend was feeling the same thing. The sound of his breath sawing in and out of his lungs was almost as loud as his own.

"You smell divine, love," Atticus growled quietly.

Jasper wisely kept his mouth shut—the thoughts in his head were far dirtier than a simple "divine." He would have told Nicole how his mouth was watering to strip her naked right there in the backseat and run his tongue over every curve. He would have told her how he was dying to hear the little whimpers she would make when he was fucking her with his fangs in her throat.

No, it was better for Atticus to take the lead. He was too tactful to voice the hunger gnawing at his own belly.

The car rolled to a stop in a long driveway, headlights shining on a house that hadn't seen better days since before Nicole was born.

"Thanks for the ride," she said quickly. "It was... great."

Nicole opened the door and hurried up the driveway. The two vampires watched her wave from the porch and disappear into the dilapidated house.

They waited in silence, neither acknowledging the shock and hunger that was plaguing them both. A light clicked on in an upstairs window.

"Can we keep her?" Jasper asked quietly.

He didn't want to abandon his best friend if he didn't agree, but for the first time in two hundred years, he was seriously considering it. Now that he'd had a taste of her luscious scent, Jasper wasn't sure he could live without it.

"I intend to." Atticus shot him a wicked grin and put the car in reverse.

Jasper took one last look at the shadow moving in the lit window and breathed a sigh of relief. Nicole had no idea what was coming for her.

5

NICOLE

Nicole stared at the ceiling. The black abyss of her bedroom matched her dark mood. Last night was a disaster. First, the date, then, the demise of her car—even a ride home with two seductive vampires hadn't been enough to lift her spirits.

Was it too much to ask for a couple of hot monsters who desperately wanted to pay her bills, spoil her, and got along like best friends? Okay... that probably was too much to ask for, but two out of three? Nicole would happily settle for two out of three.

Sighing, she started to put together the day's to-do list in her mind. Bills and errands fought for the top spot. And the contractor—oh God, the contractor—that was going to put a hefty dent in her savings.

Pinching her nose in the dark, Nicole sighed. Her dire financial situation wasn't exactly soothing her anxiety. Quickly shoving it down into the depths of her spiraling mind, she fumbled in the dark for her phone.

So the first date had been a disaster, it wasn't like the next one could be as bad. If the bar was already in hell, there was nothing left to do but step over it.

Squinting at the bright screen, Nicole flipped open MONSTR and stared at a blue-skinned demon with horns longer than her forearm. Her soulmate—or soul monster—could still be out there.

Could she handle horns? Or was that too outside the box for her?

Shaking her head, she swiped past the profile. The last thing she needed was some jacked-up demon gouging holes in her ceiling. Her house was already a wreck; she didn't need help making it worse.

CHRIS

Hey baby girl. Wanna take a walk on the wild side?

Gag. Where were they getting these awful lines? Whatever happened to "hello"?

CHRIS

Hey baby girl. Wanna take a walk on the wild side?

NICOLE

No thanks, I'm not much of a hiker.

She stifled a laugh and deleted the match. No loss there. She'd never seen a vampire with such shrimpy fangs before—and if his fangs were small, who knew what else was.

Flipping through more profiles, the different kinds of monsters made her brain spin. Werewolves, bear shifters, dryads, yetis, chupacabras; the list went on and on. The longer she swiped, the more she'd never heard of.

"What the hell is a selkie?" Nicole muttered. Pulling up the internet browser for the umpteenth time, she did a quick search. "A seal shifter? We don't even live by the ocean."

Her phone buzzed again. Sighing, she closed her eyes

and counted to ten in the hopes that the notification would go away. If she had to look at one more random dick pic before breakfast, her phone was going straight into the nearest trash can.

What had happened to flirting without close ups of a guy's business? Romance wasn't just dead—it was dead, embalmed, and buried somewhere in the Bermuda Triangle.

"Just get it over with, and then you can have coffee," she promised herself.

Nicole tapped on the notification. Atticus and Jasper, the vampires from the date from hell, had messaged her again. Clearly, they were masochists who enjoyed suffering.

Or, with her luck, she had left her dingy wallet behind in their fancy car.

> **ATTICUS & JASPER**
>
> Good morning, sweet Nicole.
>
> Jasper and I enjoyed our evening with you last night—with the exception of the actual dinner, of course. It was truly a pleasure to meet such a lovely creature. We were hoping that you might be inclined to a more intimate dinner with just the two of us. We'll be retiring shortly for the daylight hours, but please do let us know if you so desire. Tomorrow night?
>
> I'll be dreaming of you. - Atticus

Nicole stared at the invite. If she hadn't known he was a vampire already, the flowery text in her inbox would have been a flashing neon sign. She'd read sonnets written with less care.

How was last night not bad enough to drive them away? Dinner had been nothing short of a disaster... but then again, that steamy drive home had been closer to what she had been hoping for when she'd spent an hour and a half agonizing over her outfit last night.

A shiver crawled down her spine. Sitting in their fancy car, the plush leather against the back of her thighs as they snuck glances at her, she'd been fidgeting in her seat for the entire drive. And that was before her accidental paper cut had made them both look like they were dying under a desert sun and she was the only bottle of water for miles.

The two vampires had looked at her like they had wanted to eat her up... and not in the fangy way.

Her fingers hovered over the keyboard. As fiery as the short drive had been, hesitation knotted her stomach. A little voice in the back of her mind wondered if this was all just an elaborate scheme to nibble on her—and *not* in the fun naked way.

She could practically hear Ashley's voice in her head, admonishing her for being a big scaredy cat. Wasn't this exactly why she had signed up for this dating app? The interest on her student loans wasn't exactly decreasing while she laid in bed.

Fuck it. She was doing it.

Nicole typed out a quick message, her finger hovering over the send button.

"Just do it," she grumbled to herself. "Stop being a weenie."

Her alarm blared, and Nicole jumped, her heart pounding in her chest. Glancing quickly at the clock on the nightstand, she winced. The first contractor would be there soon to look over the house and give her an estimate. If she didn't stop giving herself useless pep talks and get a move on, she was going to be greeting him in her pajamas.

Nicole quickly sent the message and leaped out of bed before she could waste more time worrying. Dragging on a hoodie and a pair of leggings, she raced downstairs to start the coffee maker. She had just dumped an unhealthy amount of creamer into her mug when someone pounded heavily on the front door.

Coffee sloshed onto her sweatshirt as she ran. She cursed under her breath and ripped the door open. A stooped old man with enough wrinkles to give a shar-pei a run for its money waited on the other side.

"Is your husband home?" he grunted.

Nicole blinked. "What?"

"Your husband," the gruff old man huffed. "I'm here to do an estimate for some work. I need to talk to the man of the house."

She couldn't stop the annoyance from seeping into her frown. Seriously? The "man of the house"?

"I'm not married," Nicole said as pleasantly as she could manage.

"Boyfriend, then. Whatever." The old man pulled out a clipboard and started to scrawl on his forms. "Go get him, sweetheart. I want to get on with this."

"There is no boyfriend," she growled. "You can deal with me."

Looking up, he finally met her eyes. The contractor looked her up and down, his frown pulling at the wrinkles on his face. Apparently, she didn't meet with the ancient mummy's approval.

"Fine. I'll look around." He turned away without another word and started inspecting the outside of the house.

"Don't I need to tell you what kind of work I'm looking for?"

"I think I can figure it out, girlie."

Anger pooled, hot and devastating, in her belly. Nicole wasn't the type of woman to slug an old man for his misogyny, but if he called her one more pet name, he was going to find out just how little patience she had.

Ignoring his dirty looks, she slammed her feet into her shoes and followed him around the side of the house. If he thought she was letting him out of her sight, he had another thing coming.

Her phone buzzed in her pocket. Nicole tugged it out and glanced at the message.

> SVEN
>
> Hey there, cutie pie. How about I take you out for ice cream?
>
> Or hot chocolate?
>
> Anything, as long as I get a chance to lick it off you ;)

Nicole gritted her teeth. Maybe it was the rude old man she was forced to trail after, or her frustration still lingering from last night's disastrous foray into online dating, but she was feeling anything other than "sweet."

> SVEN
>
> Hey there, cutie pie. How about I take you out for ice cream?
>
> Or hot chocolate?
>
> Anything as long as I get a chance to lick it off you ;)

> NICOLE
>
> How about no.

"I need to take a look at the inside of the house, darlin'." The contractor waved his clipboard back toward the front porch. "Or are you too busy texting?"

"You know what? I don't have time for this today." Nicole jammed her phone back into her pocket and waved him to his truck. "Go ahead and just assume the house needs to be gutted and write up your proposal from there."

"But—"

"You can email me my quote," she said cheerily. "Good luck with your next client."

Grumbling under his breath, he turned on his heel and stomped back to his truck. The slam of the door echoed in the quiet morning air, and Nicole scowled as the truck kicked up gravel, digging grooves in the driveway.

Well, she definitely wasn't going with the crypt keeper.

She turned back to her front porch. Maybe another cup of coffee would make her feel a little less murderous. Her phone buzzed in her pocket. Clenching her jaw, she turned her face up to the sky and forced herself not to scream.

If it was another shitty pickup line or weird monster dick pic, she was going back to bed and starting her day over. Nicole fished her cellphone out and squinted at the screen through the glaring sunlight.

> WES
>
> Good morning, babe. I managed to find another alternator in the garage last night. Swing by at any time to pick up your car. I'll be waiting ;)

She glanced at the time. If she called a rideshare, she might have just enough time to pick up her car from the werewolf and get back before the next contractor arrived. But that would definitely mean saying 'no' to a second cup of coffee.

So much for turning her day around.

6

NICOLE

Nicole nervously smoothed a hand over her messy bun. She definitely wasn't as polished as she had been for their group date, but hopefully, the werewolf wouldn't mind. Besides, he'd already fixed her car, so it wasn't like he could rescind the offer in light of her coffee-stained sweatshirt.

She hurried into the garage before she could change her mind and give in to the wild voice whispering for her to just abandon the car, change her name, and move to another city. Obviously, that was a terrible idea... even if it *was* appealing.

Studying the explosion of tools and parts she couldn't even begin to name, Nicole looked around for any signs of life. A desk sat empty against the closest wall. An explosion of paperwork covered every inch of free space. Wes wasn't much of a secretary, that was for sure.

"Hello?" Nicole called softly. "Anyone here?"

"Hey there, gorgeous."

The werewolf wove through the tools scattered on the floor, a rag in his hands. She blinked at the tight tank top stretched across his chest. If she squinted, she could almost make out the outline of his abs through the stained material.

Not that she was looking or anything.

Wes swiped at the grease on his hands and flashed her a grin. Any semblance of rational thought fell out of her head as she watched his muscular arms flex.

"Don't mind the mess. Tony is in over his head on a Volkswagen, and the day has gone to shit."

Nicole wasn't sure who Tony was, but in the presence of Wes' dazzling smile and carved biceps, it didn't matter much. Her stomach rolled, turning somersaults as she tried to form a coherent sentence. Golden eyes watched her, and the handsome bastard's smile grew.

It wasn't fair. In fact, it was outright criminal.

No one should look that good covered in grease and dirt. She was pretty sure she still had smudges of last night's makeup under her eyes, and the sly monster was playing with cars looking like *that*?

He'd even managed to make coveralls hot. Her eyes dropped to the baggy outfit tied around his narrow waist, and the knots in her stomach tightened.

"Nicole?"

"Uh huh?" she murmured.

"Do you want to see your car, or do you want to keep checking me out?" Wes asked, his dimples flashing with his grin. "I'm good with either."

She hated him. With every fiber of her being, she despised that he had ambushed her with his silly dimples and liquid gold eyes. Wasn't it bad enough that she had to show up looking like a trash goblin who'd just rolled out of bed? No, the wolf had to look like a Greek god come to life.

In that moment, Nicole wasn't sure if she wanted to sink into the floor or push him back onto the hood of the nearest car and find out just what was waiting for her under those coveralls. Of course, with her luck, they'd dent the hood of the car, and she'd have to pay for it.

The horrifying thought of her empty bank account dragged her back to reality.

"Right, my car... lead the way."

"This way, beautiful." Wes stepped back and waved her forward.

Eyes locked on the minefield of tools as she stepped past him, Nicole made a point not to stare at his tanned arms. She needed to get her shit together. They still needed to negotiate payment, and there was no way she was going to get a good deal with her head in her panties.

A warm hand gripped her elbow, and spicy cologne tickled her nose pleasantly as the werewolf steered her through the messy garage. She gritted her teeth. If Nicole started trying to sniff him, there was no way she would walk out of there with a shred of dignity intact. Not that she had much left anyway.

"Wes! This fucking timing belt is off!" a muffled voice shouted.

Rolling his eyes at the car next to them, he kicked a pair of boots poking out from underneath.

"I told you to stop messing with it. You're going to break it beyond the point that I can fix it."

"I can do it!"

"Tony, step away from the damned Volkswagen."

Nicole jumped back as the infamous Tony came rolling out from under the car. Sitting up, he glowered at Wes and scrubbed a hand over his horned head. She blinked at the gray-eyed demon.

Why did he look so familiar?

"I can fix this, you interfering mutt—" He choked on his words as he caught sight of her wide eyes. "Um... hi."

"Tony, Nicole," Wes introduced them. "Lemme get her

squared away with her car, and then I'll come fix whatever you just fucked up."

Ignoring the introduction, Tony cocked his head to the side. "Have we met?"

Nicole shook her head. "I don't think so, but you do look awfully familiar."

"Oh, shit! We matched on MONSTR!" Tony laughed. Jumping to his feet, he scrubbed his greasy palm on his pant leg and offered her his hand. "I said 'feelin' horny?' but you didn't respond. Get it? The horns?"

Oh... shit.

Her stomach dropped. This wasn't super awkward or anything.

"Uh, yeah. Super busy week and all that," she muttered. "Didn't get a chance—"

"Anyway," Wes interrupted. His hand gently settled on the small of her back and nudged her past the grinning demon. "We should get you on the road."

She waved goodbye and didn't let her sigh of relief slip until they were well out of earshot.

"Thanks," Nicole whispered.

"Sorry about that. He's a bit of a horndog, but he's harmless." Wes steered her to the back of the garage, his warm hand lingering. "I should have figured he would have been on MONSTR too."

"It's okay. That's definitely not your fault."

They came to a stop next to her rusty old sedan and still, his hand curled against her back.

"Feelin' horny?"

Nicole blinked. "Excuse me?"

His carved muscles and wolfish grin were definitely doing something to her, but that was a bit forward, especially with her being a customer—

"Tony's pick-up line," Wes laughed. "That was just terrible. Zero originality."

"Oh! I thought you were—" She snapped her mouth shut. Nope, she'd made enough of an ass of herself already without admitting that she thought he was trying to get into her pants.

The gleam in his eyes lit with hunger as he studied her flaming cheeks with a slow, satisfied smile.

"Trust me, babe. You deserve better than a line like that." He leaned in close, his lips brushing her ear. "But if I were going to hit you with a crass pickup line, it would be a lot better than 'feelin' horny?'"

A shiver rolled down her spine as he leaned away. Nicole breathed out; she needed to get the hell out of there before she melted on the spot.

Cold metal pressed into her hand. She blinked down at her car keys. The werewolf tucked them into her shaking hands and took a step back. Her heart held a small memorial service for her desperate body as his hand fell away from the small of her back.

"Um— the bill—I, I mean—how much do I owe you?" Nicole stuttered.

The werewolf shrugged. "Let's say one hundred."

She frowned at the casual way he thrust his hands into his pockets and glanced at the floor. He might be hotter than sin, but Wes couldn't play poker to save his life.

"There's no way an alternator and labor only cost one hundred dollars."

"Are you a mechanic now?" One eyebrow lifted even as his teasing smile brightened.

"No," Nicole admitted. "But it's like one of two car parts that I know, and they definitely cost more than that. And that's not including labor, the tow, or the fact that this was so last minute."

"Let's call it the 'Beautiful Woman Who Had to Suffer Through a Terrible Dinner' discount."

Pity parts. Lovely.

Eyes narrowing, she stared down the stubborn werewolf. "You're not going to let me pay a penny more than that, are you?"

He barked out a laugh. "No, definitely not. I'm struggling to charge you even that much."

Damn it. Nicole glanced down at the time and winced. She didn't have time to argue with him. When she'd set foot in the garage, she'd never thought she'd be urging the flirty werewolf to charge her *more*.

"Okay, I'm not going to argue," she surrendered. Not that she thought it would do any good. "But only because I'm running late for a meeting, and I fully intend to pay you back with coffee or dinner or something."

"I'll hold you to that, gorgeous." Stepping around her, Wes opened the bay door. "You'd better get going. I don't want you blaming me for being late. Not this time, anyway."

He winked and waved for her to back the car out. Nicole jumped behind the wheel and started the engine. She blinked for a stunned second at the warm purr. The werewolf had done a lot more than fix the alternator—she didn't know how to prove it, but she was sure of it.

Waving goodbye, she pulled the car onto the street and peeked at the rearview mirror. Wes waited in the open bay, his hands tucked in his pockets as he watched her drive away.

A small smile stretched her lips. Maybe last night hadn't been a complete disaster after all.

Dragging her eyes away, she stepped on the accelerator and headed home.

Time ticked by as speed limits quickly turned into

suggestions. There was no way around it... Nicole was going to be late.

"Shit, shit, shit," she muttered under her breath as she turned down her road. Hopefully, the next contractor wasn't the type to jack up the price for making him wait.

Nicole slammed on the brakes in her driveway and jumped out of her car.

"I'm so sorry!" she said quickly. Stumbling over the uneven ground, she thrust out her hand. "I had to pick up my car from the mechanic, and I thought I had enough time. I hope you weren't waiting long."

The contractor pushed the bill of his hat up with the end of his pencil and laughed. Nicole stared at the familiar face.

"I think after one date, we're probably okay to move past the handshake stage." Drake grinned.

She gaped at the were-cougar. As a fairly logical person, Nicole had never been a big believer in fate, but as she stared at yet another one of her dates, she couldn't help but feel the universe was playing a joke on her.

"Right, definitely." She pulled her hand back.

"If you wanted a second date, you could have just asked," the hulking shifter teased. Drake looked up at her house, and his smile dimmed. "Then again, this place is gonna take more than a few dates to get straightened out."

Fire burned in her cheeks. Nicole wasn't sure what she wanted to defend more: herself or her house.

"Let's get this quote started, shall we?" Drake waved her forward. "You show me what you want fixed, kitten, and I'll start crunching numbers."

Kitten? Nicole opened and closed her mouth. Nope, she was already late to their meeting. She'd lost the right to complain about cutesy nicknames when she'd come screaming up the driveway.

"This way."

Drake followed her, always one step behind as they toured the house and the yard. He lingered at her back like a shadow. If he moved any closer, his chest would have brushed her back.

Nicole shivered from her perch on the kitchen counter. Every teasing laugh and smoldering look was pushing her closer to the edge. Drake was being perfectly professional, asking all the right questions and taking notes in his careful scrawl, but there was something in his eyes that had her squirming.

"Have you lived here long?" he asked, measuring her kitchen cabinets.

"A couple months," Nicole said. She looked at the room with fresh eyes and winced. Why hadn't she tidied up a bit yesterday? "I inherited the house from my great aunt."

"She must have loved you a lot. It's not too difficult to imagine why."

"I think you mean hated," she laughed. Waving at the stained countertop and sagging drywall, Nicole grimaced. "Clearly, I was not her favorite relative."

"It's not that bad," the cougar argued, his deep voice rumbling in the quiet kitchen.

She raised her eyebrows.

"Okay, it *is* that bad," he admitted. Pocketing his tape measure, he straightened up and caught her with his calm, gray-eyed gaze. "It might need some work, but it has good bones."

"Good... bones?" Nicole was really hoping he was being metaphorical because if she stumbled on a body somewhere in the dilapidated house, she would burn it down to the foundation and walk away.

"Maybe this isn't a punishment or an old lady's revenge." Drake shrugged and bent over to take a look under the sink.

"Maybe she wanted you to start over and build something new."

Nicole was sure he was trying to be deep and inspiring, but it was really hard to focus on any of the words coming out of his mouth when his ass looked that good in jeans.

At least the were-cat hadn't worn his tool belt. Her self-respect was pretty much nonexistent as it was.

"Can you pass me my pencil?" he muttered. "I think I left it on the counter."

Pencil. Right, she could definitely do that.

Nicole scrambled to grab his pencil and pass it over. His storm cloud eyes rose from the tape measure to her face as he took it from her hand. For the briefest moment, they stared into each other's eyes in contented silence. Drake's eyes flicked down to her coffee-stained chest and back up to her face.

"Thanks."

Fire bloomed in her cheeks. Damn it. She was trying to keep her cool, and blushing like a total dork because she thought his eyes were pretty was definitely not "cool."

Drake scribbled down some numbers and straightened up. "Okay, I think that's about it."

Without another word, he turned and headed for the front door. She blinked at his back. Was she supposed to follow him?

Nicole hurried after the cougar. Rushing out the door, she wasn't prepared for him to stop right in her path. She slammed into his back and rocked back on her heels. Drake spun quickly, catching her hips in his tight grip.

"Careful, kitten. I don't want to have to add a trip to the emergency room to this quote."

He steadied her and took a step back. Eyes dropping to the numbers on his paper, he carried on with his calculations as if his hands hadn't just made her tingle all the way down to her toes.

Biting her lip, Nicole stared past him into the trees. The sooner she got the were-cougar out of her house, the better. In fact, it would probably be better if she found another contractor altogether.

The longer she was in Drake's presence, the more she was going to make a fool of herself, and she wasn't sure how much more humiliation and yearning she could take before she imploded. For all she knew, he kept staring at her because he was judging her stained sweater.

"All right, I think I got it all." The monster ripped the sheet free from his notepad and passed it to her. She took a deep breath and braced herself.

If it was bad, she could always burn the old place down for the insurance money.

Calming at the thought of a little arson, Nicole looked down at the number he had circled. She stared at the estimate. Was he serious, or was she having a stroke? Did she care?

"You're hired," she blurted before he could change his mind.

"Excellent. I'll get a contract printed up." Drake picked up his toolbox. "I'm just going to take a second look at the electrical box before I go. It didn't quite look right to me, and I don't want to get a call in the middle of the night that you lost power."

Nodding, Nicole was only half listening. She was too busy staring at the way his broad shoulders moved under his shirt and thanking her lucky stars he had terrible business sense.

"I need to meet some friends; will you be okay to finish up on your own?" she asked. Nicole was bursting to tell

Ashley and Miri about her morning. Maybe her luck was changing after all.

The were-cougar shot her a thumbs up and hefted his toolbox. "I'll see you tomorrow, kitten."

Nicole watched his muscular back disappear around the side of the house. Covering her face, she silently screamed into her hands and jumped up and down.

"Thank fuck!" she breathed.

Had Drake low-balled the quote to get in her pants? Probably. Did she care? Not in the slightest.

Between Wes and Drake's horny generosity, she was actually going to be able to afford groceries this month—and not just dented cans and discount boxed dinners, but actual food. When was the last time she cooked a vegetable that hadn't started out in a can?

Ashley was a genius, a pushy, crazy genius with a coffee addiction. If Nicole didn't love her friend like a sister already, she would have declared her undying devotion in gratitude of this crazy scheme.

Resisting the urge to skip, Nicole hurried to her car. She had just enough time to stop for "thank you macchiatos" on the way to the farmers' market. Smiling to herself, she backed her car out of the driveway.

Ashley and Miri were going to lose it when they heard about this. She wasn't sure if one could be thrown out of a farmers' market for excited shrieking, but Nicole was about to give it her best shot.

7

NICOLE

"I'm sorry, I'm sorry, I'm sorry," Nicole began her usual mantra before she had even jumped out of the car.

She wasn't usually this late—okay, she was—but the line at the coffee shop was out of hand. No, it wasn't even the understaffed coffee shop's fault. The blame lay squarely on the shoulders of the two hunky monsters still occupying her mind.

The fact that they wanted to flirt with her after their horrible group date was borderline miraculous. How bad were monster dates usually if their shitshow hadn't seemed so terrible? It was a question she pondered as she jumped out of the car, the tray of coffee clutched to her chest.

Nicole wove through the crowded parking lot. Where the hell were they?

Bright red curls poked out of a baseball hat ahead of her. Beelining for the redhead answering emails on her phone and the tall blonde patiently applying her lip gloss, she had to stop herself from running forward and blurting out her news.

"Finally!" Ashley laughed as she closed the distance.

"I'm sorry, I'm sorry, I'm sorry," Nicole chanted.

"What took you so long? The good bakery stand is going to run out of the turtle cookies." Miri snagged her coffee and took a deep sip. "Never mind. Forget the cookies; *that* is perfection."

"You would not believe my morning!"

"Please tell me you spent the evening as the center of a giant monster sandwich," Ashley teased hopefully.

"Not quite. The date was a disaster, and my car broke down. The vampires had to give me a ride home while my car was being towed," she said, punching a straw into her own coffee. "But the hot werewolf mechanic insisted on fixing it—and for a heavy discount, I might add. I picked my car up this morning, and there was definitely some flirting involved."

"How are you gonna thank him?" Miri wiggled her eyebrows.

"Oh, I'm not done!" Nicole laughed. "So, I get back to the house and the contractor I'm supposed to meet with? The were-cougar!"

"No!" Miri choked on her coffee.

"Yes! And he was looking at me like he was ready to tear my clothes off right there in the driveway."

Ashley swiped a pamphlet off a produce stall and started to fan herself.

"Babe, you are living the dream." She looked Nicole up and down like she was trying to find a way to crawl inside her skin. "Can I be you? Just for, like, two days? I would love to be at the center of a shifter cream puff."

"Cream puff?" Miri raised her eyebrows. "How would that—"

"Don't," Nicole cut her off. The last thing they needed was to get banned from the farmers' market before they'd even found the cookie stall. "Just let me live in financially independent bliss for two minutes before you start talking about monster threesomes."

"Maybe we should look for a thank-you present while we're here?" Miri suggested. She picked up a hand thrown ceramic bowl from a display.

Ashley took it from her hands and put it back on the shelf. "Trust me, the only 'thank you' they want is a big old bowl of Nicole."

Nicole snorted. Before this morning, she would have thought Ashley was full of it, but the way the vampires had looked at her last night? The way Wes and Drake were practically drooling over her today? She was starting to think monsters had very low standards.

They were willing to share her. *Her*. It wasn't like she was some kind of supermodel or super rich and successful. She wore socks with holes in them because she didn't want to buy more, she never drank enough water, and her car had had a mix tape stuck in the tape deck for at least five years now. To say she was a shitshow was putting it lightly.

And they still looked at her like she was best thing since sliced bread.

"Nicole?"

She glanced around the crowded farmers' market, but no one looked familiar. A mass of tentacles waved. Were they talking to her?

"Nicole! I thought that was you. It's me, Tim!"

Her eyes widened. Oh, she remembered him all right. She had unmatched from him so fast, she could have broken a land speed record. The unsolicited tentacle pic in her inbox had nearly put her off sushi for life. At least buy a girl coffee first.

The tentacle monster shuffled closer to her, and it was all she could do not to jump back. Her stomach rolled.

Nicole wasn't prejudiced about monsters with tentacles, but the suction cups made her skin crawl.

Especially when she found them in her inbox with the caption, "On a scale of one to ten-tacle, how bad do you want me?"

"I'm so glad I ran into you. The app glitched and unmatched us," Tim scoffed. "I was going to take you out to dinner?"

There wasn't a chance in hell of that happening.

"Oh, no. That's really sweet, but— but I can't," Nicole said.

Ashley and Miri gaped beside her. Clearly, they were going to be no help at all.

"Why not?" Tim demanded.

"Um—"

"There you are, honey!"

Nicole jumped as a muscled arm wrapped around her shoulders. Squinting into the sun, she blinked at the smiling face beside her. She almost didn't recognize the fae with the sunshine glinting off his pale hair.

Hawthorne squeezed her gently. Right, get with the program.

"Sorry, babe. I ran into a friend and got to chatting."

"Hi, I'm Hawthorne... Nicole's boyfriend." He offered his hand to shake.

Tim took one look at him and ambled away, muttering under his breath about lying hoes. Talk about dodging a bullet... or a tentacle.

Hawthorne's arm dropped away, and he took a quick step back. A light pink flush tinged his cheeks and the tips of his pointy ears as Nicole turned to thank him. Miri and Ashley studied him curiously.

"I thought you might need some help there," he said, his

ears glowing red against his silver hair. "You looked like you wanted to run away as fast as possible."

"You couldn't possibly be more correct," she laughed.

"Bad MONSTR match?" he guessed.

"Unfortunately." Nicole shuddered. "It was the unsolicited tentacle pics. So... um... do you come here often?"

The fae laughed. "Actually, I have a stall further down the row."

"Ooh, what do you sell?" Ashley asked eagerly. She lifted her bag, giving it a small shake to make sure she still had room.

"I own a landscaping business, and I grow my own flowers and plants in greenhouses. Anything left over from my landscaping jobs, I bring to the market on weekends to sell."

"Ooh, plants!" Miri walked right past him to find and ransack the stall.

"I'll go rein her in." Ashley took off after her.

Between the shopaholic and the plant queen, Hawthorne would be lucky to have anything left. Nicole shook her head. Hopefully, he had some extra bags they could use.

"Those were my friends, Ashley and Miri. We'd better follow them," Nicole laughed. "Otherwise, you're going to have nothing left but buckets of dirt by the time they're done."

"Nicole!" Ashley's voice floated through the market. "You have got to see this!"

They followed the sounds of Ashley and Miri's excited chatter to the end of the row. She stumbled to a stop, her eyes widening as her jaw dropped.

Enormous flowers covered every inch of the stall. She squinted at the fabric of the tent and raised a tentative hand.

There were so many plants tucked inside the small tent that it looked like it was woven together out of leaves.

Leaning forward, she sniffed a bright yellow daffodil. Never in her life had she seen flowers so big and vibrant.

"These are the *leftover* plants?" she gasped.

"You'd be amazed at how many flats of flowers I go through in a week." His face flushed pink. "Maybe— maybe I could show you my greenhouses some time."

Nicole beamed at the shy fae. "I would love that!"

He looked away quickly, his flush coloring his ears. She swallowed a giggle. That cute blush of his was absolutely killing her. Every time Hawthorne's pointy elf ears turned pink, she had to resist the urge to reach out a hand and trace them with her fingers.

"So... which ones are you favorite?" Nicole asked.

"The sweetfern and the peonies."

He waved at some innocuous looking greenery and baskets of peonies that had yet to bloom. She studied the plants, positive she was missing something. They just looked like plants to her.

"Why those two?" she finally asked.

"Because they're a bitch to grow."

A laugh burst out of her at Hawthorne's disgruntled growl. It was the first time Nicole had heard him say anything that wasn't sweet or quiet, and it was because he had a grudge against house plants.

"I like the challenge," he admitted with a smile, for once not blushing under her gaze.

Hawthorne pulled a pink peony stem out of a bunch and cupped the blossom in his hands. As he muttered something under his breath, the runes on his arms flared a brilliant blue. Nicole blinked at the flash of light. What the—?

He opened his hands and she gasped. The delicate

peony had bloomed from a tight bulb into a work of art. Fluffy, vibrant petals fanned in gorgeous pink spirals.

She looked up at the fae, an awed smile lighting her face. He pressed the flower into her hands.

"For you."

"It's beautiful," she whispered.

Fire burned her cheeks, and Nicole didn't need a mirror to know that her face was redder than the roses in the stall. Apparently, it was her turn to be flustered.

"Nicole!"

She jumped as Miri called her name. The redhead bounced up and down, her eyes glowing in delight. She pointed at a basket overflowing with pale purple flowers.

"These would look so good on your porch!"

"Begonia tuberosa," Hawthorne said quietly. "They come in other colors if you don't like purple."

Nicole's eyes crept upward to his hair. In the shade of his overflowing stall, the pale silver hair pulled back from his face in a loose bun was the same shade of lavender as the hanging basket.

"I like the purple just fine. Can you show me some more?"

Stepping back, she followed Hawthorne as he pointed out which plants would be best for her house. By the time Miri was struggling under her armfuls of house plants, Nicole and the fae had composed a jaw-dropping order.

Miri and Ashley paid for their plants and stepped outside for a breath of fresh, un-perfumed air. Nicole fumbled in her bag for her wallet. Hopefully, it would go through. It was going to be her turn to be flustered again if it declined.

Hawthorne waved her down when she offered him her credit card. "Don't worry about that yet. I need to double check if I have more hydrangea shrubs first."

"I ordered a lot more than hydrangeas, Hawthorne."

"We'll square up when I drop them off in the next couple days," he promised.

Nicole watched his ears turn bright red and knew he was lying. There was no way the elf was going to let her pay; she could already tell. What was with these monsters trying to spoil her after one date?

"We *will* talk about it then," she said stubbornly. She would get the fae to take some kind of payment even if it killed her.

As she turned to leave, Hawthorne caught Nicole's hand. He tugged her back a step and raised her fingers to his lips, pressing a soft kiss to her knuckles before he let her go.

Ashley and Miri were giggling as she hurried to catch up. Nicole looked over her shoulder one last time to catch a glimpse of the sun shining off his silver hair. The fae offered her a quick, shy smile and disappeared into the mass of flowers.

An elbow dug into her ribs, and she turned to find Miri's grin filled with mischief.

"Girl, if you don't fuck that tall drink of water, I will!"

"First off, you just got mean-mugged by a granny and a toddler." Ashely laughed, her own bouquet of lilies clutched to her chest. "Secondly, stop eyeing her dates!"

"She didn't even want them!" Miri reminded her.

Nicole looked down at the delicate peony stem twisting in her fingers. Flashes of Hawthorne's shy smile, Drake's quiet smirk, and Wes' teasing wink played in her mind. Jasper and Atticus watched her hungrily from the depths of her memory.

Miri was right—she hadn't wanted them. But did she want them now?

8

DRAKE

Drake tapped his fingertips on the steering wheel to the beat of the radio. As much as he loved a quiet morning, just him and the swaying trees, he would much rather be in bed. There wasn't enough coffee in the world to turn him into a morning person.

He turned the truck into the driveway and parked. Peering up at the dark windows, the were-cougar wondered if Nicole was still sleeping. The cat inside of him was jealous.

Maybe he could find a nice sunny spot for his break later and catch a nap.

Coffee in one hand and his toolbox in the other, he climbed out of his truck and headed around the side of the house. There was no use whining about it. He had promised Nicole he'd get her house in decent shape.

A promise that was going to take every bit of skill Drake possessed. She hadn't been kidding when she said her house was a wreck. It was going to take weeks, if not months, to get the house up to his standards. The were-cougar had almost turned down the job the second he'd seen the property.

If it hadn't been Nicole's, he would have. But spending weeks hanging around her? Teasing her and flexing his muscles until her cheeks turned that delightful shade of pink? Smelling her luscious scent everywhere he went?

How could Drake possibly say no?

He hadn't even let any of his workers take on the job. It was his or no one's.

Putting his toolbox down on the rusted air conditioning unit, he filled his lungs with clear, morning air. The faint curl of Nicole's scent still lingered from their conversation the day before.

Prickles rolled down his arms, and Drake shook his head. It was time to work, not let the cat out to play. He would never live it down if Nicole walked out to find him furry and rolling around on her lawn.

Grabbing his tools, he got to work and did his best to put the tempting human out of his mind. Not an easy task when her scent still lingered in the air.

Hours passed as Drake forced himself to work on various problems around the yard. At some point, he was going to have to knock on the door and wake her up. Not yet, though—not until he was ready to be blasted by her sweet scent again.

Maybe someday, he would become immune to the temptation, but today definitely wasn't that day.

"How's it going?"

Crap. He took a deep breath, and Nicole's flowery wine scent punched him in the nose. Resisting the urge to spin around and press his body against hers, he schooled his face into a careful mask.

Drake smiled at her over his shoulder. "Gimme one sec."

Drilling one last screw into the panel, he set the drill down and turned to give Nicole his full attention. She stood huddled in a thick cardigan and clutching a cup of coffee for dear life.

A fresh wave of her sweet scent washed over Drake and had him swaying on the spot.

He cleared his throat. "Good. It's going... good."

She moved to get a closer look, and soft hair brushed against his arm. Gritting his teeth, the shifter started counting down from ten in his head.

There's no way the tempting woman wasn't doing this on purpose. She had to know what her scent was doing to him. How could she not? Nicole smelled like sin and flowers —and right then, Drake didn't give a flying fuck about flowers.

He forced himself to breathe through his mouth. She was definitely going to shred their contract if he gave in to his urge to lick her throat.

Nicole looked up at him and caught his hungry eyes. Biting her lip, she took a step back and focused on the coffee in her hands.

"You look good—I mean—it," she mumbled. "*It* looks like you're doing a good job. I need to go get ready."

Nicole turned away, her cheeks flushing bright pink as she hurried back toward the porch. Drake grinned at her retreating back. At least he wasn't the only one feeling it.

The cougar couldn't help but wonder what she was doing as he worked. Was Nicole in the shower? Or was she putting her make up on? Standing in her closet in a tiny bath towel, and picking out an outfit?

He jammed headphones into his ears and cranked up the volume on his music. If Drake couldn't keep his head clear, at least he could drown out his horny thoughts for a while.

"Pull it together, man," he hissed at his wandering mind.

If Drake kept this up, the tempting human was going to

come back to find him with an erection hard enough to hammer nails with.

The front door shut hard enough to rattle the wall. Heels clicking on the porch, Nicole waved to get his attention. He blinked at her trim skirt and silk blouse. Her dark hair had been smoothed into neat curls curving over her shoulders.

Drake ripped his headphones out of his ears. It wasn't like he could hear the music anyway, not with his heartbeat hammering in his ears and all the blood in his body rushing away from his brain.

"I have a job interview I need to run out for," Nicole called out to him. "Will you be okay on your own for a bit?"

"Ygh—" Drake cleared his throat—"Uh, yeah. I'll be fine. Good luck!"

"Thanks!" Smiling brightly, she waved and hurried to her car.

He watched her every step, his eyes flicking between her heels on the uneven ground and the way her ample ass moved under her skirt. Suddenly, the pinch this job was going to make in Drake's accounts didn't bother him at all.

Not one bit.

Her car backed out of the driveway and disappeared down the street. The sudden urge to rip off his clothes and let the cougar out nearly overwhelmed him. The feral need to run after Nicole clawed at his gut.

He had to give the cat something before it tore him apart from the inside. Drake eyed the porch. If he marked just one support post, that wouldn't hurt anything—and it might be enough to keep that insufferable werewolf away.

He took a single step forward before the logical half of his brain kicked back in and stopped him dead in his tracks. The last thing he needed was for Nicole to come home because she forgot something and find him peeing on her front porch.

Shaking his head, Drake walked around the side of the house. If he was going to go all furry, it would be best to do it in the backyard, where none of Nicole's neighbors would catch a glimpse and go tattling to her.

He skidded to a stop, a creeping unease skittering up his spine. Drake looked around. The fuck?

His eyes landed on the electrical panel he had repaired the day before. It hung open, swaying in the light breeze picking through the trees.

"What the hell?"

Drake opened the panel and stared at the wires. Half the coiled lines hung slack inside, shredded and severed worse than before. He studied the damage carefully.

There was no way Nicole had done it. She knew he was coming by today, and she was the one who was footing the bill for the repairs.

Small scratches lined the edge of the panel. Could an animal have pried it open?

Drake hissed, frustrated and confused at the work he was going to have to redo. Grumbling under his breath, he set to work repairing what had already been done the day before—and made a mental note to install some kind of lock on the panel.

A loud rumble cut through the music in his ears as he was finishing up. Drake tugged an earphone free just as a shining black motorcycle growled up the driveway.

He started around the house and blinked at the sight in front of him. The cocky werewolf from the other night sat up front, a tight t-shirt molded to his skin as the wind played with his hair. A small figure swimming in a leather jacket sat behind him. Thin arms wrapped around his waist, hanging on for dear life.

"Nicole?" Drake called. He hurried over to the motorcycle, worry seeping into his gut.

The wolf started to stand but abruptly thumped back onto the seat as Nicole tightened her grip. If she clutched him any tighter, she was going to fuse herself to his back. Drake did his best not to hiss. He wanted to be the one she was pressing up against like her life depended on it.

"You can let go now," Wes said gently.

The human koala shook her head. "I don't think I can move my arms."

Carefully holding her wrists, he pried himself loose from Nicole's death grip. Drake quickly closed the short distance and wrapped his hands around her waist. He lifted her off the back of the motorcycle, holding her upright until she was steady on her feet. He ignored the wolf's irritated frown.

Now they were even.

"What happened to your interview?" Drake asked as Wes slipped the helmet off her head.

She blinked, the color slowly coming back to her pale face.

"I never made it. My car broke down," she muttered shakily. "I made it about halfway there, and then the engine died."

Anger burned like a wildfire through his veins as Drake turned to glower at the werewolf. If he didn't think it would terrify Nicole, he would choke the life out of the smug prick.

"I thought you fixed her car, Fido?" he spit.

"I did!"

"Obviously, not well enough."

What if her car had gone off the road? Or the engine caught on fire? She could've been on the highway, in the middle of traffic. Nicole could have been seriously injured because the mutt hadn't done the job right the first time.

Two seconds, that's all Drake wanted. Two seconds for

the sweet human to close her eyes and plug her ears, and then he could wallop the furry moron.

"I replaced the alternator and anything else that looked worn out," Wes insisted. "There was nothing wrong with the engine when I sent her home yesterday."

"Clearly, she needed a second opinion!"

The wolf's golden eyes flashed. "Like you can do better, pussycat? I didn't see you stepping up to help her when it was crunch-time."

Drake took a step forward. Maybe she would forgive him one swing. The puffed-up twit definitely deserved a broken nose.

"*Enough!*" Nicole interrupted. They each took a turn wilting under her glower. "As I was saying... I pulled over and called Wes at his garage. He came and picked me up and arranged to have my car towed again. And then he was kind enough to give me a ride home."

She turned her blistering frown on the shiny, black motorcycle parked innocently behind her. Drake had a feeling motorcycle riding lessons were not in her future.

"And he rode without a helmet on, I should add."

Shooting a cheeky wink in her direction, Wes scrubbed a hand over his windblown hair. "And muss my luscious locks?" he teased. "I think not."

Drake snorted. What an idiot.

"It's okay, kitten," he told her. "A little road rash won't kill a werewolf... sadly."

Instead of easing Nicole's concern, his words only made it worse. He could smell the worry pouring off her in sour waves.

Damn it. He wasn't trying to scare her.

Wes leaned past him and pet her helmet-mussed hair back into place.

"Seriously, don't worry about it. Nothing short of a

throwing me into a woodchipper is going to make a dent in this gorgeous physique." Flexing his bicep, he struck a pose. "Monster, remember?"

Drake rolled his eyes. He wasn't sure what bothered him more: that the werewolf had made her smile... or that *he* had made her sad.

Making a mental note to buy a woodchipper—for totally valid, non-werewolf related contracting reasons— Drake gritted his teeth and once again reined in the cougar. As much as he wanted to claw Wes, that definitely would *not* make a good impression.

"Besides, didn't I look so much cooler with my hair blowing in the wind?" Wes kept teasing.

Maybe that's why he hated the bastard so much. The wolf was handsome—even Drake could admit that—but he didn't have to strut about like a peacock to show it off.

"If you weren't so busy looking in the mirror, maybe you would have fixed her car properly," he hissed.

A low growl rumbled from the werewolf. "I did fix it properly. The fuel line was perfectly fine when she left yesterday."

"The fuel line?" Drake's heart dropped. Why did he suddenly have such a bad feeling?

"Yeah, why?"

"Yesterday, I found some wiring that didn't look right on the house's electrical panel. I was checking something when I came back today, and some of the wires that I replaced are shredded."

Wes frowned. "Shredded?"

"I thought maybe I hadn't screwed the panel on tight enough and an animal had managed to pry it open, but if there was something wrong with her fuel line too..." Drake trailed off, unwilling to voice the worry on his mind.

"Show it to me," the wolf growled.

Wes set off in the direction of his pointing finger. Every few steps, he stopped and took a deep sniff. Nicole looked between him and Drake curiously.

He just shrugged. The less she thought about them playing bloodhound, the better. If Drake's hunch was right... Nicole had bigger problems.

The werewolf stopped where Drake had been working the previous day and recoiled. "Did you have any other workers here today, or did you fix this yourself?"

"Just me."

Wes shook his head. "Someone else was definitely here."

Elbowing past him, he crouched down and breathed deeply. His face darkened; the prick was right.

Drake rose to his feet. He felt less like punching the wolf than he did himself. He'd been so caught up in relishing Nicole's sweet scent all over the house, he'd completely missed any that didn't belong.

"What's going on?" she asked, her worried eyes flicking between them.

"Between your car and the electrical panel... I think someone's trying to sabotage you, kitten."

9

NICOLE

Sabotage? He had to be joking.

Nicole was a grad student—well, an unemployed graduate, but still. She was absolutely nobody.

Shaking her head, she opened her mouth to tell him just how wrong he was, but she clicked it shut as Drake reached for the hem of his shirt and started to peel it up his body. She stared in awe as she was treated to a front-row view of his tanned abs.

"What are you doing?" she finally gasped.

Drake didn't say a word. His shirt dropped to the ground, and he started working on his pants. Eyes wide, she tried to look away.

Just a peek, the little voice in her head urged.

No. Absolutely not, Nicole argued with herself.

If he didn't want you to look, he wouldn't be stripping right in front of you.

Who could argue with logic like that?

Nicole peeped from under her lashes as his pants hit the ground. She could feel the blush creeping up her neck and taking over her cheeks as her gaze slid up his thighs, higher and higher until—

A nose pressed against her hair. Nicole jumped, a flash of shame burning her from the inside out as she was caught staring. Wes raised his eyebrows and sniffed her again.

"Why are you—?" Her question cut off as she caught sight of Drake... except it wasn't Drake.

No, it was something else entirely. Part human, part cat, part nightmare. Her jaw dropped as the man standing naked in front of her jerked and twisted, his limbs morphing until he dropped to all fours. An enormous fluffy cougar sat in his place.

Did that really just happen? Or was the stress of defending her dissertation, inheriting a dive of a house, and juggling too many hot monsters finally causing her mind to break?

Drake gave himself a quick shake and started sniffing the ground.

"What the fuck? What the actual *fuck*?"

Nicole couldn't tear her eyes from the lethal cat wandering around her driveway. What the hell had she been thinking? Dating monsters? How the hell had she ended up like this?

Was joining a convent and declaring a vow of abstinence really that bad?

Drake padded closer to her, and her heart leapt into her throat. She squeaked as he buried his nose into the back of her knee. A warm tongue flicked across her skin before he darted toward the house.

"Really?" Wes rolled his eyes. "Even my human nose is better than yours, kitty cat."

Drake flicked his tail and didn't bother to look back. The werewolf followed after him, grumbling with every heavy thump of his boots.

Nicole stayed where she was. Swaying on her feet, she was left reeling as the two monsters disappeared around the side of the house without a backward glance.

"What in the actual fuck is my life?" she murmured.

First, she'd gotten an eyeful of Drake's admittedly impressive dick, and then he'd turned into an honest-to-god cougar. A cougar.

Swiping through monster dating profiles was one thing, but seeing one actually do something monstrous in person was a whole different ball game. What the hell was she doing? She was human.

Sure, Nicole wasn't particularly good at being human. She regularly forgot to feed herself, she couldn't balance a checkbook to save her life, and her diet mostly consisted of boxed macaroni and cheese and expensive lattes... but she sure as hell didn't turn furry at the drop of a hat!

Pressure weighed on her chest as air sawed in and out of her lungs. She bent at the waist and braced herself on her knees. Was this a panic attack? There was no way Ashley and Miri were going to let her live it down if her first look at a dick in over a year made her hyperventilate.

"I'm fine," she muttered. "He's just a shifter... a naked, well-hung shifter. It's still Drake."

Nicole straightened up and forced herself to breathe slowly. She could freak out later, preferably when two monsters weren't playing detective in her backyard.

A truck pulled into the driveway. A yowl echoed over the property, alerting her to the new arrival—as if she had somehow missed the vehicle parking right in front of her. Nicole ignored the screeching cat and the werewolf presumably arguing with him.

She was more concerned with cracking open a bottle of wine and rewinding her mind back to when Drake had first started to strip. To before the lovely view that had gone sideways.

The driver's side door swung open, and a silver man-bun glinted in the light. Nicole relaxed. Finally, someone she was on equal footing with.

Hawthorne waved cheerfully and grabbed a flat of flowers from the back of his truck. "I got your order done early!" he called.

And he'd brought it to her personally. The corner of her mouth curved. He was such a sweetheart... a sweetheart who wasn't about to do a striptease and turn into a giant cat.

He carried the first batch of flowers to her, the smile fading from his lips as he studied her face. "What's wrong?"

"What?"

"Your eyes." Hawthorne gestured at his face. "You're tense. Is everything okay?"

Damn perceptive elf. "Not really."

"What's going on?"

"Well, I was on my way to a job interview, and my car broke down, so yay me!" Nicole laughed. If it sounded a little unhinged, he was polite enough not to mention it.

"I thought the werewolf was going to fix your car?"

"Oh, he did. But now, according to Drake, somebody might have sabotaged it." She shrugged. That she was on the brink of a mental breakdown after watching the werecougar dick swing into an actual cat seemed like the more pressing problem. "Personally, I think it's bullshit. Now, they're off inspecting the house because Drake's convinced somebody sabotaged the wiring too."

His pale brows wrinkled into a frown. "You don't sound too worried. What if they're right?"

"No, I'm more worried about the fact that I just saw Drake naked and melting into a house cat with claws bigger than butter knives." Nicole sighed. "That's what's going to keep me up tonight. Some shredded wires? Nah. I once found a squirrel chewing through the plug to my toaster. This house isn't a wreck for nothing."

Hawthorne looked past her to the old house behind her. "Are you sure you're safe here?"

"Because of the squirrels?"

He blinked like she was crazy. It wasn't her fault. The squirrels had been living in the walls long before Nicole had inherited the house.

"No, because someone might be sabotaging your life. On the off chance the shifters are right, you might not be safe here."

"She will be," Wes cut in as he returned from his explorations around the back of the house.

"What does that mean?" Nicole asked, her eyebrows soaring.

The last thing she needed in her life was a werewolf dogging her every step. There was no way she was going to get a job that paid well enough to cover her student loan payments with a grease-covered wolf as a bodyguard.

"It means I'm sleeping on your couch tonight."

"Excuse me?" Nicole glowered at his casual tone.

The hell he was. Who was he to just invite himself over to sleep on her couch? That was her couch. It might be older than her and sagging in the middle, but it was *hers*.

Drake darted around the side of the house, his clawed feet silent on the gravel. He padded up to them and brushed against her legs before his body started to shake and twist once more.

Nicole turned her eyes up to the sky. One stomach churning shift was enough for her today. Though she did peek a little bit as he dragged his pants up his legs.

She was only human.

His arms crossed over his broad chest, his shirt hanging uselessly from his belt. Nicole blushed furiously. Was nudity a common thing for monsters, or was it just shifters?

Drake raised his eyebrows at the fire burning her cheeks. The corner of his mouth curved up into a small smile, but he wisely kept his mouth shut.

"We're both staying."

Nicole stared helplessly at the two stubborn shifters. At what point exactly had her life spiraled out of her control? Was it before or after she had downloaded a monster dating app? Or was it the moment she agreed to celebratory shots with Ashley and Miri?

Frankly, she was starting to wonder if it was the moment she was born.

"That is not happening."

"It is," Drake said breezily before nodding at Hawthorne. "Do you need help with those flowers?"

"Sure, that would be great."

The three monsters walked away, leaving Nicole staring at their backs. In two days, she had gone from barely scraping by to getting lavished with attention by monsters, then back to tearing her hair out in frustration. She'd been on rollercoasters that were less exciting.

Wes and Drake filed past her, their muscled arms overflowing with plants. Hawthorne hurried up and pressed a quick kiss against her cheek.

"I have to make a couple more deliveries still, but I'll be back tomorrow to get those planted and grown!"

The fae was already in his truck when Nicole found her voice again.

"Bye," she mumbled. "Wait... what do you mean *grown*?"

The truck backed out of the driveway, and she was once

again alone with two pushy shifters and no more answers than she had started with.

"Are we supposed to water these?" Wes asked.

"I think he would have told us if we needed to."

"Right... that makes sense. Do we put them in the sun?"

Drake shrugged. "I'm sure the porch is fine."

Nicole shook her head hard to clear it. Right. Pull it together and send the monsters home. Easy peasy.

"Time to go!" Stomping up the steps, she took Drake's shirt out of his belt and shoved it into his arms. "Time to put on your clothes and get going. Both of you."

"But I'm already wearing all my clothes." Wes looked down at his t-shirt. "I can take it off if you want me to."

It was like pulling teeth with these two.

"What I want is for you two to *go home!*" Nicole stressed. "You know? Your own homes... with your own couches... and your own food... where you live!"

"For tonight, this is home." Drake patted her shoulder. "Sorry, kitten."

Wes opened the door, and the two monsters disappeared into her house. She glowered. Every day, she was one step closer to burning the old house down. If today was the day she snapped and two monsters got caught in the blaze, there wasn't a jury on Earth that would convict her.

"Is this a monster thing, or are you two just overbearing in general?" she called at their backs.

"Both," they said in unison.

Oh, great, they'd finally found something to agree on. Too bad it wasn't grabbing their shit and leaving her house. If they hadn't given her hefty discounts, she would call the police and let the officers drag them out by their fur.

Damn them and their stupid discounts.

"I don't have time for this," Nicole sighed in defeat.

If she didn't get a move on, she wasn't going to have

enough time to fix her frizzy helmet hair for her date tonight. Ignoring the two intruders, she walked into her home and took the stairs two at a time.

Nicole had a date with two vampires, and if today was any indication of monster etiquette... they wouldn't be keeping their clothes on either.

10

NICOLE

Nicole glared at her reflection in the steam clouded mirror. It was difficult to feel cute, calm, and collected when all she could focus on was the two shifters moving around her house like two furry pinballs.

Were they moving furniture? Why did they need to make so much noise?

She gritted her teeth. Drake and Wes were seriously ruining her zen. Didn't they realize that the hours before a date were prime meditation time? This was supposed to be her time to put on her makeup, magically find the perfect outfit, and walk down the stairs feeling like a bombshell. It was a sacred ritual as old as time itself.

And two stinky boys were ruining it for her.

Nicole picked up her eyeliner. The shifters were *not* going to ruin her date with Atticus and Jasper. If that meant winged liner sharp enough to draw blood, then so be it. So help them if their continued noises made the wings crooked. They were already on paper thin ice.

Slicking on mascara, she was determined not to think about Drake and Wes anymore. She needed to focus—not an easy task when flashes of the were-cougar peeling his clothes off kept dancing through her mind.

Why did he have to have *so many* abs? And why did she so desperately wish she'd had a chance to reach out and run her fingers over them?

Nicole threw down her mascara. Clearly, her makeup zen wasn't going to happen today. Stomping into her bedroom, she ripped open the closet and rifled through her clothes.

Her makeup was a bust, and her hair was bordering on frizzy. If her outfit wasn't immaculate, she might as well just crawl into bed and call the whole thing off. If Nicole had to walk into a restaurant with two suave and sexy vampires, she damn well wasn't going to be a hot mess.

Flipping back and forth between a sunny yellow sundress and a rose red number just short enough to make any nosy grannies clutch at their pearls, she bit back a growl. What if the yellow was too yellow and made Jasper and Atticus miss the sun? What if they looked at the red dress and decided to eat her for an appetizer?

What if she was being absolutely ridiculous and they didn't give damn about what was on her body?

"Why is this so hard?" Nicole moaned.

She dragged both dresses off their hangers and threw them on her bed. Eyeing them critically, she pinched the bridge of her nose.

"I'm overthinking this."

It was just a dress—albeit a dress she was going to wear to God knows where with two monsters who looked like their suits were tailored by sin itself—but still, just a dress.

Maybe she should ask Drake and Wes what they thought?

Nicole took one step toward the door before she stopped herself. No, they didn't deserve an opinion. Not tonight. As ecstatic as she'd been with them yesterday, they were in the doghouse.

Besides, it's not like she didn't know what they would say. They would take one look at the minidress and try to lock her in her room.

Before she could reconsider, Nicole grabbed the deliciously short rose dress and slipped it over her head. She wiggled it into place and smoothed it down with her hands.

There. Now she was ready... so why didn't she feel ready?

"Stupid shifters," she grumbled to herself.

A sharp buzz dragged her out of her cloud of self-pity. Grabbing her cellphone off the nightstand, she clicked on the waiting message.

> ATTICUS & JASPER
>
> Two minutes to sundown and then we'll be on our way to you, pet. I can't wait to see your beautiful eyes again. - Jasper

Nicole took a deep breath and let it out slowly. She wasn't going to let Drake and Wes and their idiotic worries over nothing ruin her evening. Jasper and Atticus deserved better than that.

In fact... they deserved a lot better. Maybe the shifters needed a little reminder who was really in charge under her roof.

Tossing her phone on the bed, she dug through her nightstand. It had to be there somewhere. It's not like it was her favorite or anything, but she was on a time crunch—

"Aha!" The small bullet vibrator rolled into her hand, and a sly smile twisted her painted lips. "Perfect."

Nicole flopped backward onto her bed. Wriggling her hips, she pushed her skirt up over her hips. She nudged her panties to the side and stroked her pussy. Fingertips dipping into the wetness, she glided her fingertips up to her clit.

Two hunky shifters teased her distracted brain; first Wes with those carved biceps flexing constantly, and then Drake... naked... smirking Drake.

Nicole bit her lip to hold back a groan. It hadn't been fair springing all those muscles on her like that and not even giving her ample time to admire. He was a sadist, clearly.

But she certainly wasn't.

Her fingertip circled her clit in slow circles as flashes of the were-cat's cut abs and strong shoulders danced in her mind. What she wouldn't give to see his tool belt wrapped around those slim hips. Until then... Nicole could certainly imagine it.

Fumbling for her vibrator, she replaced her impatient fingers with silicone. The first gentle buzz was a bolt of pleasure through her body. She tapped the button to speed up the vibration.

As lovely as it would be to take it slow and romance herself a bit, Nicole was on a deadline.

Her hand glided up her body and squeezed her breast. The tiny bite of pressure fanned the flames in her belly, threatening to turn her quick bonfire into an inferno. Her fingers plucked at her nipple through her dress.

Her gasp filled the empty room. As she moved her vibrator in little circles, a whimper escaped her lips. If Nicole didn't find some way to keep quiet, she was going to have two shifters getting one hell of a surprise when they came bursting into her room.

Blindly grabbing for a pillow, Nicole dragged it over her face. Damn monsters. It was a little difficult to enjoy her looming orgasm when she was forced to smother herself. The only thing she wanted on top of her in that moment was a certain were-cougar.

Or werewolf. She had only gotten a glimpse from his MONSTR profile pictures, but what she had seen had promised a set of abs to rival Drake's. For a brief second, Nicole considered how incredible it would feel to be pressed between the two of them, and then it was over.

She fell over the edge, her orgasm taking her by surprise. She groaned into the pillow as pleasure scorched her from the inside out, burning under her flesh in sharp, teasing waves.

Nicole lifted the vibrator from her clit and let the air saw in and out of her lungs. Well, that was... different. Damn shifters. They were even butting into her orgasms now.

She shook her head. No, they didn't deserve to be the cause of her coming before she climbed into a car with Jasper and Atticus. She wanted a do over.

Letting the pillow drop down over her face, Nicole pressed the vibrator against the sensitive flesh between her legs and cranked up the power. This time she refused to think of Drake or Wes. The next one would belong to the two sensual vampires who looked at her like they wanted to lick her from head to toe.

From their fascinating blood red eyes to the polished lines of their luxurious suits, every gliding step they took promised her the darkest of sins. The gold rings on Atticus's hands had fascinated her. How would that cool metal feel on her skin?

Nicole bit down on her pillowcase as her moans grew louder. The strong buzz circling her clit was drowning her in pleasure. Gone was the inferno, replaced by a monsoon drowning her in crashing waves even before she came.

A flash of Jasper's wicked grin teased her mind. Those fangs... At some point she would feel them on her throat. Would it be tonight? Tomorrow? How long would they make her wait before the two vampires consumed her in every way?

The orgasm hit her hard, sweeping her away before she realized it was coming for her. Nicole screamed into her pillow. The soft weight swallowed the sound and took the brunt of her digging fingernails.

She flopped back on to the bed, her mind twirling in dizzying circles as aftershocks teased her body. Now *that* was an orgasm...

Head buried under her pillow, Nicole almost didn't hear the doorbell ring. She bolted upright, and her sanity rushed back like a splash of water to her flushed face. Cursing under her breath, she jumped off the bed and tugged her skirt back into place.

She might have gotten a little carried away and lost track of time. If she didn't hurry up and get her shoes on before all-out war broke out between the vampires and the shifters, there was no telling what in her ramshackle house would end up as collateral damage.

"I'm coming!" Nicole called from her bedroom door.

Technically, she already had. Twice.

A faint flush still burned in her cheeks as she snatched her wrap off the bed and hurried down the stairs. She paused mid-stride as her brain caught up with the rest of her.

Jasper and Atticus waited on the porch, just as breathtakingly delicious in their sleek suits as she'd been imagining. Blocking the doorway with his broad shoulders, Wes waited with a dark frown on his handsome face. Atticus flicked a piece of lint from the cuff of his jacket; he and Jasper looked utterly unbothered by the stormy werewolf doing his best to stare them down.

Someone cleared their throat. Nicole leaned over the railing and caught Drake looking up at her. Leaning against the wall, he smirked when she caught his eye. Clearly, she wasn't the only one enjoying the show.

"Don't be rude, Wes," Nicole ordered. She descended the stairs slowly, her heart hammering in her ears. She might not feel calm, but she was determined to look it.

As if he was reading her thoughts, Drake raised an eyebrow. Nicole watched his nostrils flare as she drew closer, and a slow grin stretched across his lips. Moving slowly for her eyes to follow, he reached down and adjusted the front of his gray sweatpants.

Fluttering her lashes innocently, she walked past him without a second glance. Drake barked out a laugh. He pushed off the wall and walked out of the room, leaving her with two patient vampires and one pissed off werewolf.

All three of them stiffened as Nicole walked to the door. The sharp click of her heels was the only noise in the silent hall. She stopped beside them and motioned for Wes to move out of the way.

Ignoring her, the wolf leaned in close and inhaled her scent. His eyes gleamed.

"Why are they here?" he growled.

Nicole bit her lower lip before an evil grin could give her away. She passed her frilly shawl to Wes and turned to let him wrap it around her shoulders.

"We have a date," Jasper answered for her.

"Why do they get a second date?" The werewolf's words were tight, but his hands were gentle as he settled her wrap over her shoulders.

"Because they asked for one," Nicole said smoothly. She turned around and patted his arm. "You didn't."

He gaped. "But—"

"Dibs on tomorrow night!" Drake called from the kitchen.

"You can't dibs—" Wes argued.

93

"Just did!"

Atticus cleared his throat before their argument could turn into a shouting match. "We didn't realize this was going to be another group date..."

"It isn't," Nicole assured him. Squeezing past the immovable werewolf, she stepped onto the porch. "You said you wanted some alone time with just me."

The vampires exchanged a look and raised their eyebrows at the scowling monster standing over her shoulder.

"In case you weren't aware, pet... you have a werewolf and a were-cougar in your house," Jasper laughed. "It's not exactly 'alone time' if they tag along."

"Oh, I'm very aware, which is why they're staying here." Nicole waved at Wes over her shoulder and threaded her arms through Atticus and Jasper's. "Goodnight, Wes."

"But—"

"You wanted to keep an eye on the house, so feel free to keep an eye on it." She smiled brightly at him. "I never said I would be staying in."

Walking away on the arms of two vampires, Nicole felt more badass than she ever had in her life. Fuck pre-date rituals. Vibrators and dramatic exits were the only confidence booster she'd ever need again.

11

ATTICUS

Atticus took a deep breath of Nicole's candied scent. Even with all aromas of the trees and flowers of the dark night, she overpowered everything with her tempting presence. His mouth was watering by the time they climbed into the back of the limousine.

"A limo?" she raised her eyebrows.

Was it overkill? Undoubtedly, but Atticus was going to spoil her rotten... and he didn't want to argue with Jasper about who got to sit next to her in the car tonight.

He raised her hands to his lips and brushed a kiss over her knuckles. Thank the stars they did. He would've ripped Jasper's head off for a chance to sit next to her smelling like a lusty treat.

How the werewolf had stopped himself from grabbing her before she walked out the door, he had no idea. He was clenching his fists to stop himself from burying them in her hair and tipping her head back for better access to the cleavage teasing from her low neckline.

"You look stunning, love."

Her cheeks flushed. "Thank you."

"I hope you like French food." Jasper smiled and took

her other hands in his. "Café Bleu has the best wine selection in the city, and it's not too far from here."

"I don't actually know," she laughed, the sound chiming in the quiet limousine. "I don't think I've ever had French food."

"It's to die for," Atticus promised.

The fascinating human snorted. "Maybe not the most comforting thing to hear on a date with two vampires."

All three of them laughed. Fair enough.

"Maybe that wasn't the best choice of words," he agreed. "Though you have nothing to fear from us, love. In fact, we fully intend to spoil you rotten."

Her dark brows raised. Nicole looked like she wanted to ask what exactly that would entail, but the car pulled to a stop outside the restaurant at that moment.

Atticus generously allowed Jasper to help her from the car. Nicole threaded her arm through his as he slid out of the limo to stand beside them, her warm curves pressed against his side. If he were a less vampire, he might consider dragging her back to the car and having his way with her in the backseat.

But he was a gentleman, and the evening had only just begun.

He led them inside. The hostess smiled brightly and greeted them by name. Leading them to their usual table in the back of the restaurant, she passed a singular menu to Nicole.

She raised her eyebrows as she took a seat. "You two must come here often if they know you well enough not to bother giving you menus."

Jasper shrugged. "Once or twice a month... for two generations."

Nicole choked on a sip of water. "Two generations?"

Laughing, Atticus took his hand in hers and stroked his thumb over her knuckles.

"We're over two-hundred years old, love. We've had a good deal of time to kill."

Jasper shook his head, the corner of his mouth turning down. Right, maybe don't causally use words like "kill." Bagged blood hadn't always been an option—something neither of them wanted Nicole to focus on.

"Two hundred?" Her mouth gaped open. "I can't even imagine the things you must have seen. You were right there in the middle of world events."

"The bad thing about world events is that they don't always seem important until they're over," Jasper laughed. "That's how Atticus got stuck in Greece in 1821... right as they declared their war for independence. He thought it would be over in a week and ended up trapped on an island for almost a decade."

"In my defense... I was only in my thirties at the time, and Mykonos was lovely."

Nicole laughed. "I would say at least you had plenty of beach time, but..."

Atticus snorted. She wasn't wrong. Spending a decade on a sunny island in the Aegean wasn't all it was cracked up to be when you were trapped inside all day. He couldn't even work on his tan.

The waitress walked by and placed a bottle of wine on the table. They didn't even have to ask what they wanted anymore. It was nice to be a regular.

"What can I get you, honey?" she asked Nicole.

"Um." She glanced down at the menu. "Honestly, I have no idea what any of this is."

"How about the coq au vin? It's the chef's specialty."

"Sounds great."

Nicole waited until the waitress was out of ear shot

before she leaned in and whispered to the two vampires. "What exactly did I just order?"

"Chicken stew." Jasper grinned. "You could have just asked her."

The delectable human shrugged. "I'm trying to step outside my comfort zone more."

Atticus poured the wine into three glasses. So that was why she was on a dating site for monsters. He and Jasper had been curious after they'd met the sweet little flower—she didn't exactly seem the type who frequented such services.

It wasn't long before they had finished off the first bottle of wine. The waitress flitted by, settling Nicole's plate in front of her and replacing the empty bottle with the next selection.

Atticus watched in fascination as she swirled her spoon through the dish and spooned the first bite into her mouth. The tip of her pink tongue swiped over her lips, and Nicole made a satisfied noise and went in for a second bite.

He looked up at Jasper and saw the same hunger he felt gnawing at his belly reflected in his red eyes. Every little noise and happy sigh was a shock to his body. He shifted in his seat, his cock hardening.

Nicole was halfway through the meal before Jasper put his wineglass down with a little too much force. Atticus shot him a look. She looked up curiously, her eyes lingering on the cracked glass.

"Sorry, pet," the vampire said sheepishly. "But you're driving me crazy."

"What?"

"The sounds you're making." A wry smile had the vampire reaching across the table and raising her hand to his lips. "It's more than a little bit tempting."

"Tempting?" Nicole glanced back and forth between them. "What do you mean?"

"Jasper—"

Ignoring the warning, his old friend dragged his tongue over her knuckles and watched her face with fiery eyes. "You have no ideas what those little sounds are doing to my cock, pet."

Cheeks turning red, she looked down at her plate. "I was just eating."

"Yes, and I like the way you eat."

Jasper gave her knuckles one last kiss before replacing her hand on the table. Shaking his head, Atticus topped off his wine. Two-hundred years old, and the fool still couldn't control himself. If he ruined this for them, Atticus was going to stake the idiot out on the lawn for the sunrise to find.

Nicole only took a couple more bites of food, her cheeks burning red with every spoonful. Her enticing scent bloomed around them, and Atticus stiffened in his seat.

Okay, maybe Jasper hadn't ruined it after all. The smell of her lust washed over them, teasing and tormenting in a way her precious little sounds never could.

The dinner ended quietly, both vampires focused on not climbing over the table and dragging the sweet human into their laps. They walked Nicole out to the limo and climbed into the backseat, but as soon as the doors closed, Atticus knew it was a mistake. Inside the car, there was no relief.

"You're killing me, pet," Jasper groaned.

"I didn't do anything!"

"You don't have to do anything," he sighed. "Just sitting next to you is making my cock hard."

Nicole frowned as the vampire's head rocked back against the seat. She looked over at Atticus, and her pink lips parted as she met the hunger in his eyes.

"We can smell you, Nicole. Every passionate thought,

every time you squeeze your thighs together, every time you look at us like you're undressing us with your eyes. We can smell the desire pouring off you."

Her breath hitched in her chest, her breasts straining against her tight dress. His eyes fluttered shut as he savored the heady scent filling the car. The soft slide of silk tickled his ears. He opened his eyes and looked down at her tanned thighs rubbing together under her skirt.

Glancing over Nicole's head, he caught Jasper's eye. He grinned wickedly. Good, it was always easier when they were on the same wavelength.

He placed his hand on her knee, and Nicole jumped. Blinking up at him, she couldn't hide her soft gasp as his fingers glided up her thigh.

"I told you earlier, love." Atticus leaned close enough to smell the blood pooling in her blushing cheeks. "We have every intention of spoiling you rotten. You don't even have to ask."

Jasper's hand stroked her other thigh. "And by 'spoil', he means that he has no intention of letting you leave this car before you've come all over his fingers."

Her wide eyes flicked back and forth between them. "You don't have to—"

Atticus laughed; he couldn't help himself. She was sweeter then even she knew.

"Have to? Love, I've been thinking about this since you walked down the stairs in this tiny scrap of a dress." Fingers petting further up her thigh, he watched Nicole's chest rise and fall. "If you want us to stop, tell us, and we will. You have my word."

Her mouth opened and closed. Biting her lip, she glanced once more at Jasper before nodding quickly. Nicole shifted in her seat and spread her legs wider.

Not wide enough. The two vampires each cupped a

hand behind a knee and draped her thigh over their own. Silky skirt riding up to her hips, nothing but a tiny scrap of lace hiding her from them.

Atticus licked his lips. It was taking every shred of restraint not to drop to his knees and replace Nicole's tiny panties with his tongue. That would be too much for their precious human.

The last thing they wanted to do was scare her away, not when they craved her as badly as they did. No, Atticus planned to lure her in with kisses and gifts and gentle touches. By the time Nicole realized she was well and truly claimed, she would already be the center of their world.

He nodded at Jasper. The blond vampire cupped her jaw and turned her face to capture her lips. Jasper devoured her mouth, his tongue teasing her own.

As much as he hated to tear his eyes from the delectable sight, Atticus had waited long enough to touch her, and he was done waiting. His hand glided up her open thighs. Gently tugging aside her panties, he traced a fingertip over the seam of her tempting pussy.

Nicole gasped against Jasper's mouth, tipping her face back for Atticus to watch as he planted wet, sucking kisses under her jaw. Atticus had a front row view of her moaning lips when the first fingertip brushed her clit.

The sweet human jerked like she was being electrocuted. Gasping, she rocked her hips forward for more. He smiled and rewarded her with a kiss. It was his turn to taste her moan as his fingers moved deeper into the silky wetness between her legs.

Nicole watched him, eyes wide and gleaming. Fingers plucked desperately at their pantlegs as the first waves of pleasure washed over her. Jasper laughed against her throat.

"Such a needy little human." Licking the line of her jaw, Jasper captured her mouth.

Atticus carried on with his teasing. Each frenzied jerk of her hips was rewarded with a slow stroke to her throbbing clit, just enough to push her one tiny step closer to relief but never enough to let her come. No, Nicole would come with his fingers deep inside of her, or not at all.

He dipped his fingertips into her center, and her wanton moans filled the silent car. Her quiet panting peppered the air.

"P—please!" she gasped.

Jasper pinched her nipples through the front of her dress. "I think she wants to come, Atticus. What do you think?"

"I'm not sure she's ready." He pressed his fingers deeper into the dripping heat of her pussy. Stroking slowly, he reached for that special spot that would drive her mad. "Are you, Nicole? Are you ready to come for us?"

"Yes!" the sweet human whimpered. "Please!"

Atticus nuzzled her flushed cheeks. He had promised to spoil her, after all.

Thumb working her clit, he stroked her g-spot with his fingertips. Nicole arched off the seat. Pressing her back down, Jasper caught her lips and plundered her loud moans.

Atticus smiled as her pussy clenched around his fingers and he was rewarded with a fresh rush of moisture. He continued to tease until her legs trembled.

"Good girl," he praised.

The car pulled to a stop, and the vampires' heads shot up to glance out the window. Parked in her driveway, a part of him mourned the loss that would soon be coming when they said goodbye for the evening.

Still glassy-eyed, Nicole didn't even look up as they opened their doors. Atticus gently lifted her from her seat and steadied her on her feet. He smoothed her dress back into place. The shifters might smell the sweetness between her legs, but they didn't need to see it. What had happened in the back of the limo was only for Nicole, Jasper, and himself.

Tucking her under his arm, Atticus led her up the driveway. Jasper appeared on her other side, his hand stroking her back as they walked her to her front door and waited until she opened it wide. Stroking her jaw, Jasper kissed her hard and whispered something in her ear.

Nicole turned to him, still more than a little dazed from her crashing orgasm. Atticus raised his hand to his mouth and licked his fingers clean. She watched him, her teeth teasing her lip, and a fresh wave of her rich, lusty scent filled the dark night.

Atticus leaned forward and kissed her. Tongue swiping across the seam of her lips, he hoped at least of a little of her sweetness was left behind for her to taste. He pulled away and nudged her through the door.

Bright, glowing eyes watched her from the darkness of her home; the shifters, awake and ever watchful. They gave her a sniff and Jasper smirked.

"Goodnight, pet."

They waited until they heard the lock slide home before they turned back to the driveway. The two old friends walked in silence back to the limo. It wasn't until they were both seated and once again enveloped in the cloud of Nicole's scent that they dared speak.

"She's perfect." Jasper sighed. "I'm even willing to share her with the damn shifters."

Hell, Atticus would share the precious human with every monster in town, so long as a part of her belonged to him.

"Whatever it takes."

12

HAWTHORNE

Hawthorne was definitely *not* being creepy. Nope, not at all. He was just dropping off breakfast. That was totally normal when you'd only been on one date with a woman, right?

Or maybe it wasn't. But who wanted normal anyway?

Besides, creepy or not, it wasn't Hawthorne's fault. If Nicole didn't want him to worry about her wellbeing, she shouldn't have casually told him that someone was sabotaging her house. Maybe she didn't fully believe it, but he had seen the look on the were-cat's face. Someone was messing with her.

He parked his truck in the driveway. Carefully balancing a small bouquet of flowers on the box of pastries, Hawthorne took a deep breath. Hopefully, Nicole didn't mind the pink roses he had mixed in with the wildflowers. Roses could be polarizing, especially mixed with something like wildflowers, but they reminded him of her blushing cheeks and...

"Stop stalling," the fae muttered to himself.

Sure, the werewolf and the cat had stayed the night, but

that didn't mean she didn't like him too. He was just overthinking it again.

Hawthorne climbed out of the truck and jogged up the sagging porch steps before he could talk himself out of it. He knocked on the door. Trying not to fidget while he waited, he stared at the vibrant flower petals.

Maybe he should have left the anemones out...

The door swung open, and Nicole blinked at him from the other side. Hawthorne stared at the tiny, winged piglets on her pajama pants and the tangled hair falling out of her messy bun. She raised a chipped coffee mug to her mouth and took a sip of coffee.

He opened and closed his mouth. Every anxious thought had tumbled right out of his head at the sight of her. Gorgeous. Absolutely gorgeous.

Hawthorne had thought she was beautiful dressed up for that first group date, as well as when she'd been laughing and clutching her iced coffee at the farmers' market, but fresh-out-of-bed Nicole was a whole other level of adorable.

"Is that a pickle?" he finally managed to ask.

The sleepy human turned her battered mug to study the green blob painted on the ceramic. "Yes. I'm kind of a big dill," Nicole yawned. "It says so on the mug."

Hawthorne didn't know whether to laugh or pour her another cup of coffee. He had a feeling she wasn't going to remember most of this interaction once her brain was fully awake and if she did, she would be cursing herself.

Might as well make the best of it.

He leaned forward and pressed a light kiss against her smooth cheek. The tips of his ears burned hot as he stepped back. Worth it.

"I brought you flowers," Hawthorne said to cover the silence as he thrust the bouquet into her arms.

She smiled at the petals tickling her nose. "They're beautiful—"

A car door shut behind them, and they both turned to study the dark luxury car parked beside his dirty truck. The two vampires slid out from the front of the car and grabbed matching leather bags from the backseat.

Hawthorne's pale brows soared as they strolled toward them. Were they even aware the sun was going to rise over the horizon any minute now? Did they care?

"Cutting it kind of close, aren't you?" the fae said drily.

"We're two hundred years old," Jasper yawned. "What's immortality without a little risk?"

The two vampires each pressed a kiss against Nicole's cheek and stepped neatly around her into the house. Hawthorne was too busy grumbling to notice her frown. He'd bet the contents of every one of his greenhouses that they had layered their kisses on top of his on purpose.

"What are you doing?" Nicole asked, drawing him out of his head.

Atticus tucked an errant strand of hair back into her messy bun and smiled gently.

"You didn't really think we were going to trust the house pets to keep you safe, did you?"

"We'll be in the attic if you need us." Jasper winked and headed for the stairs.

"There's no sabotage, for fuck's sake!" Nicole shouted at their backs. "And don't touch the squirrels!"

Shaking his head, Hawthorne bit his lip to keep from laughing. The pretty little human was going to need to up her game if she wanted to roust them all from her house. Once a monster found a home it liked, they were harder to get out than termites.

"You have squirrels for house pets?" he teased.

"Of course not. They moved into the attic all on their own."

Woodland pests aside, Hawthorne didn't sense any other animals in the house. What—?

"The shifters?" he laughed as it hit him.

"Drake and Wes took it upon themselves to move in permanently," she grumbled. "What started as them taking the couch to 'keep an eye on me' has ended with them staking claim to their own bedrooms this morning. I was in the middle of trying to throw them out of my house when you drove up."

He glanced at the pastry box he was still clutching to his chest. It was a good thing he'd gotten the big assortment. If Nicole wasn't careful, the furballs would eat her out of house and home.

"And now, Atticus and Jasper," she sighed. "At this point, maybe I should just give up."

"Well, it's not like you can kick the vampires out right now anyway."

Her eyes narrowed. "What?"

Hawthorne pointed over his shoulder. The sun was just rising over the horizon and turning the sky pink—the same pink of her cheeks as she glared at the sky.

"Those tricky bastards. They timed it like that on purpose, didn't they?"

"Probably."

Honestly, he wouldn't put it past them. The fae hadn't gotten to know them very well on their disastrous group date, but he didn't get the impression that much got in Atticus's way when he wanted something. Especially with the sly-eyed Jasper at his back.

She scrubbed a hand over her tangled bun and sighed. "I didn't even invite them in. I thought vampires had to be invited over the threshold or something."

"That's a myth."

Hawthorne was definitely going to have to give her some tips if she didn't want to be steamrolled by the horde of monsters at her door. Maybe over coffee. Nicole was definitely going to need a refill to get through the morning with her sanity intact.

An enormous cat came hissing out the door. It took one look at him and settled, the fur on its back smoothing out. Apparently, Drake wasn't a morning person either.

The cougar shifter rubbed against Nicole's legs until she gave him a scratch behind the ears. Satisfied, he went bounding off the edge of the porch. They watched his fluffy tail vanish into the trees in silence.

"If you want the shifters out of your house, you're definitely going to want to stop petting them," Hawthorne advised. "They're never going to leave if they know they can bully you into ear scratches."

"Well, fuck." Nicole pinched the bridge of her nose. "Do you want to move yourself in? Everyone else seems to be making themselves comfortable."

"I thought you'd never ask," he said quickly.

Pushing the box of pastries into her hands, Hawthorne started back to his truck.

"I was joking!" she called behind him.

He ignored her. Monsters didn't do take-backs. She was as stuck with him now as she was the shifters and vampires. Whether Nicole liked it or not, she had just stumbled her way into five monster roommates... all of whom were already obsessed with her.

Hawthorne fished in the back of his truck for the stained overnight bag he kept for emergencies. *Prepare for anything.* That was the Elf Scout motto, and he'd been the number one badge earner for three years straight in middle school.

Not that he was about to tell anyone that.

Dragging the bag out from under a pile of dirt-covered pots, he tossed it on the hood of his truck and unzipped it. If he was going to be stuck around that werewolf for a while, he was going to need some allergy meds. A *lot* of allergy meds.

"Is everyone moving in?" a deep voice growled from the dark.

Hawthorne nearly jumped out of his skin. Clenching his fists, it was all he could do not to curse Drake into a bush as he came walking out of the foliage around the house. It would serve the naked bastard right.

"It looks like it," the fae grumbled. "The vampires showed up right before sunrise."

"Good. The more of us keeping an eye on Nicole, the better." The solemn were-cougar nodded toward the yard. "I need your opinion on something."

Sighing, Hawthorne shouldered his bag. He followed after Drake and kept his eyes firmly on the sky and not his swinging dick.

Fucking shifters. What, were they allergic to pants?

Hawthorne stumbled to a stop before Drake did. There was something wrong with the backyard. His head shot up. He was already bristling when the cougar started to explain.

"Someone dumped weedkiller on the back lawn," Drake growled. "A couple gallons at least."

A shiver crawled down the elf's back. So that's what he was feeling: the death of thousands of blades of grass.

Dropping his bag on the ground, Hawthorne followed the feeling to an enormous patch of uneven lawn. The sharp smell of weedkiller stabbed his nose.

"Can you stop it from dying?" Drake asked quietly.

"Some of it, but not all." He raised his eyes from the dying grass and met his gaze. "Why?"

"I don't want Nicole to freak out." His thick arms crossed

over his chest. "Someone is screwing with her, and we'll take care of it as soon as we can find the bastard, but I don't want her to be scared."

And from the dark look on the shifters face, Hawthorne didn't have to wonder how he would "take care of it." The fae was feeling a little murderous himself at the moment.

He peeled off his flannel shirt and tied it around his waist. It was his favorite shirt, and if the magic grew too strong, the glyphs tattooed on his arms would burn little holes in the sleeves.

He'd learned that lesson at an early age.

Crouching down, Hawthorne buried his fingertips in the ground. Magic spilled outward, moving beneath the earth in gentle waves. He was farther from a ley line than he would have liked, but he could still save some of it.

"I can revive most of it, but the patch with the most concentrated poison is a total loss."

It was a good thing Drake had chosen to go for a morning run in his fur. If they had caught it any later, Nicole would have lost her entire lawn.

"How large of an area is a goner?"

Hawthorne nodded at the patch of grass.

"I can handle that part." Drake waved him on. "You do your bit."

The blue glyphs on the fae's arms glowed as he channeled the energy into the right spots and started to chant quietly. It wouldn't be perfect, but he could always spread a little grass seed on the brown patches.

"That should do it," he sighed. Dragging his fingers from the earth, he severed the link to the plants around him. A sharp pain pulsed in his temple. "Ooof. I definitely should've eaten something first."

"Come on." Drake scooped up his bag and led him to the house. "We need to make sure Nicole eats anyway."

Hawthorne smiled. He wasn't sure how their sweet human would feel about being babied, but today, he really didn't care. Someone had poisoned her lawn.

His smile faded. By the time he was sitting at Nicole's kitchen table, he was silently freaking out. A thousand worries were running through his head.

Why would anyone want to ruin her lawn? Or sabotage her house at all? That was how they had ended up laying claim to her house after all. Someone was messing with Nicole, even if she didn't realize it yet.

Drake placed a jug of orange juice and a full pot of coffee on the table. Thank Gaia, he had found some sweatpants. Hawthorne didn't want to see any kind of sausage at the breakfast table... especially if it were attached to another man.

He grabbed a danish out of the box before thoughts of shifter dick could ruin his appetite. Raising the pastry to his mouth, he paused as Nicole walked into the room. The flying piglet pajamas had been replaced with sleek leggings and a t-shirt, and her sleepy eyes were bright—if somewhat apprehensive— as she took a seat at the table.

The pretty human frowned. "Did anyone see where my lucky mug went?"

Waving the empty pickle cup, Drake filled it with coffee and took a small sip. He passed it to Nicole and dropped into the seat next to her.

"You'd better grab your food before the wolf gets in here," Hawthorne warned her. He'd been serious about shifter appetites. They made his grocery budget look like a pittance.

As if summoned by his words, Wes walked into the room rubbing a towel over his wet hair. Nicole quickly grabbed a croissant from the box and shot the fae a grateful smile.

His belly warmed even as the tips of his ears started to

burn again. If pastries and flowers were enough to get him smiles, Hawthorne would bury her in pain au chocolat and daisies.

The conversation around the table settled into the occasional yawn and muffled chewing, and his mind began to wander back to the dead grass in the yard.

"I'd like to grow the hedges a bit," he interrupted Wes and Drake's growling argument about orange juice pulp. "I think it would be better if the house was harder to see from the road."

Nicole paused, her coffee cup halfway to her mouth. "You're going to what?"

"Grow them."

That's what fae did. They spoke to the Earth and helped it reach its full potential.

"He's going to stick his hands in the dirt and sweet talk the bushes into growing," Wes snorted.

Her soft brown eyes lit up. "Seriously?"

"In short, yes."

It was probably better not to overwhelm her with the nitty gritty of forest magic. Nicole had looked like she was magic trick away from bolting all morning.

"Can I watch?"

His ears burned bright red. Hawthorne said a silent prayer to Gaia that his hair was covering the tips. Could he even channel energy with Nicole watching him so intently? He'd have to find a way when the time came.

"Of course," he promised. Like he was going to say no?

"Oh my God, that's going to be so cool!"

They all smiled at her excited words. Hawthorne was pretty sure that if she asked for the moon, they would find a way to get it for her. Five dangerous monsters, all ensnared by one sweet little human.

She might not know it yet, but they were hers.

13

NICOLE

"And again, thank you so much for doing this over video call," Nicole said gratefully.

The interviewer on her screen waved away her thanks. The company she had been on the way to interview with had been surprisingly understanding when she'd told them she was having car trouble.

"Honestly, we're so desperate for help, you could have crashed your car through the lobby, and we still would have given you a sign on bonus," Marta laughed.

A bonus. If she didn't think it would scare the kind Human Resources manager, Nicole would have burst into tears.

"Do you have any more questions for me?"

"Just one. When can you—?"

A loud crash from the living room interrupted the interviewer, and the knots in Nicole's stomach tightened. She had no idea what Drake and Hawthorne were doing down there, but they were one more interruption away from being buried alive in her backyard.

"*Will you shut up?*" A loud voice boomed from the attic. "*Some of us are trying to sleep!*"

Nicole pinched the bridge of her nose. Dead. They were all dead to her.

"Um... is everything okay?" Marta asked.

"My roommates," she sighed. "It's a long story, but let's just say working from home won't be in the cards for me."

"Not a problem. Can you come in tomorrow?"

Her heart stopped. "To-tomorrow?"

"For paperwork." Marta smiled. "The job is yours if you want it."

Okay, now she really was going to cry. Nicole nodded, not trusting herself to speak.

"Excellent. I'll email you the details and the offer letter, and I'll see you tomorrow!"

The screen went black as Marta waved goodbye. Nicole stared at her reflection, her mouth still gaping like a fish. She got the job.

She got the motherfucking job!

Nicole jumped out of her seat and screamed into her hands. Over a decade of work, countless hours studying and pulling all-nighters on term papers, and *she got the job*!

Loud voices carried from downstairs, and a tiny cloud passed over her glee. Apparently, the monsters in the house hadn't understood what "be quiet for the next hour or you're all dead" meant.

Nicole hurried down the stairs. Hawthorne stood across from Drake and Wes, his arms folded over his chest. The shifters glowered back at him. If they started a brawl in her living room, there was no way her sagging couch would survive it.

"I demand a recall," Hawthorne growled.

"No—"

"Not a chance—"

"What the hell is going on?" she interrupted.

"The fae is pouting that he wasn't informed about the dibs system," Wes answered.

"Dibs system?"

"For dates. Drake called first dibs after the vampires, then me. That leaves Hawthorne, and he's demanding a redo since he wasn't there."

They had to be fucking with her. There's no way they were seriously arguing about this when she was supposed to be in the middle of a job interview. Not even one of them had asked her how it went yet.

"All dibs are revoked," Nicole snapped.

"What—?"

"But—"

"Excellent."

"You're all in the penalty box until further notice. No kisses, no handholding, nothing." If they couldn't behave and act like gentlemen, she was going to treat them like the scoundrels they were. "The interview went great, by the way. Thanks for asking."

All three sucked in a breath. Wes had the shame to look down at his shoes.

"Did you get the job?" Drake asked carefully.

"Yes," she snapped. They were seriously dimming her triumphant buzz. "No thanks to you three yelling and banging things around down here."

"If we apologize and order pizza...will we be forgiven?" Hawthorne asked.

Nicole's arms folded over her chest. She wasn't sure how long she was going to make them suffer yet, but it was hard to be annoyed when all three monsters were looking at her with puppy dog eyes.

"Pizza might shorten your sentence."

How much remained to be seen.

The three men shot her one last apologetic look and

disappeared in different directions. Flopping onto her couch, she sighed. Finally, some blessed silence.

A wave of euphoria crashed through her, and she started to giggle.

She had a job. An actual, grown-up job with health insurance and a retirement plan. Hell, she even had dental now.

Nicole was one step closer to wriggling out from under her crushing debt. One step closer to buying name brand toothpaste and being able to breathe easily when her credit card bill came in the mail.

She wasn't sure how long she lay there and stared at the ceiling in blissful silence, but it wasn't long enough. A knock pounded on the front door. Nicole raised her head and sighed.

Back to reality.

She dragged herself upright and padded down the hall. Tripping over someone's muddy boots, Nicole yelped. Pain stabbed at her toes. She cursed under her breath and ripped open the front door.

"What?"

Miri blinked, her hand still raised to knock again.

"I'm really loving that murderous glint in your eye," she deadpanned. Using her free hand, she brushed her bright curls off her shoulder. "You just need to practice balling up your fist and yelling at the neighborhood kids to get off your lawn, and then I think you can officially deem yourself a 'curmudgeon.'"

Nicole sighed. "Sorry. It's been a... day... week... I don't even know anymore."

Her car breaking down, monsters moving in, possibly being sabotaged by a stranger. All that on top of job interviews, and she was lucky that she hadn't had a nervous breakdown.

Her gaze dropped to the tight leggings barely restraining her friend's curvy hips and the yoga mat slung over her shoulder. A knot formed in her stomach.

"Did we have plans?" In all the chaos of having five monsters bustling around her house at all hours, she could barely remember if she brushed her teeth, let alone made plans. "I'm sorry— wait, a minute. It's a Wednesday. Shouldn't you be teaching some kids long division or something?"

Miri squinted at her. "I teach... kindergarten."

"Do they not learn long division?"

"More like finger painting and their ABCs. And no, we didn't have plans," Miri reassured her. "It's an inservice day. My meetings are done for the day, so I thought I'd do a quick yoga class."

And yet somehow, Nicole wasn't any less confused than she had been when she opened the door. Had someone put decaf in the coffee maker or was her brain just running slow?

"A yoga class... in my living room?"

"No, you donut." Laughing, Miri raised her rolled up mat. "I have a giant tear in my yoga mat and haven't had a chance to replace it yet. I just wanted to see if I could steal yours for today."

"Oh! Why didn't you lead with that?"

She shrugged. "You opened the door like an avenging fury. I wanted to see where you were going with it."

Nicole shook her head. Why couldn't she have normal friends? Preferably friends who texted before they showed up at her door and purloined her belongings.

"Come on in. It'll take me a minute to find mine."

Miri followed her into the house, and her sharp eyes immediately landed on the dirty boots waiting by the door.

Ignoring her questioning look, Nicole opened the hall closet and started digging.

"I know it's in here somewhere," she muttered as she pulled out a broken umbrella. "It's not like I've used it since the last time you tried dragging me to hot yoga."

A dust bunny landed on her nose, and Nicole sneezed. Would it kill her to do some spring cleaning? Maybe she could convince Hawthorne and Wes that they would earn her undying devotion by decluttering her closets. Honestly, it would probably work.

Nicole wasn't too proud to admit that she would happily jump into bed with the first person who gave her house a proper dusting.

"Aha!" Raising the yoga mat over her head in victory, she spun back to an inexplicably empty hallway. "Um, Miri?"

"Kitchen!"

Nicole followed her voice down the hall. A bemused smile on her freckled face, Miri stood beside a pair of muscled legs poking out from under the sink. From the bare abdomen and tools scattered around the narrow hips, she was guessing it was Drake.

Fixing her sink, apparently. She hadn't known there was anything wrong with it.

Miri cocked her head to the side and studied the golden hair sprinkling his abs and disappearing under the edge of his boxers.

"Hand me that big, red wrench, will ya?" the cougar growled.

Nicole stepped past her and snatched the heavy tool off the ground. Catching his bemused gray graze under the sink, she shook her head and dropped it into his hand.

When she looked back at Miri, the cheeky teacher was watching her with a sly grin.

"So… last night's dinner date went well?" She flicked her

eyes back to Drake and bit her lip. "Or maybe he was breakfast?"

"Out!"

Nicole shoved the yoga mat into her arms and dragged her laughing friend back to the front door. She could just make out the sound of the cougar chuckling behind them.

Damn her. Juggling five of them was hard enough without Miri giving the monsters fodder to tease her with.

Nicole opened the door. "Goodbye, Miri."

"God, those jeans look painted on." She swooned against the door frame. "On a scale of one to ten, how big is *his* wrench?"

"*Goodbye, Miri!*"

Her laughter followed her through the door and down the driveway. Oh, wait. She almost forgot.

Nicole tugged open the door and poked her head outside. "*I got the job!*"

Miri honked her horn and cheered before pulling out of the driveway. Smiling to herself, Nicole closed the door and started shoving the closet debris back into place.

By the time Nicole made it back to the kitchen, Drake was upright and bent over the sink. She paused in the doorway; that man really liked to test the structural integrity of denim. If his jeans stretched any tighter over his muscled ass, they would split wide open.

It was really difficult to be annoyed with a view like that.

"Can you hand me that blue hose, or do you need a little longer to admire my ass?" the cougar asked.

Nicole's stomach yo-yoed. How did he...?

"I need another thirty seconds."

There was no point pretending. She was already caught, and all her monsters owed her one today.

Drake laughed. "If you pass me the hose, you might even be allowed to touch... if that's allowed in the penalty box."

Smart ass.

Rolling her eyes, Nicole grabbed the hose he pointed at and pressed it into his hand. Drake tossed it in the sink. A callused hand caught her wrist and tugged her in close. He pressed her back into the counter, his hips pinning her in place.

She looked up into his gleaming eyes and swallowed. Why did the world suddenly feel like it was spinning off its axis?

14

NICOLE

Heart hammering in her chest, Nicole didn't dare turn away as his face lowered. Soft lips slanted over hers, the minty taste of his gum teasing her tongue as her lips parted. The were-cat nibbled at her lower lip, sinking every bit of his hunger into the all-consuming kiss.

Fuck. If she'd known the cougar could kiss like the devil, she wouldn't have dragged her feet about letting him move himself into her house. She would have hauled him through the door by his belt buckle.

Nicole pressed against him as her hands skimmed up his bare chest to clutch at his shoulders and drag him closer.

"Ahem," a throat cleared on the other side of the kitchen. "I guess pizza really did shorten our sentence."

She pulled away, their lips parting with a pop. Someone had a death wish.

Drake growled, the rumbling sound vibrated between them as Nicole squirmed away. She craned her neck and looked over his broad shoulder.

Hawthorne stood awkwardly by the back door, a stack of

pizza boxes balanced precariously in his arms as he waited for her to untangle herself from the shifter.

"You have terrible timing," Drake growled, his warm hand smoothing down her back.

Stepping back with a sigh, he took the boxes from Hawthorne and set them on the kitchen table.

"That was fast. Did you sprint to the pizza place?"

"No, I had already ordered it before we messed up Nicole's interview." He smiled apologetically before turning back to the grouchy cat. "Next time, text me if you're getting handsy. I'll take a lap around the block to give you more time to earn us some extra forgiveness."

Nicole ignored the satisfied grin on the cougar's face and grabbed a stack of plates. She had no idea why she was embarrassed. She was a grown woman. The monsters had known what they were getting into when they moved themselves into her house.

So why did she feel like she needed to taste Hawthorne's lips to make it even?

"Who's getting handsy?" Wes asked as he followed the smell of pepperoni into the room.

"The cougar."

He turned and fixed the shy fae with a sympathetic look. "Just say 'no,' Hawthorne. He's not worth the heartbreak."

"I definitely am," Drake said breezily.

He leaned around Nicole and started flipping open pizza boxes. His bare abs brushed her back. Biting her lip, she swallowed her tiny moan at the hard length pressing against her ass.

Hawthorne really did have terrible timing. Terrible, terrible timing.

"Leave me some peppers and pineapple," the inconvenient fae grumbled.

"Don't worry, bud," Wes laughed. "That's all you and Nicole."

She studied the pile of meat covered slices appearing on Drake's plate. The wolf wasn't joking. Most of the pizzas were laden with pepperoni and sausage. A singular pizza was left untouched for the vegetarian elf.

It's a good thing they didn't eat nearly as much as the shifters. The grocery bill was already climbing high enough with two of them under her roof.

"You're a garbage disposal." Hawthorne shook his head at the depleting boxes. "By the way, you need to let me know what you want for the gazebo. I have some Persian ivy and lilac cuttings that would do nicely."

"Who me?" Nicole looked around. "Wait, what gazebo?"

"No, me. We're putting a gazebo in the backyard," Drake said around a mouthful of pepperoni.

"But that wasn't in your quote."

A tendril of guilt wormed its way deep into her gut. They were starting to go overboard with all these discounts.

Sure, that had sort of been the point of this whole mess, but they were so damn sweet about it. She didn't even care if they were doing it out of pity or concern that her house was going to collapse right on top of her head. They were doing too much.

Drake shrugged and piled more pizza onto his already towering plate.

"I should have enough scrap laying around, and elf boy can magic up some plants easily enough."

He made eye contact with Hawthorne over the pizza box, and a silent look passed between them. Eyes narrowing, Nicole studied them both. She had no idea what was going on, but she was pretty sure she didn't like it. Hawthorne caught her suspicious frown and quickly jammed a slice of pizza into his mouth.

She definitely didn't like it. It was one thing when they were all working separately to woo her, but this was starting to feel like collusion. If all five of them decided to gang up on her, Nicole would never survive it. She was barely hanging onto her self-control around them as it was.

Who knew living with five monsters could turn a girl's libido up to maximum overdrive? She sure as hell hadn't.

Wes reached around them to grab the rest of the meat lover's pizza and slapped the cougar on his meaty shoulder. "Maybe you can work on a giant litter box for yourself next, pussycat."

A sigh of relief slipped out of her. That was more like it.

For a second there, she had been worried. If they banded together, they would steamroll her.

Grabbing her plate, she bypassed the kitchen table and flopped onto the couch. The monsters trailed after her like little ducklings. Hawthorne settled on the couch beside her while the shifters sprawled on the floor. Plates balanced on their stomachs, they consumed their pizza at alarming speeds.

"How have you two not choked to death by now?" Nicole questioned. It had to be a supernatural skill.

Drake shrugged. "Shifters need a lot of calories. You get used to it."

She was pretty sure she would never get used to watching two men vacuum up a buffet's worth of food in one go, but sure.

"You sure you don't want some of this, Hawthorne?" Wes waved a slice laden with bacon and sausage.

The fae wrinkled his nose. "Hard pass."

"You're missing out."

"He's really not," Atticus said as he strolled into the room. He pressed a kiss to Nicole's cheek and raised his wrist. "Will you fasten my cufflinks, love?"

Ignoring the urge to blush, Nicole wiped her greasy hands on a napkin and carefully adjusted the vampire's pressed shirt cuffs. If she got any pizza on his shirt, he wisely kept it to himself.

"Jasper and I have some urgent business tonight, so we'll be leaving not long after the sun goes down and will be gone long after you're in bed."

He sighed apologetically, like it was the most devastating news he could have given her. Fighting a smile, Nicole crooked her finger to bring him closer.

"Then I guess you both need a goodnight kiss now."

Carefully keeping her greasy pizza hands to herself, Nicole pressed her lips to his. His tongue swiped over her lower lip before she pulled back.

"What's this about kisses?" Jasper asked absently as he walked into the room, scrolling on his phone.

"We get goodnight kisses early since we have to leave," Atticus said gravely.

The blond vampire's head shot up. "You have my attention."

Nicole laughed and waved him over. For two-hundred-year-old men, they were absolutely ridiculous. She gave him a quick kiss and shooed them out of the room to get their work done.

If she let them linger, they would never leave.

The rest of her monsters grumbled about being left out but quickly settled into a lively discussion about football. Nicole tuned them out. It wasn't difficult—she wouldn't know the difference between a yard line and a yardstick with a gun to her head.

She ran through her clothing options for her first day of work. Slacks, maybe... Did she even own slacks? A dress... or was that trying too hard?

Nicole grew increasingly incapable of relaxing as the

evening dragged on. By the time the shifters had transitioned their argument to basketball, she had given up entirely.

"I think I'm going to head to bed early tonight."

She was too anxious about starting her new job to be any good at small talk. Plus... sports bored the hell out of her.

Grabbing the stack of plates, she disappeared into the kitchen. Nicole eyed the mess of pizza boxes. She should clean those up... or she could leave them for the monsters who had made the mess.

She voted for the latter.

"Goodnight, boys!" Nicole called into the living room.

"Oi! What about our goodnight kisses?" Wes called. "The bloodsuckers got kisses, so we should too!"

"Penalty box!" she reminded them. Climbing up the stairs to a chorus of grumbling, she grinned to herself.

Maybe managing a horde of monsters wouldn't be as difficult as she'd imagined. They might be overbearing and messy, but a kiss here and there, and they were putty in her hands.

Nicole made her way into the bathroom and brushed her teeth. Her smile had quickly vanished as she faced the reality that tomorrow would be the start of the rest of her post-university life. She had a job, one she had to make a good first impression at tomorrow—something she was historically terrible at.

Grumbling under her breath, she crossed the hall into her bedroom and fished pajamas out of her dresser. She dragged them on and clicked off the light.

Nicole started to climb onto her bed and paused. A small box with a sleek black ribbon waited on her nightstand. She tugged it into her lap and eagerly tugged at the bow. The heavenly scent of chocolate teased her nose and filled the small room as the lid slipped free and tumbled onto the bed. A folded slip of paper rested on the rows of gleaming chocolates.

Unfolding it, she squinted at the neat handwriting in the darkness.

Have a taste and dream of me.
Good luck tomorrow, love.
- Atticus

Nicole popped a chocolate into her mouth and settled the lid back into place.

Who cared if she'd already brushed her teeth? When a vampire who made you think of dirty, sinful deeds just by walking into the same room gave you chocolates, you ate a damn chocolate. It was the law.

Relishing the sweet taste on her tongue, she lay back on her pillows. A slow smile spread across her face. Ashley might need to reconsider her career and take up life coaching. Had she expected five monsters to be completely obsessed with Nicole? Probably not, but talk about a happy accident.

Her tongue swiped a dot of chocolate off her lip, and a hint of pleasure curled in her belly. It wouldn't be long before things started to get spicy in her dilapidated house—there was no point denying it anymore. They might drive her a little bit crazy, but Nicole could see the hunger in each of her monsters' eyes.

It was the same hunger reflected in hers.

It was only a matter of time now... and a question of who. Which monster was going to tempt her over the edge first?

A sharp howl split the night. Nicole rolled off the bed

and hurried to her window. Quickly shoving it open, she poked her head out into the cold evening air.

A large wolf stood in the backyard. His furry head thrown back, he howled at the pale moon peeking over the horizon. She chuckled quietly to herself.

Wes howled again, the eerie sound painting goosebumps up and down her arms.

Another window burst open beside hers. Hawthorne stuck his head out, his long hair falling tangled around his face. The silver burned bright in the dying light as he scowled at the werewolf.

"Keep it down, fuzzball!" he shouted into the shadowed yard. "Some of us have to get up early for work!"

Slapping her hand over her mouth, Nicole choked on her giggles as Wes looked up at the steaming elf and let out the longest howl yet. A polished shoe sailed high through the air and smacked against his furry face.

"I'm on a work call, moron!" Jasper yelled. A second loafer followed the first.

Kicking at the grass, Wes gave them his back and loped away into the trees. Nicole wasn't sure if a wolf could look smug, but she would swear on her life he was smirking.

She closed the window and crawled back into bed. Another round of giggles pealed out of her in the dark. Her roommates were so weird.

Her eyes were just starting to drift closed when the door creaked. Squinting into the shadows, Nicole could just make out a dark shape creeping across the floor. She opened her mouth to scream, and a handful of fur brushed her mouth.

Smacking it away, she leaned back and reached for the lamp. A heavy weight turned in a circle and settled peacefully across her legs.

Her heart hammered, and her hand shook as she inched toward the light. What the hell kind of monster was in her bed? It certainly wasn't the half-naked variety she had envisioned.

A gentle purring filled the quiet room. Nicole paused, her fingertips on the lamp switch. Purring?

"Drake?" she whispered.

A heavy paw tapped her thigh over the blankets. That motherfucker.

She opened her mouth to give him the world's most scathing lecture about sneaking up on poor unsuspecting humans, but she snapped it closed as the comforting weight settled across her hips.

Nicole flopped back and stared at the ceiling through the darkness. They were going to have to have a serious talk about boundaries. Yawning, she curled into the soothing purrs that lulled her to sleep.

Tomorrow. They would talk about it tomorrow.

15

DRAKE

Drake stumbled into the kitchen and glared at the bright eyed fae. Why did he look so damn awake? Did Hawthorne understand that mornings were unholy?

Shaking his head, he swiped a granola bar from the pantry and jammed it into his mouth as a pre-breakfast snack. He loaded up the coffee maker and started his morning mug hunt. Finding his prize in the sink, he washed it out and stared impatiently at the slowly filling pot.

He blinked tired eyes and yawned. It was going to be a long day. Maybe he could sneak back into Nicole's bed after she left for work and take a quick nap.

He filled his cup and looked around for the sugar.

"Sugar?" he grumbled at the fae. Drake could probably sniff it out, but that was strictly a post-caffeine type of activity.

"Yellow canister with pink flowers." Hawthorne waved a spatula in the right direction.

The were-cat scooped a spoonful into his drink and raised the pickle mug in salute. Drake raised it to his lips and sipped his coffee. He had no idea why, but it just tasted better from Nicole's dill mug. Something they had all noticed by now. It was a daily struggle to see who would get to the cup first in the morning.

As the superior monster, he was obviously the victor.

And today, he needed to be. Their sweet, little human was going to need an extra-large hit of caffeine this morning. She had tossed and turned all night. He'd been smelling her nerves since she'd opened her eyes and remembered that today was her first day at her new job.

Drake wasn't the only one feeling her tension. The monsters had moved around the house in silence that morning, none of them needing to voice aloud the cloud of nerves hanging over them all. They were practically tying themselves into knots as she got ready for work.

Nicole was going to have a good day. She had to... otherwise the five of them were going to become someone else's nightmare.

Sipping his coffee, he leaned against the counter and waited patiently for her to come downstairs. He was a cat. He could wait all day if he had to.

Hawthorne was far less patient. The fae shuffled around the kitchen, his pale eyes flitting to his watch from time to time, no doubt putting off going to work until he could confirm for himself that Nicole had eaten a decent breakfast.

After what felt like a century, Nicole came padding into the kitchen with her heels tucked under her arm. "The hall shower is draining slow," she mumbled sleepily.

Drake made a mental note to take care of it... and add more bathrooms to the house plan. Between her thick head of hair and two men who could turn into furry woodland creatures, they were going to shed a lot.

Thumping into a kitchen chair, Nicole shoved her feet

into her shoes and yawned. She blinked at the vase overflowing with elegant red roses in the center of the table.

"The bloodsuckers had to get to bed early, but Jasper left those for you for your first day," Hawthorne told her. He slid a plate of toast and scrambled eggs in front of her and kissed the top of her head. "Wes had to leave early too, but he made your lunch and left it in the fridge."

"He made me lunch?"

"It's a shifter thing," Drake said.

Nicole's sleepy face morphed into a frown. "That's my lucky mug."

"I know."

Pushing off the counter, he drained the last of his coffee. Drake grabbed the coffee pot and filled the mug to the brim with sugar and caffeine. He took a tiny sip to make sure it was just right and put it in her waiting hands.

He bent low and dropped a teasing kiss under her jaw. Swiping an orange from the bowl on the table and taking his place back at the counter, Drake pretended not to notice the pink flush spreading across her cheeks.

He adored that silly blush. It never failed to make a quick appearance after one of them kissed her. Even when it was a chaste peck on the cheek, Nicole's warm scent always flowed in waves until the pink faded away again.

Such a sweet reaction over a simple kiss. And all the while, she had no idea they would all have her stripped naked and never let her cute little feet touch the ground if they could. Nicole might have something to say about that… but it wasn't easy to win an argument against five stubborn men, most of whom had fangs.

Drake looked her up and down as she picked at her food. It was a good thing the wolf wasn't home to see the way her skirt was stretching over her curvy hips. She would never make it out the door.

It was all the cat could do to keep the brash idiot in check. If Wes had his way, Nicole would live between his sheets... or the dog's idiocy would scare her off completely.

Hawthorne took her lunch bag from the fridge and set it on the table. Frowning down at her uneaten breakfast, he caught Drake's eye. What was the shy fae up to?

The cougar sat back and peeled his orange.

Shoving her plate out of reach, Hawthorne grabbed Nicole's hips and lifted her out of her chair. Her ass thumped down on the table. Drake raised his eyebrows as the quiet elf pushed her skirt up her thighs.

"What are you—?" Nicole gasped.

"Helping you relax."

The fae nudged her onto her back and slid his fingertips under her panties. The scrap of lace slid down her legs and landed on the floor.

"What—?" she squeaked as her thighs were placed on his shoulders. Her protests turned into a surprised gasp as Hawthorne's face disappeared between her legs.

Huh. Drake wasn't sure the quiet fae had it in him. Go figure.

Nicole's head dropped back with her first moan. Hands gliding down her body, she gripped the hem of her skirt and pulled it up even higher. Drake chuckled. As much as their delectable little human argued and stubbornly pushed back at the monsters in her house, he wasn't surprised at how quickly she gave in to the elf's ministrations.

Anyone with eyes and more than three brain cells could see the hunger she hid behind that sweet blush of her... so that pretty much only excluded Wes.

Leaning against the counter, Drake caught her gleaming gaze and winked. As tempted as he was to join in, Hawthorne had staked his claim first. He calmly peeled his orange and watched the show.

Nicole trembled, a shaking, moaning mess as the fae licked her pussy. Popping an orange slice into his mouth, the were-cougar watched the silver head feasting between her legs. Her tiny hands fisted in her silky shirt. A whimper tore her lips as whatever Hawthorne did hit all the right buttons.

Her head tipped back in a moan, the wanton sound parting her pink lips. Dark lashes fluttered open. Drake stared into her eyes and sucked on another orange slice. Keeping eye contact, Nicole slipped her hands under her shirt and squeezed her breasts. Generous cleavage flashed for him as she manhandled herself.

The wet sounds of Hawthorne's fingers joined the litany of her delicious whimpers. Drake grinned. The fae must have some kind of skill if he had her legs shaking like that.

Shifting on his feet, the were-cat adjusted his aching cock. He was tempted to unzip his pants and stroke himself to the sound of Nicole's pussy being eaten out on the breakfast table. He eyed the flush darkening on her cheeks and reconsidered.

She was close to coming. If Drake was fisting his cock when she came, he wouldn't be able to stop himself from coming on the tits peeking out from under her wrinkled shirt.

He ate another orange slice and ignored the ache in his pants. He had all the time in the world to handle it later.

"Oh, God. I'm coming!" Nicole moaned.

Hands fisting in the elf's silver hair, she ground her pussy against his mouth. Tremors wracked her curvy body. Not even the elf's strong hands on her thighs could keep her still. Her chest heaved with each desperate pant.

Nicole lay limp on the table as the orgasm finished tormenting her. Gently untangling her fingers, Hawthorne pulled her hands free from his hair and straightened up. He shot the cougar a satisfied grin and licked his lips.

Lucky bastard.

Drake sighed. He shook his head and chewed his last orange slice. Next time Nicole was anxious, it was his turn to make her moan. He didn't care who he had to step over to make it happen—the next time she was coming all over the breakfast table, it would be because of him.

Hawthorne gripped her elbows and hauled her upright. Scooching her off the table, he placed her carefully on her high-heeled feet. A stab of jealousy jabbed at Drake as the fae smoothed Nicole's clothes. If he'd thought a little faster this morning, it could have been him licking her pussy for breakfast. It could have been him stroking his hands over her body to put her back together.

But then again... watching Nicole come undone had been well worth standing by. While Hawthorne had done the work, Drake had been the one rewarded with the view of her pink lips moaning for more.

The fae kissed her and pressed her lunch into her hands. Nicole stumbled toward the door, still more than a little bit dazed by her crashing orgasms. Drake caught her chin as she passed close to him. He tilted her head back and kissed her deeply, his tongue sweeping over her lips for even a tiny taste Hawthorne might have left behind for him.

Stepping back, he patted her ass and watched her walk out the door on wobbly legs. A colorful flash of lace caught his eye, and Drake bent down and swiped Nicole's bright pink panties off the floor. He tucked them in his pocket. They would come in handy later when he was stroking his cock to the thought of her flushed cheeks and desperate whimpers.

Drake stole Nicole's abandoned toast and sat down across from the fae.

"So... I'm thinking cedar for the gazebo. Thoughts?"

16

NICOLE

Nicole shadowed Marta, the kind human resources manager who had interviewed her for the job. They walked around the office as she introduced her to everyone and showed her to her tiny office.

She was a total sweetheart—short and curvy, with a mane of smooth dark hair that Nicole would sell her soul for. Everyone seemed to love her as they bounced from department to department, learning everyone's name.

Nicole did her best to keep up, but all she could think about was breakfast—or her lack thereof.

Shy, quiet Hawthorne had picked her up and put her on the table next to a plate of eggs and devoured her pussy like it was nothing. He'd been head and shoulders under her skirt like it was his favorite vacation spot. And Drake—calm, stoic, smirking Drake—had stood there and watched the whole thing while he nibbled on orange slices.

Never in her life had she had a breakfast quite like that. She'd dreamed up a couple, but they hadn't been anything like the reality.

Nicole had been reeling ever since she walked out of the house. It had only been a matter of time before the sexual tension in the house boiled over... but Hawthorne? *Hawthorne?* If there had been a betting pool, no one would have put their money on the shy fae being the first to peel her panties off.

And it had been good. Like mind-melting, leg-shaking, soul-leaving-her-body good. Hawthorne had more talent in the tip of his tongue than some of her past lovers had in their entire bodies.

Nicole shook her head as she waved at yet another employee Marta was introducing her to. A part of her felt dirty. Wandering around behind her new friend, she was stuck in her head, thinking about how one of her new boyfriends had managed to find a way into her panties.

Panties she had never managed to put back on. She squeezed her thighs together. Going commando her first day of work wouldn't have been her choice, but if it increased her odds of a repeat performance, Nicole would never wear panties again.

Of course, if her underwear was still waiting for her on the kitchen floor when she got home, she might have to reconsider. Assuming she didn't die on the spot.

There were five monsters in her life. *Five*. Keeping them all satisfied was going to be a nine-to-five job on its own. Then again, if this is what they had planned for her every day, well, who needed a job anyway? Nicole could spend the rest of her days happy and curled up in bed, getting her pussy licked.

If that was what the universe had planned for her... who was she to try to thwart the universe?

"Goodness, we've covered a lot!" Marta beamed at her, her sunshiny demeanor dragging Nicole out of her dirty thoughts. "How about we take a break for lunch?"

Nicole snapped out of her reverie as her stomach rumbled. She never actually did eat breakfast. Her plate of eggs and toast had been left abandoned as Hawthorne had eaten *his* breakfast.

Marta laughed as her stomach grumbled again. "Perfect timing. Normally, I would offer to take you to lunch for your first day, but unfortunately, I have a call scheduled with my divorce lawyer during my break."

Her bright smile drooped slightly. Nicole had no idea what the story was behind her divorce, but anyone stupid enough to leave such a sunshine-y human deserved to die alone.

"Rain check?" her new coworker offered.

"Sure. That would be great."

Nicole wasn't about to say it, but she was actually grateful for some quiet time to pull it together. If she didn't get her head out of her panties, her first day of work was going to be a horrible first impression for all her coworkers.

Not the mediocre first impression she had anticipated.

Nicole left Marta outside the Human Resources office and hurried to the break room. Grabbing her lunch from the refrigerator, she darted back to her small office. She sat down at her empty desk and opened up the brown paper bag.

Eyeing the food Wes had selected with interest, she got ready to judge his selection. A turkey sandwich on some kind of homemade bread—she didn't even know where he'd gotten it. Nicole certainly hadn't made it. There was a container of grapes already plucked off the stem, strawberry yogurt, and a chocolate snack cake.

Part of her felt like an elementary school student who had been put on the bus and sent to school that morning with her lunch in hand, but another, much larger part of her was just grateful she didn't have to pack her own damned lunch. How many kisses would it cost her to get him to keep packing it every day?

Knowing the horny werewolf... not many.

She reached for her sandwich and a folded piece of paper slipped out from underneath the bag. Nicole picked it up and unfolded it.

Have a great day, babe. I can't wait to hear all about it tonight!
- Wes xoxoxoxo
(which ones are the kisses again?)

Nicole smiled. Reaching for her phone, she sent him a quick text.

NICOLE

> Thank you for lunch! I hope you're ready to hear about a lot of people whose names I will never remember.

> And the x's are the kisses, silly wolf xxxx

A soft knock on the door caught her smiling at her phone. The smile faded a bit as someone poked their head into her office. She frowned at the familiar man, iridescent scales dotting along his hairline and behind his ears. Had Marta introduced them?

She cocked her head to the side. Oh, shit.

He was the scaly guy with the tongue. The tongue Nicole had joked would reach her lungs if things got sexy. She had swiped left on him on MONSTR on that very first morning.

"Hi, I'm Jeff!" He waved cheerfully. "I didn't get a chance to say hi when Marta was taking you around and giving you a tour. I just thought I'd pop in real quick."

"It's nice to meet you. I'm Nicole." Definitely not the same Nicole who had swiped past him for shooting a peace side and waving around a fish.

"Oh, great! I have the office next door."

Shit. There would be no avoiding him now. Hopefully, he didn't recognize her from the dating app... but with her luck, he was already writing her love notes and doodling her name on his desk calendar.

Nicole's phone buzzed on the desk, drawing both their attention.

Jeff waved goodbye. "I'll just let you get that. See you later!"

Close call. Nicole sighed in relief as the door clicked shut and snatched up her phone. The message wasn't from Wes—it was Jasper checking up on her.

> JASPER
>
> I didn't get a chance to see what you wore out the door this morning, but I'm sure it was sexy. Can't wait for a peek later ;)

She raised her eyebrows at the flirty text. That vampire was incorrigible. Wait...

Nicole glanced at the time. It was the middle of the day; shouldn't he be fast asleep? For some reason, she assumed vampires keeled over asleep as soon as the sun was in the sky and didn't wake up until sunset.

Shaking her head, she made a mental note to ask Miri if she knew anyone who had textbooks about the history of monsters. She was working with a middle schooler's knowledge and it clearly showed.

> JASPER
>
> I didn't get a chance to see what you wore out the door this morning, but I'm sure it was sexy. Can't wait for a peek later ;)

> NICOLE
>
> Aren't you supposed to be asleep right now?

He didn't respond, but the smile on her face wouldn't go away. Lunch, flowers, cute texts... pussy licking. They were trying to kill her with this cute ass bullshit. How was she supposed to stay focused her new job—or anything, for that matter— when all of these men were doting on her?

Nicole was one love note away from melting into a puddle of goo.

Shaking her head, she peeled the bag off her sandwich and took a bite. She blinked and studied the sandwich. Was that pesto? Where the hell had Wes gotten pesto? Not from her fridge, that was for sure.

Picking through her lunch like some kind of cafeteria archaeologist, Nicole tried to figure out exactly where Wes had gotten all the components. Was he breaking into her neighbor's house and swiping their food? She wouldn't exactly be mad. That judgey hag in the yellow house on the right was a total bitch.

Marta poked her head through the door. "Are you ready to wrap up the last of the paperwork?"

"As ready as I will ever be."

Nicole swept her trash into the paper bag and threw it away. She made sure to tuck the scribbled note into her skirt pocket.

Looking up, she beamed at Marta. "Lead the way!"

Three hours later, she was convinced the Human Resources Manager was part robot. Nothing human had that kind of stamina. She studied the short, curvy woman from the corner of her eye. Marta certainly didn't look like any kind of monster she'd seen yet, but as Nicole was becoming increasingly aware, she was no expert.

Nicole scribbled her signature for what felt like the millionth time. How was Marta not cramping up yet? The woman could paperwork with the best of them.

"Annnnnnd, I think that's the last of it!" she said brightly, signing the last page with a flourish. Marta fixed her with a bright smile. "Now you get to get out of here and go home! Oh, and do you like chocolate? I was going to bake brownies tonight, and I can bring you in a couple tomorrow. My way of saying sorry for abandoning you at lunch today."

"Marta, I don't want to alarm you," Nicole deadpanned. "There is a very good chance that I'm in love with you."

The Human Resources Manager laughed and shooed her out the door.

Nicole wasted no time grabbing her purse from her office and shrugging her jacket on. The sooner she made it to her car, the sooner she could get home and put on sweatpants. Her bed was calling her name, and she was ready to answer.

She glanced at her phone, and she moved to throw it in her purse. No new texts from her monsters, but she had missed a call. She pulled the voicemail from Ashley waiting in her inbox and raised her phone to her ear.

"Hey, girlie. We're having dinner at your house tonight. No lallygagging after work; we're starting this party with or without you!"

Dinner at the house? *Her* house? Nicole's eyebrows soared. What mischief had her friends gotten her monsters into?

17

NICOLE

Throwing her purse on the table, Nicole peered into the empty kitchen. Where the hell was everybody?

The quiet sounds of arguing floated through the air. Lights flickered through the open back door, casting shadows on the kitchen wall. She followed the sound of raised voices into the backyard.

Stumbling to a stop, Nicole blinked at the scene in front of her. There was a gazebo standing in her backyard, covered in ivy and flowers that hadn't been there yesterday. The smoking grill that rested not too far from it was also brand new. The familiar cougar flipping burgers, not so much.

Miri and Ashley sat at a table under the gazebo. Hawthorne and the vampires sat beside them, laughing at whatever story Miri was telling.

Nicole stared. And now there was patio furniture? Her jaw dropped open as she eyed the heavy table and squishy-looking chairs. What store did they rob on the way home from work today?

A large paper banner hung from the roof of the gazebo.

The word "congrats" was spelled out with tiny, colorful handprints. Nicole grinned. Miri must have shanghaied her class into making her decorations. How had she explained that to a room full of five-year-olds?

They were there to celebrate her and her new job. Warmth glowed in her belly. For a long time, Nicole hadn't had very many people in her life at all. Her mom was off in Florida living her own life, and her dad wasn't even in the picture.

Really, all she had were Ashley and Miri... and now she had five monsters too.

Miri caught her eye from the gazebo and waved enthusiastically. Heads turned in her direction and started to cheer. Wes whipped out a party popper and let a tiny cloud of confetti fly. A blush fired up her face.

They were absolutely ridiculous, and she loved it.

Careful of her heels, Nicole picked her way across the lawn. Jasper was the first to catch her in a tight squeeze. He kissed her lips and nipped at her lip with the point of his fang, and Nicole gasped. He let her go as quickly as he had grabbed her.

"At least let her get comfortable," Atticus admonished him.

His cool hand rested on her lower back as he led her over to an empty chair and placed a drink in her hand. The bossy vampire kissed the top of her head and waved them on with the conversation.

"I hope you like burgers!" Drake called from his post at the grill.

"I love them!"

"Good," Hawthorne sighed. "Can we switch seats? I think I'm downwind of the grill."

He did look a bit peaky. Trying not to giggle, she

swapped seats with the queasy elf and gave his hand a squeeze as she passed. Poor thing.

"I hope Drake is making something edible for you." Nicole glanced at the meat covered grill with worry.

"Veggie kebabs for the fae," Drake grunted. "I cooked them in their own pan."

"Thank you, Drake!" Nicole blew him a kiss.

Hawthorne looked relieved. The shy fae had probably been intending to keep his mouth shut and nibble on chips all night just to keep the peace.

Glancing around at the gazebo, she eyed the arching vines and blossoms. Nicole sat there in awe. She completely ignored Miri and Ashley as they peppered her with questions about work, too focused on the transformation of her backyard.

"When the hell did I get rose bushes back here?" Nicole gaped at the huge pink blooms in her planter boxes.

"This afternoon," Wes shrugged.

"But they're huge!"

Drake pointed over at Hawthorne. "Fae, remember?"

Right. The elf could just stick his hands in the earth and will them to grow—something she still had not had a chance to see. Frankly, if he hadn't made the peony bloom for her at the farmers' market, Nicole would have thought they were messing with her.

Nicole shook her head. Studying all their improvements, she tried to catch hold of her reeling mind. Ashley waved her hands in front of her face to get her attention.

"Hello! Forget the roses, Nic." The blonde grinned, her eyes gleaming in the pale evening light. "Let's talk about the hunks throwing barbecues in your backyard!"

Nicole laughed. What more could they possibly want to know? It's not like she and Miri hadn't been texting her constantly over the last few days.

"Which one's the best kisser?" Miri asked.

"No, better question," Ashley interjected. "Which one's got the biggest... you know?"

Absolutely not... and she didn't know yet.

Nicole raised her hands to her fiery cheeks. "You're being so rude! I am not answering any of that."

"Oh no, they're fine." Wes grinned and walked over to plant a kiss on her burning cheek. "This is their payment."

She eyed the grinning werewolf suspiciously. "Payment for what?"

"For answering all of our questions about you. They've been here for over an hour now."

"*What*?" She turned to glare at her two friends. Traitors.

The werewolf walked off in the other direction, laughing maniacally. That motherfucker.

"When were you going to tell us you had a tattoo?" Drake teased from the grill.

Nicole glared at her two best friends. "You're both dead to me."

The monsters burst out laughing as Miri laughed into her drink and Ashley looked far too smug for her own good. Sure, it was all fun for them; they weren't the ones who had five monsters to contend with on a daily basis. The boys did not need more ammo to tease her. She gave them more just by existing within arms' reach of them.

Drake walked around the table and put a paper plate in her hands. He bent low and pressed a kiss under her jaw in the one place that drove her crazy. Nicole shivered.

Maybe a barbecue wasn't the worst idea. It got them all together and getting along, and she got food out of the deal. She had had plenty of worse days.

Ashley wiggled her eyebrows as he turned back to the grill. She pointed at the cougar's back and raised her hands to measure. "Say when."

No, this evening was definitely a terrible idea. Ashley and Miri did not belong in the same vicinity as her new monster paramours. Nicole quickly scooped up her burger and took a bite out of it to avoid answering any more questions.

Drake bumped into Wes as he was walking back to the grill, and the wolf's drink spilled in the grass. He looked up at the were-cat with a glower on his face and shoved him back a step.

"Watch it."

Nicole sighed. So much for getting along. How long had that been, fifteen minutes?

"Seriously? I'm trying to cook, and you're being an ass."

"I'm not the one stomping all over other peoples' feet!"

Damn it. Couldn't they behave for one evening?

Nicole put her plate on the table and rose to her feet. She took two steps forward to intervene when a strong arm grabbed her around the waist and tugged her back against a hard chest.

"Never get between two angry monsters, pet," Jasper murmured in her ear.

Atticus stood beside them, his arms folding over his chest. He frowned imperiously at the two shifters who had just started throwing punches.

"Oh my God, stop!" Nicole yelled. The two shifters ignored her.

Waving at the two morons wailing on each other's faces, Atticus turned back to the fae. "Hawthorne, would you mind?"

Putting his food down with a sigh, the elf came around the table. He crouched low and dug his fingers into the earth. The blue glyphs on his skin glowed bright. Nicole blinked as the hard ground liquefied and rolled like waves on the ocean.

Drake and Wes sank hip-deep into the earth. Hawthorne jerked his hands back and the ground hardened around their legs, trapping them in place. They froze, Drake's arms wrapped around Wes in a headlock.

"Are you done?" Atticus snapped.

Wes turned his head up to glare at the cougar, and Drake frowned right back. He released the werewolf and leaned away as far as the ground would allow.

"Yes," they said begrudgingly.

"Good." Atticus waved for Hawthorne to release them.

He crouched down again, tattoos glowing, and the shifters climbed out of their earthly prison.

"Drake, go get more drinks from the cooler," Atticus ordered. "Wes, take over the grill and shut up."

The two monsters turned to glare at the commanding vampire while Nicole glared at them both. If they started throwing more punches, they were both banished from the barbecue. Wes took one look at her face and stepped back.

"Bossy bloodsucker," Drake muttered under his breath.

Wes bumped his shoulder in agreement and walked in the other direction.

Oh, sure. Now they agreed on something. Nicole shook her head and leaned back against Jasper's chest, surrounded by overgrown children.

"Animals," Atticus snorted under his breath.

Jasper released his iron hold on her waist and nudged Nicole back to her seat.

Miri and Ashley sat exactly where she had left them, wide-eyed and clutching their plates for dear life. Miri had her burger halfway raised to her mouth, her lips still gaping open.

"That was—"

"Hot as hell!" Miri cut in. "Are they always like that?"

"The arguing, yes." Nicole shook her head. "The punching, no. I'm just glad everyone kept their clothes on and no claws came out."

"Speak for yourself," Ashley muttered.

"That actually wasn't too bad. They're really toning down their more feral natures for you, love. We all are," Atticus said. He swirled his glass of wine and glanced thoughtfully after Drake's retreating back. "Normally, there would have been at least a little bloodshed... or kissing. It was actually rather tame for a shifter argument."

Hawthorne beamed at her. "Congratulations, you've domesticated us."

Nicole stared. That was *tame*?

"Thank you?" she said hesitantly.

Chewing on her burger, she was still bewildered. That was a mere argument? To any human, it would look like they were trying to kill each other. Wait... kissing? Did Atticus say *kissing*?

Nicole's head pivoted to stare back and forth between the two grumbling shifters. Did she wanna know? The conversation picked up at the table, and she decided that no, she certainly did not want to know. Not tonight.

Their fight barely a blip in the evening, conversation and laughter rolled on unhindered. Nicole finished her food and moved to a squishy love seat. She curled up next to Hawthorne and the fae slung his arm around her shoulder, cuddling her in the chilly evening air. She listened to the sound of laughter and good-natured ribbing amongst her friends and monsters.

Her phone buzzed in her lap, and she glanced down at a message from Jeff at work. She didn't read it. Looking up at her monsters, Nicole smiled. She deleted the message and clicked the icon to snooze her MONSTR profile.

She was pretty sure she wasn't going to need it anymore.

18

WES

Grabbing his jacket, Wes yawned and headed for the bedroom door. He had a long day of engine tune-ups and prepping for the upcoming winter rush ahead of him. His heavy boots clunked on the floor with each step.

They really needed to get some throw rugs. Of course, then the fae would have something else to complain about wolf fur sticking to.

It wasn't his fault. Werewolves always shed when the seasons changed. Everyone knew that.

A sharp sound pricked his ears. Wes paused outside the hall bathroom and pressed his ear to the door. The off-key singing echoing from the steaming shower could only belong to one person—his favorite person in the house.

He listened to Nicole caterwaul for a few minutes and couldn't help the grin that curved his lips. His sensitive ears might hate the sound, but listening to it made his heart skip a beat every morning.

The werewolf cracked the door and popped his head into the steamy bathroom.

"I'm heading out, babe," he called. "Your lunch is in the refrigerator!"

The edge of the shower curtain peeled back, and Nicole's soapy head poked through the gap. Soap suds dripped down her neck and shoulders and disappeared out of view. Wes blinked hard. He definitely wasn't imagining what was behind that thin shower curtain... soaking wet... and within his reach.

"Thank you!" Nicole blew him a kiss. "Have a good day!"

Not good enough. He needed more than an air kiss today.

Throwing the door open, he crossed to the shower curtain and cupped her wet cheeks in his hands. His lips slanted over her, the taste of her toothpaste and sweet Nicole scent brushing his tongue. The wolf licked her lips and backed away before he gave in to the urge to rip the shower curtain aside and climb under the spray with her.

"See you later, baby."

Wes turned his back on the tempting sight and forced himself to get going. He couldn't stop smiling as he closed the bathroom door and headed outside.

For once, the wolf was perfectly calm.

Everything about Nicole made him feel at peace—from the top of her sweet-smelling hair to her tiny painted toes. He didn't even mind sharing her with four other monsters. As long as she let him have a piece of her heart to himself, he could share the rest of it.

The smile faded from his face as he walked onto the porch. A familiar scent pricked his nose, just barely lingering in the air. Their mystery guest had been poking around the driveway recently.

Wes leapt off the porch, skidding to a stop on the gravel as he caught sight of what the saboteur had done. Every tire had been slashed—his motorcycle, Drake's truck, Nicole's tiny rust bucket, Hawthorne's truck overflowing with bags of soil. Even the vampires' sleek luxury car hadn't been spared.

Rage boiled deep in his gut. The wolf clawed at his skin, desperate to free itself and maul something. Gritting his teeth, Wes shoved the feeling down. He needed to keep his human form for a little bit longer. After he'd handled things, he could go furry, but not a second before.

He eyed the four flat tires on Nicole's small car. It was only her second day of work and her tires were slashed. She was going to be pissed.

Oh, God. What if she cried? Wes was terrible with tears.

His hands balled into fists, claws biting into his palms. What the werewolf wouldn't give to rip something to pieces right about then—preferably the prick who was making their life difficult.

It might not make Nicole feel better, but he would certainly find it soothing.

"Drake!" he shouted. "Get out here!"

This was one problem Wes couldn't fix on his own, not with all of them about to be late for work.

The cougar came slinking out of the house in nothing but gray sweatpants. His bare feet padded silently over the gravel driveway. Wes looked him up and down, his eyes lingering a little bit too long on his muscled chest as anger mixed with something else deep in his belly.

He shook his head. That was a problem for another day... or never. Wes might occasionally swing in that direction, but the condescending cat was definitely not his type.

Drake's steps picked up speed as he caught sight of the look on his face. "What's up?"

"Someone slashed all of our tires." Wes stepped back and waved at the deflated vehicles.

A dark storm gathered on the were-cat's face. He tilted

his bearded face back and sniffed the air. "The scent is weak," he growled. "Could they still be here?"

The wolf shook his head. If they were still there, he'd currently be fertilizing the elf's rose bushes with their blood.

"There's no one in the woods, and no one is in the house who doesn't need to be." A frown wrinkled his brow. "There were new scratches all over one of the bedroom door frames, but they've been there since yesterday, so I doubt it's related."

A surprising blush colored Drake's face. "That was me... I'll fix it."

He snorted. Fucking cats. They couldn't help but sharpen their claws on anything that would hold still long enough. Wes had sworn off were-cats years ago after an ex had used his guitar as a scratching post.

The instrument had been vintage, for fuck's sake.

"Any ideas?" he sighed.

Drake shrugged. "Replace the tires?"

"No shit."

Apparently, it was "National State the Obvious Day," and no one had penciled it into his calendar. Wes glowered at the moronic cat.

"I meant about the prick who is sabotaging our lives."

"Find him. Get rid of him."

His eye started to twitch. "Are you being an asshole on purpose, or is this what happens when you haven't had your coffee yet?"

"I don't hear you offering solutions, pretty boy," Drake growled.

Wes gritted his teeth. He was over the stuffy cat and his condescending bullshit about his looks. It wasn't his fault he was good looking. If that made the hulking brute insecure or horny or whatever the fuck he was feeling, that was his problem.

"Keep being a dickhead, and I'll tell you exactly where I'm going to stick those solutions!"

"That doesn't even make sense," he yawned.

That's it. Wes was going to murder him.

"Maybe if you stopped focusing on how pretty you think I am, you could use your three brain cells—"

"I thought you left already?" Nicole called from the porch.

They both whirled to face her, cheeks flushed. Drake shot him a small glare as they banished their irritation for her sake.

"Something came up," Wes sighed. "You're going to need to—"

His words trailed off as the words fell right out of his head. Eyes laser focused on the pretty human, he watched her curves sway as she walked down the steps in a tight skirt and flowered blouse. His gaze dropped to the bare stretch of leg leading down to her high heels.

Was she trying to kill them? How was he supposed to let her walk out the door when all he wanted was to study the way her breasts moved under the thin fabric? How were any of them?

Every inch of her made Wes dream of dirty things that would make her scream. The wolf inside him howled to bend Nicole over and fill her with cum until she was round with his pups.

Wes shook his head hard. He might recognize the hunger in her eyes every time she looked at him, but the sweet little human might have a problem with getting railed in her driveway.

Maybe in the future. Hawthorne had mentioned growing the hedges a bit more, and the cat could always put up a nice, tall privacy fence. No one deserved to see Nicole coming on the front lawn except for them.

A sharp elbow drove into his ribs. Wes glared at the were-cat at his side.

"Tell her."

Fuck, there was no way around it. He was good, but there was no way Wes could seduce her into not seeing dozens of slashed tires.

"We've had another visit from the saboteur," he said shortly.

"What happened?" she gasped.

"The vehicles." Drake nodded at the ruined cars behind them. Wes winced at the flat tires hanging off his motorcycle rims. Those were vintage too.

A low growl rumbled from his chest, the claws digging into his palms dug deeper. Drake's head shot up as the faint scent of blood floated on the wind.

Wes opened his hands and glowered at the red punctures on his hands. Damn it.

"Walk it off if you have to," the cat hissed.

Nicole bumped his hip with her own. "Are you okay?"

Choking down the growl that welled in this throat, he offered her a nod. The faint smell of her perfume tickled his nose. The wolf settled. He pressed his face into her hair and breathed deep.

She said something about being worried, but he was too focused on inhaling everyone bit of her scent.

Wes looped an arm around her Nicole's waist and dragged her tight against his side. If a little of her scent was good, a lot would be better. The werewolf buried his face against her throat.

She relaxed against his side, her stiff muscles melting into his. His fingers petted over her hip. Better. Much, much better.

He raised his head and nodded at Drake. He was okay now.

"Do you have any idea who could be doing this?" the cat asked her.

Nicole shook her head. "It's not like I have enemies. The worst thing I've ever done is steal a handful of grapes from the bag at the grocery store."

"Before you weighed them?" Wes shook his head. "And we're the monsters?"

She elbowed him. "Seriously! I don't have any enemies. My PhD is in Computer Science and Information Systems! It's not exactly a cutthroat program."

"Do you have any family that hates you?" Drake asked.

"Drake!" Wes growled. Though, if she insisted on explaining what "computer science and information systems" was at every holiday get together, he could see why that might the case.

"I'm just asking."

"My mom lives in Florida, and I see her once a year," she said drily. "Other than that, I have a cousin I haven't seen in over a decade. That's pretty much it. No evil twin to worry about."

Way to go. He shot a glare at the cat over her head. The tires weren't upsetting enough; let's bring up her non-existent family too. Maybe kick Nicole in the shins for good measure.

Damn cat.

"None of that matters right now anyway," the wolf interjected. "We're all going to be late for work."

"It's only my second day," she groaned. "They're going to hate me."

"I have the old tires for my truck in the shed." Drake jerked his thumb over his shoulder at the ramshackle hut in the backyard.

Nicole blinked "You do?"

"There was room." Drake shrugged.

Apparently, they were moving *all* their stuff into the house. No one had given him the message.

"I couldn't even get the damn door open," Nicole grumbled. "I thought it was empty."

"I'll take you to work and Wes to the garage, and we'll start working on getting these all replaced." He caught the werewolf's eye. "Do you have tires for her car? Then we can drop it off at her work later."

"I'm pretty sure I have some. I'll have to double check."

Taking charge, Drake started barking orders. "Go let the elf know what's up and grab my keys, and we'll get the tires swapped over while you're inside... please."

Nicole raised her eyebrows at the hastily tacked on concession and the pink glow of the cougar's cheeks but didn't say a word. Wes gave her one last squeeze before letting her go.

Drake and Wes worked in silence, changing over the tires as quickly as they could. Every now and then, the wolf would look up to catch him giving him an odd look. He didn't know what the cat was staring at. *He* wasn't the one half naked and wielding a socket wrench.

Gritting his teeth, he refused to look at the difficult shifter. They had work to do.

By the time Nicole came running back, they were tightening the lug nuts on the last tire. She passed Drake his keys and a shirt with a smirk, and he glanced down at his bare chest in surprise.

It was all Wes could do not to roll his eyes. Sure, he'd "forgotten" that he was prancing around half-naked. Subtle.

They piled into the front seat of the truck, Nicole hugging her lunch bag to her stomach. Sandwiched tightly between them, she was tense against his side. Wes glanced at her from the corner of his eye. A troubled wrinkle twisted her brow while her teeth worried at her bottom lip.

The werewolf sighed. If he got his hands on the bastard who was making them all so anxious, he would tear his arms off. The prick deserved that and more for worrying his sweet Nicole.

Wes curled his hand over her thigh and squeezed gently. Everything was going to be okay. He would make sure of it.

19

NICOLE

Nicole hurried out of the office, her head down. If she moved fast, she could avoid another awkward conversation and romantic overture from Jeff. Apparently, he wasn't great at taking hints. Not even telling him she was seeing several other men had gotten him to back off.

At some point, she was going to have to be aggressively straightforward. Maybe if she told him she was in a serious relationship, he would stop talking to her about fish.

Because that's what was happening, right? A relationship... or five.

Were the monsters living in her house her boyfriends? At no point had they talked about it or even approached the subject. It had to happen, but how the hell was she supposed to bring up that conversation?

Nicole snorted. She could picture their horrified faces vividly. She would gather them around the kitchen table and ask them as a group "so... what are we?" and then sit back and watch them unravel.

As entertaining as it would be, there was no chance in

hell of that happening. All it would take would be one of them saying they were just in it for fun, and she would probably start crying. In no time at all, the vampires, shifters, and fae had become important of her life.

Nicole shook her head. This was *so* not the time to be worrying about any of this.

Someone was actively trying to sabotage her life—a fact she was begrudgingly coming to terms with. She was going to have to tell Drake and Wes they were right... but not any time soon. Wes didn't need the ego boost, and Drake was already plenty smug.

Nicole climbed into the waiting car. The guys had certainly delivered on the new tires. She couldn't remember the last time her old beater had new tires. Probably before the car had come into her possession.

And now, some dickhead trying to ruin her day had forced her to rely on Wes to replace them. It was bad enough that he and the others spoiled her so thoroughly; she didn't want to cost him a ton of money. Tires weren't exactly cheap.

Sighing, she started the engine. Nicole was stressed enough without giving in to her mounting guilt. One crisis at a time was plenty.

Her phone buzzed in her purse. Fishing blindly, she dragged it out of the bag.

WES

Hey, baby. Can you pick me up at the garage on your way home? I'm still sourcing new tires for my motorcycle. There will be plenty of kisses in it for you ;)

NICOLE

On my way <3

Nicole winced. He loved that damn motorcycle. Now her drama was becoming their drama, and she hated that. Never in her life had she enjoyed asking anyone for help—Ashley had practically had to browbeat her into this little plan of hers—and now, it seemed to be all she was doing lately.

Her stormy mood rode shotgun all the way to the werewolf's garage. By the time she pulled up outside, Nicole was in a pitiful mood.

> **WES**
>
> Hey, baby. Can you pick me up at the garage on your way home? I'm still sourcing new tires for my motorcycle. There will be plenty of kisses in it for you ;)
>
> **NICOLE**
>
> On my way <3
>
> I'm here
>
> Wes?
>
> Weeeeeeeeees????

Grumbling, she threw open her door and trudged into the garage. If the wolf was going to request a ride, he could at least be ready when she showed up.

"Wes?" Nicole called into the cavernous space.

"In the back!"

Of course. Picking her way through the maze of scattered parts, she hunted for her werewolf. A pair of greasy coveralls were bent over an engine, and a smile curved her lips. She would know that muscled ass anywhere.

He stared under the hood with a handsome frown.

Biting his lip, the wolf focused on whatever was in front of him. A light sheen of sweat covered his muscular arms as he turned a wrench. Nicole had no idea what he was doing, but he sure made it look good.

Walking up behind him, she smacked his ass. "Hey, you."

Wes shot upright, his head banging into the open hood of the car. Wincing, Nicole slapped her hands over her mouth to hold back a laugh. The werewolf rubbed his head and glowered at her, the wrench in his hand forgotten.

"Sorry," she giggled.

"Make more noise when you walk," he growled.

That was rich coming from him. Between Wes and Drake, she was sure she was going to develop heart palpitations from how often they snuck up behind her.

The wolf pouted, his hand still dramatically rubbing his scalp.

"What if I kiss it and make it better?" Nicole teased.

His golden eyes lit up. "I guess that would be fine."

Wes dropped his head and pointed at the offending spot. She leaned in, prepared to kiss the top of his head, but at the last second, his head shot up and she kissed his lips instead.

Hand curving around her neck, he held her tight and swiped his tongue over the seam of her lips. She smacked his shoulder and shoved him away.

"Sneaky wolf," Nicole laughed. He must have been a hellion as a kid.

Wes grinned. At least he wasn't rubbing his head anymore. For a second there, she had worried she'd broken his skull.

Tossing the wrench aside, he grabbed the front of Nicole's jacket and towed her in close. His nose pressed into her hair and inhaled. When he pulled back, the gold in his eyes seemed brighter.

Nicole squinted as his face. Were his eyes glowing? Before she could ask, Wes buried his face in his neck and inhaled again.

"Stop that!" she shimmied out of the way. "That tickles!"

Plus, the press of his hard body against her was doing things to her, things she had no business feeling in the middle of grease-covered garage.

"Is that all?" Wes raised his eyebrows. Hands tightening on her jacket, he dragged her forward a step. "Because I smell something else."

"And what would that be?"

"Your pussy."

Nicole stared at him. He did *not* just say that. For a brief second, she was tempted to smack the hood of the car down on his head again.

He ignored the fire in her cheeks and stroked his hand down her back. His palm curving over her ass, he gave her a light squeeze through the thin fabric of her tight skirt.

"This is the second time you've walked into my garage smelling like a lusty treat," Wes teased. He looked down, his eyes lingering on the cleavage peering out of her shirt. "If there's a third time, you don't get to leave without letting me have a taste."

She raised her eyebrows. "Is that a rule?"

"Company policy."

"Poor Tony," she deadpanned. "I bet he dreads getting turned on at work."

Wes barked out a laugh. Shaking his head, he nuzzled the top of her head. "Stop trying to ruin my boner."

It was Nicole's turn to laugh. "I'm pretty sure nothing I could ever say would make you less horny."

"True." Leaning around her, he slammed the hood of the vehicle closed. "You hit all the right buttons for me, baby."

It was mutual. Would it kill the werewolf to wear long

sleeves in the garage? Every time she saw him flex, it was a new exercise in self-control. It was a miracle he didn't have random women throwing themselves at his dick all day.

Wes took another deep breath and groaned. "You're killing me."

"Then do something about it."

Nicole's own boldness shocked her. The words had left her mouth before she could think them through, and now, she was staring into the glowing eyes of a horny werewolf.

Strong hands gripped her hips, a squeak escaped her lips as her ass thumped down on the hood of the car behind her. Wes loomed in front of her.

Apparently, all a werewolf needed was the tiniest hint of permission and he was off to the races.

Wes caught her lips again. Pressing kisses down her jaw, he tilted her head back and kissed her throat. Nicole shivered; every teasing kiss was like he was hitting speed dial on her pussy.

He tried to step between her knees and paused. Looking down at her tight skirt, he growled. Nicole watched him reach for the fabric and grabbed his wrists.

Bright wolfish eyes looked up at her.

"This is my favorite skirt," she warned. "If you rip it, you're definitely not getting any."

Wes eyed the dirty garage and frowned. "If I take it off of you in here, there's no way that it's not getting grease on it."

Damn it. So much for getting laid. Today really did suck.

"I still want a taste."

"What—?"

Hooking his hands behind her knees, he tipped her back and wiggled the hem of her skirt as high as it would reach up her thighs. He paused and growled at his dirty hands.

"Wait here."

Wes vanished into the shadows of the garage. Nicole

propped herself up on her elbows and stared after him. What the fuck was he doing? *Now* was really the moment he wanted to catch up on paperwork?

The werewolf came jogging back, wiping his freshly washed hands on a towel.

"Grease." He shrugged, as if that explained everything.

Nicole opened her mouth, her questions transformed into a gasp as his hand slid up the inside of her thigh and tugged her panties aside in one deft move.

Wes leaned over her, his mouth finding her throat once again. His rough fingers brushed over her clit, and Nicole was seeing stars. He teased the sensitive bud with firm strokes until she was a panting mess. Stroking his fingers through her slippery folds, he moved on to torturing the rest of her pussy.

"Oh, fuck!" she gasped as the first thick finger slipped inside her.

His thumb worked her clit even as a second finger slipped inside. He worked her pussy with steady thrusts, and she bit her lip to keep from coming as his thumb circled her pulsing clit and his fingertips teased at her g-spot.

Nicole's hands rose to tangle in his messy hair, but Wes ignored her tight grip. He was too busy kissing and licking his way down her chest and into her cleavage.

"That's it, baby. Come on my fingers."

His tongue slicked over the curves of her breasts and she shuddered. Hand moving faster, Wes pressed his thumb harder into her clit, and the stars in her eyes exploded, showering her in sparks of bliss.

Nicole slumped against the hood of the car, and the werewolf raised his head to watch her face as he slipped his hand free. Raising it to his lips, he licked his fingers. Wes sucked them clean one by one, a wolfish grin on his face.

"Definitely the best thing I've had in my mouth today."

He dragged her off the car and onto her feet. Still in a daze, Nicole barely noticed him peeling off his coveralls and turning out the lights. Wes wrapped his arm around her shoulders and locked up the garage behind them.

"Keys." He held out his hand.

"What?"

"I don't trust you to drive home with that look on your face."

Fair enough. Nicole tossed him the keys and climbed into the passenger seat. She definitely wasn't fully in charge of her limbs yet. In fact, if she squeezed her thighs together just right, she was fairly certain she could give herself another tiny orgasm.

Then again, Wes would probably pull over and shred her skirt if she filled the car with any more of her scent. The poor man was practically breathing through his mouth already.

They pulled into her driveway, and he walked around to open her door for her. Nicole didn't say anything. Apparently, all you had to do to turn a foul-mouthed werewolf into a gentleman was let him finger you in the workplace. Who knew?

Drake's eyes lit up when they walked into the house. Nicole didn't need him to say a word; she already knew he was smelling her from across the room. Smirking to himself, the were-cougar wisely kept his mouth shut.

Wes disappeared as soon as they crossed the threshold, probably to jerk his cock in private. Too bad... Nicole wouldn't have minded watching. Or helping.

She shook her head hard. Who the hell was she becoming?

Passing Hawthorne aggressively vacuuming the living room, she didn't need to pause and ask him why his eyes looked so red and itchy. He must have run out of antihistamines. She made a mental note to see if she could order them in bulk for the poor fae.

Still in somewhat of a daze, Nicole found herself standing in front of her dresser on the hunt for comfier clothing. And if she happened to grab a pair of pajama pants she didn't mind getting shredded... well, that was her business.

The smell of something spicy drifted up the stairs and into her bedroom. Following her nose, Nicole found Hawthorne and Wes in the kitchen making tacos. Drake waved her over to sit beside him at the dinner table, a mess of paperwork spread out in front of him, diagrams and rough sketches with measurements and calculations scribbled across them.

Nicole didn't even ask. Math was her worst subject in school.

The cougar slid her pickle mug over to her, already filled to the brim with wine, and turned back to his work without a word.

Settling in her seat, she sipped her wine from her favorite mug and listened to the werewolf and the fae argue about the proper ratio of jalapeños to salsa. A small smile curved her lips. She turned in her chair and lifted her legs to rest her feet in Drake's lap. His hand dropped to her ankle, his thumb rubbing little circles on her skin while he scribbled down more math.

The vampires glided into the room. Jasper and Atticus each paused to tilt her head back and steal a kiss before pouring their own glasses of wine and continuing their discussion about their current case.

Nicole watched her monsters and sipped her wine. She didn't know who was trying to sabotage her life, but they had better fuck right off. If they ruined this for her, they weren't going to be her problem anymore—Nicole was going to be theirs.

20

NICOLE

Nicole stared at the dark ceiling. It was too early to get out of bed, but sleep was eluding her. How was she supposed to get a good night's sleep knowing that someone was creeping around her yard at night?

Thank heavens she was dating a mechanic. The price of new tires for all of their cars would have had her fainting right there in her driveway.

"Forget this," she grumbled.

Kicking off the blankets, Nicole dragged herself out of bed. If she wasn't going back to sleep, she may as well start her morning ritual of drowning her worries in buckets of coffee.

At least she didn't have to feign energy all day at work. The weekend had arrived right in time for her anxious spiral.

She yawned and stumbled her way down the stairs. A random toolbox rested on the bottom step, nearly tripping her as she continued her sleepy quest for caffeine.

Shoving it to the side, Nicole shook her head. The men taking over her house might have abs for days and dote on her like lovesick teens, but they were also absentminded slobs.

She flipped on the kitchen light, and for the first time all week, it was blessedly silent in the house—no werewolves grumbling about condescending cougars, no vampires arguing about court documents and spitting nonsensical lawyer jargon at each other, and no elves complaining that there were leftover meatballs touching his eggplant. Just divine silence.

Setting the coffee maker, Nicole opened the cabinet, and the air deflated from her calm bubble. A frown crinkled her brow. Where the fuck was her pickle mug?

Better question, which monster had a death wish today?

"I'm buying them all paper cups from now on," she growled.

No sleep? No lucky mug? Her weekend was growing more ominous by the second.

Nicole settled for another, less lucky mug and snagged a banana from the fruit bowl while she waited for the coffee maker. She could still turn her morning around. Mind over matter and all that jazz.

Wasn't Miri always saying she needed to be more positive? Eyeing Drake's tools scattered on the kitchen table, she had to clench her teeth.

"Positive," she hissed through her tight jaw. "I am being positive."

She poured herself a cup of coffee and sighed as the first sip passed her lips. Why wasn't it as good as when Drake made it? It's not like she made it any differently than he did. The grumpy cat shifter was ruining her for any other coffee.

It had to be the lucky cup. Drake always made sure he gave her coffee in the dill pickle mug. It was lucky coffee—that was the only plausible explanation.

Grumbling under her breath, Nicole peeled her banana.

She jammed a chunk of it in her mouth and freed the rest of the peel to go in the trashcan. Her hand paused over the trash. Eye twitching, she stared at the overflowing garbage.

Her mug slammed down on the counter. Coffee splashed her hand, but Nicole didn't spare it a glance. She was too busy planning five murders.

Stomping out of the kitchen, she shouted up the stairs. "Everyone get downstairs *now*!"

The sound of thundering footsteps rumbled overhead as Nicole walked back into the kitchen and crossed her arms over her chest. Drake was the first into the room, skidding to a stop as he caught sight of her dark scowl. Wes thudded into his back.

"Have a seat," she growled.

"What's wrong?" Atticus asked urgently, his dress shirt unbuttoned and askew as he hurried into the kitchen. As much as Nicole would like to admire this casual new version of the sultry vampire, she was a woman on a mission.

"Sit," she ordered.

His dark brows rose but, like the shifters, he silently took a seat in the face of her stormy attitude. One by one, the monsters piled into a room and sat down at the table.

"Who died?" Jasper yawned.

"Probably you if you keep asking questions," Drake warned quietly.

Ignoring their questioning looks, her eyes narrowed on the familiar mug in Jasper's hand. Seriously? The vampy bastard didn't even drink coffee.

"There had better not be blood in that mug."

A sheepish smile curved his full lips. "Would it make you feel better if I lied?"

Murder was illegal, and she would not make it in prison. Maybe if Nicole reminded herself of that every few minutes, she would feel less inclined to start ripping heads off.

"There's no wine in prison," she muttered under her breath.

"I'm gonna clean it," Jasper said softly.

"I need everyone to stop talking for thirty seconds so I don't start tearing my hair out," Nicole snapped. She definitely would not look good with a bald spot.

Stomping over to the cabinet, she rifled through the junk drawer. She grabbed a pen and pad of paper and threw them on the table.

"We need a chore chart. I am not your mommy, and I am not your maid," Nicole told the gathering of fanged monsters. "The dishes are piling up, I'm out of clean underwear, and the trash pile is turning into an engineering project."

"I don't think the panties are a problem," Wes said cheekily.

From his sharp yip and the way the werewolf suddenly clutched at his leg, someone had kicked him in the shin under the table. She had no idea which one it was, but they were officially her favorite.

She picked up the pen and tapped the notepad. "Write down a chore and pass it around."

No one moved. Was she speaking in tongues? What was so confusing about housework?

The men stared at her. The more feral she felt, the wider their eyes grew. Gritting her teeth, Nicole used every scrap of self-control not to start yelling. There wasn't nearly enough caffeine in her system for this bullshit.

"Why is no one moving?" she growled. "You wanna live in this house and be my monster boyfriends, start writing!"

She couldn't be any clearer if she were drawing them a diagram. Pick up the pen, write down a chore. It wasn't that hard.

Clearly, Nicole had been going too easy on them since

they'd all bullied their way into her house. They had lulled her into a false sense of calm with their dirty words and mind-melting orgasms.

Well, the orgasm train ended here... no... that wasn't quite right. Why hadn't she finished her coffee before going nuclear over taking out the trash?

"Boyfriends?" Wes interrupted her scattered thoughts. He raised his eyebrows, a smile fighting its way forward.

"I generally don't let roommates fingerbang me on the hood of a car," Nicole deadpanned. "Pick. A. Chore."

Jasper sputtered on a mouthful of blood. At least someone was amused this morning, because she definitely wasn't.

Gently prying the pen from her clenched hand, Hawthorne slid the paper toward himself.

"That's completely fair, and we should have thought of this already," Hawthorne soothed. "How about I take care of laundry since I get the dirtiest at work?"

He paused his scribbling to eye the vampires. They might be relaxing before they turned in for the day in dress shirts and slacks, but they looked no less immaculate than usual.

"You two might want to stick with dry cleaning."

Atticus snorted. "Like I was going to let you get anywhere near my custom-tailored wardrobe with discount detergent."

Rolling his eyes, the fae slid the paper to Drake across the table. The cougar snatched the pen and quickly scribbled down his own list.

"I'll handle maintenance, trash, and recycling... and vacuuming." He shot a look at Hawthorne, who was emptying a bottle of allergy meds into his hand. "I'm going to tear out the carpet next month, so that should help."

What was wrong with her carpet?

"Wait, what?" Nicole cut in.

"Wood floors look nicer, and it will be easier to clean up any animal hair for Captain Hay Fever," Drake said as he passed the paper to Wes.

The werewolf had the decency to look apologetic before picking up the pen. "I'll do the cooking."

"You can cook?" Nicole blinked. Apparently, this morning was full of surprises. Sure, he'd done some chopping here and there, but she'd never actually seen him use a stove.

"Did you think packing bagged lunches was the extent of my abilities?" he laughed, his golden eyes twinkling. "Shifters need a lot of food. It's either learn to cook, or burn through paychecks ordering out."

Wes thrust the chore list at the ancient vampires and paused, the pen still in his hand.

"Speaking of, if we're all going to live and eat here, everyone needs to pony up for groceries and bills. We're going to need to do a big grocery run soon to restock the fridge and pantry, and it's not on Nicole to feed us all."

She stared at the brash wolf. Who was he and where was Wes? First, he pulled the fact that he could cook more than a grilled cheese out of nowhere, and now, he was managing the bills. Clearly, the sexy, happy-go-lucky man had been replaced by a doppelgänger.

Hawthorne nodded. "I'll stop at the bank and pick up some cash tomorrow."

"I have some money upstairs," Drake added. "If you decide you want a vegetable garden, let me know. I should have most of the supplies already."

Wes tapped his chin thoughtfully. "I wouldn't mind access to fresh herbs. I also have a coupon for pot roast if no one is opposed tonight."

Nicole had tripped on that toolbox on the stairs, and she

was in a coma. It was the only plausible explanation. She'd just wanted someone to take out the trash, and now they were debating an herb garden and couponing? Her monsters certainly didn't do things halfway.

"We're vampires," Jasper yawned. "We don't eat food."

Hawthorne and the shifters turned their attention on the two monsters, who had been mostly silent through the impromptu meeting.

"Do you ever plan on nibbling on Nicole?" Drake asked sharply. His serious face was hard as stone as he stared them down.

A look passed between the two vampires.

"That is between us and Nicole," Atticus answered carefully.

She raised her eyebrows. Was anyone going to ask her if she wanted to be a snack, or were they going to gloss over that bit? Not that she was opposed to a little nibble, but still... it wouldn't kill them to ask.

"Well, if there's even a chance your fangs are going to touch her pretty neck, then you need to bust out your wallet and keep her fed, leech," Wes added aggressively.

Resting her hand on his shoulder, she could feel the tension vanish from his muscles under her touch. His hand rose to cover hers, the grip on her fingers tightening and dragging her sideways. Suddenly Nicole found herself sitting in the lap of a grumpy, sleep-rumpled werewolf.

Thick arms wrapped around her waist. Someone was in a touchy mood.

"Be nice," she said softly. Her fingers stroked the arm around her ribs until she felt him relax. "It's too early for a brawl."

Eyeing her new seat, Atticus pulled a money clip from his pocket. He slipped three crisp hundred-dollar bills out of the fold and passed them across the table.

"For groceries and bills. The first of the month is coming up, and the utility bills will have risen with all of us here."

Heads bobbed around the table in silent agreement as Wes settled his chin on her shoulder. Leaning back against his chest, Nicole yawned. The spontaneous family meeting was doing a hell of job at leeching away her anxiety.

Or maybe that was the muscled body pressed against her.

Jasper pulled his wallet from his pocket and tossed a couple more bills onto the pile. "That should cover a housekeeper to come once a week and handle the rest."

"No." Drake frowned and leaned over the table. He pushed the chore list closer to them. "You still need to pick at least one chore. Everyone needs to actively participate."

"I'm two hundred years old, and I am not going to scrub —" Atticus growled.

"We will load and unload the dishwasher." Jasper gave Atticus a teasing grin and grabbed the pen. "You can wash a dish, old man."

"*Old?*"

Nicole choked on her laugh. She'd never seen a man in a shirt more expensive than her car hiss like a cat before.

Jasper passed her the handwritten chore list with a wink, and she smiled down at the notepad. If she'd known that all she had to do to force them to get along was look a bit feral and rant about the dishes, she would have done that on day one.

"Excellent." Nicole tucked the list into the pocket of her pajama pants to hang on the fridge later.

Would it be overkill to have Miri laminate it?

Now, she wouldn't be spending her days tripping over muddy boots and hunting for clean spoons. And since none of them had objected to the 'boyfriend' label, Nicole had killed two birds with one stone, and she hadn't even had a proper breakfast yet.

Speaking of...

"Who do I have to make out with to get some decent coffee?" she asked innocently.

Five monsters stood at once and beelined for the coffee maker.

21

NICOLE

Nicole screeched into the parking lot, her new tires skidding as she skipped the curb. Somewhere, she was sure Wes just had a heart palpitation.

For once, it wasn't her fault she was running late. The werewolf hadn't wanted to let her off his lap. Instead, he'd held her tight and sniffed her hair while she worked her way through two cups of coffee and flipped through a couple magazines. She barely had enough time to wash and dry her hair before running out the door to meet Ashley and Miri for lunch.

After rushing to get everyone's tires replaced yesterday, Wes had definitely earned a squeeze or two.

She parked her car and tugged her hood over her long hair. Looking anxiously for the door, Nicole made a run for the restaurant. Why did they have to choose somewhere new for this week's lunch rendezvous?

It had been a tradition for years, but now that things were heating up with the pack of monsters who had taken over her house, it was a mandatory gossip sesh. Besides, Nicole needed some non-guy time to figure things out.

Like how to get things moving in the bedroom department. Oral and what not was nice and all, but the continued presence of half-naked men in her house was making her dick-horny.

Nicole hurried into the restaurant, her face tucked low in her hood. She hid behind her dark sunglasses, eyes flitting behind the black lenses and scanning for familiar faces. She wove through the tables and dropped into the empty seat next to Miri.

"Um, hello?" Ashley snorted. "Did you double book lunch with an assassination, madame spy?"

"It's not funny," Nicole grumbled. Slipping off her sunglasses, she dropped them into her purse. "Every time I leave the house, I run into some guy with a tail or horns or whatever I didn't swipe on.

"The scaly guy with the office next to mine? I swiped left on him, and he keeps trapping me in conversations about fishing every time he spots me at the water cooler. I can't go anywhere without getting cornered by someone."

Miri laughed. "It can't be *that* bad."

Nicole looked her dead in the eye. "I was at the grocery store the other day, and some kind of yeti recognized me in the ice cream aisle and started testing out snow-themed pickup lines. Do you understand how horrifying it is to be trapped next to the frozen yogurt listening to a seven-foot fluff ball offer to show you his icicle?"

Ashley choked on her lemonade as Miri howled with laughter. "Please tell me you're joking!"

"I wish," she sighed. "I've met more monsters in the last week than I have in my entire life."

"Maybe you should delete the app," Miri gasped between giggles.

Ashley nodded, her eyes thoughtful. "You do seem pretty happy with the men you already have."

Well, she certainly wasn't about to replace one of them

with a giant yeti with terrible taste in ice cream. Pistachio? Honestly.

"I snoozed my profile so no one else sees it." A small smile tugged at the corner of her lips. "If things are still going well in a month, I'll delete it."

So far, it was going great—minus the little problem with chores, but after Nicole had had a couple cups of coffee, the situation seemed far less dire. Plus, Hawthorne had done a load of laundry. It was a lot easier to be calm about a situation when you didn't have to go commando.

"Soooo... things are going well?" Ashley aggressively wiggled her eyebrows.

She didn't have to ask; Nicole knew exactly what she meant. A blind, deaf child would have known exactly what she meant. There were astronauts on the international space station who knew what Ashley meant.

Swiping her menu off the table, Nicole raised it to hide her pink cheeks.

"Oooh! They have chicken strips!" she read.

"You have the palette of a toddler," her friend sighed.

She peaked over the top of the menu and fixed the blonde with puppy dog eyes.

"So you *didn't* already order the mozzarella sticks?"

Miri sat upright, her face sober and her laughter subsiding in an instant.

"Wait, what?"

"Of course, I ordered mozzarella sticks for the table. I'm not an idiot." Ashley shook her head at the two of them. "And stop deflecting. I didn't take the afternoon off to *not* talk about monster dick."

"It's a Saturday?" Miri raised an eyebrow.

"And I'm trying to land the firm a huge account. Saturday is the new Monday," she said primly.

Nicole rolled her eyes. For someone who was always

pushing them to "get out there" and "live their lives," Ashley was the definition of a workaholic with no work-life balance.

Maybe she wasn't only one who needed some monster dick in their life.

"When are you going to stop working so much and get some monsters of your own?"

"When I can't live vicariously through you anymore."

If anyone would enjoy being the center of a vampire sandwich, it was the long-legged blonde. Nicole had been her roommate early in college, and she knew way too much about Ashley's sexual appetite. She still had nightmares about some of the "studying" she had walked in on.

The waiter strolled up with an overflowing basket of mozzarella sticks before Nicole could push her some more. They placed their lunch orders and waited for the waiter to be out of earshot.

"Well?" Miri asked, her eyes bright behind her thick glasses. "How *is* it going?"

"It's going kinda great," Nicole admitted around a mouthful of deep-fried mozzarella.

"Details, woman!" Ashley hissed. "You've had them in your house for a week, and we need details!"

"Well, this morning, we made a chore list."

"Lame. What else you got?"

"Gee, thanks," she laughed. "I don't know. They just kind of... take care of me."

Nicole wasn't exactly sure how to describe it. It wasn't just one thing. For the first time in her life, it felt like someone was thinking about her all the time—worrying if she ate enough, if she slept well. For the first time, she felt genuinely... loved.

Miri and Ashley were great but she wasn't the center of their lives.

"Drake always takes my lucky mug so he can make my coffee in the morning. He takes a little sip out of it to make sure it's right." She smiled dreamily. Ashley and Miri exchanged smug looks and waved her on. "If I even mention something I need in passing, Atticus makes sure a brand new one is waiting for me when I crawl into bed. And Hawthorne? There's this vase on the kitchen table, and every day, he puts new flowers in it for me."

"I'm gonna cry." Miri waved at her eyes. "It's like you stack them all together to make the perfect boyfriend."

"Wes made that joke yesterday. It's like they combine into one super boyfriend... and I kind of love it."

"Okay, loving the romance." Ashley dropped a straw into her water. "But how's the sex?"

"We, uh, haven't had sex yet," Nicole muttered before cramming another mozzarella stick into her mouth.

If she'd known they were going to pepper her with questions instead of eating, she would have had a snack before she left the house.

"Pass me the ranch, please—" She trailed off at the shock on their faces.

Sitting still as statues, Ashley and Miri stared at her. Their food sat in front of them, growing colder by the second as they tried to process her words.

"It's not that big of a—"

"Nicole!" Ashley whisper shouted. "You have five men at home who look like they walked off the cover of a magazine, and you're not riding any of them? Are you dying? You can tell us; we can take it."

She rolled her eyes. Someone had woken up on the dramatic side of the bed this morning.

"Better question," Miri interjected. "You're not banging any of them, and they still want to do the laundry? They're not monsters—they're angels."

"They're being very respectful!" she insisted. Both women wrinkled their noses in disgust. Yeah, that was fair. "We've done... other... stuff."

Ashley brandished her fork threateningly. "Bitch, put down the mozzarella stick and give us the details. We're *this* close to holding an intervention on behalf of your vagina."

"Oh my God, fine!" Dropping her food onto her plate, Nicole made a show out of wiping off her hands slowly. If they were going to pry it out of her, they were going to wait until she was good and ready. "Jasper and Atticus fingered me in the car on our last date, Hawthorne went down on me at the breakfast table while Drake watched, and last night, Wes and I made out in his garage. Happy now?"

Miri clapped her hands to her chest. "I have literally never been so happy for you in my life."

"My little baby is growing up," Ashley sniffled.

"I will murder you both with a chicken strip," Nicole muttered under her breath.

They'd better enjoy the moment while they could, because the next time either one of them got a serious boyfriend, it was her turn and she wouldn't be stopping until she had their beau's social security number and shoe size.

Her purse buzzed under the table. Fishing out her phone while Ashley and Miri gushed, Nicole was already smiling in anticipation. Lunchtime, right on schedule.

She thumbed open the message, and her heart fluttered.

> JASPER
>
> The car doesn't smell like you anymore. We need to fix that, pet <3

He had to be scheduling these ahead of time. There was no way he set an alarm every single day to wake up and send her a flirty text.

Right? Because that would be ridiculous... and yet, completely in character.

"Which one is it?" Ashley teased.

"What?" Nicole looked up quickly, stuffing her phone back in her purse.

A sly smile stretched across her pixie face. "I know I'm right. Which one of your hunks has you smiling like Miri when she spots a puppy?"

Flames burned her cheeks. "Jasper."

"The blond vampire, right?" Miri questioned. "He's got that voice that just makes you wanna melt."

"He sends me a text every day at lunch."

Ashley frowned. "I thought vampires slept all day?"

"They do," Nicole said. "I haven't figured out yet if he's scheduling them ahead of time or setting an alarm and waking up to send it."

Sighing dreamily, Miri rested her chin on her hands. "That is so ridiculously cute."

Nicole was pretty sure that last text was a prelude to fingering her pussy again, but she wasn't about to announce that to the table.

"Now that the sexy stuff is out of the way, let's get real." Ashley focused on her. "How's the loan repayment plan going?"

She laughed. Typical Ashley; once the dick was out of the way, she was straight to business.

"They decided today that they'll be pitching in for utilities and paying the entire grocery bill." Nicole shrugged even as guilt started to claw at her stomach. "Between the work Drake, Thorne, and Wes have done on my house and car, things are looking a lot less bleak."

And that wasn't even taking into account Jasper and Atticus. They'd wanted to buy her a whole new car after the tire incident. They worried the sabotage was going to end in a car accident, but Nicole was just worried she was taking advantage of them.

She'd put a guilty stop to any discussion of buying her a new car. Of course, she'd still overheard Atticus talking to Wes about seat warmers later that night, so Nicole was pretty sure her words had gone in one ear and out the other.

"So, everything is going according to plan." A satisfied smile spread across her friend's face.

"I'm not sure I love the word 'plan'." Nicole cringed. "It makes me sound like some kind of gold digger."

"You're not a gold digger!" Miri reached over and squeezed her hand. "You just needed a little help with the bills. There's nothing wrong with that."

"And now you have a great job. That's going to make you feel more independent," Ashley added.

Then why did she still feel so guilty?

"I just don't want them to feel like I was using them... even though I totally was... am... I don't know."

Every time Atticus slipped a gift into her room, she felt guilty. Every time Hawthorne and Drake added another house project to the list, guilty again. Every time Jasper and Wes lavished her with attention just for existing, cue the guilt.

"Is there a point where I'm going to stop feeling bad about this?" Nicole sighed. "Should I just tell them? I mean, we're definitely past the point where this is about money. I care about them... but I also don't want to hurt them."

Ashley and Miri exchanged worried looks.

"Um, maybe don't tell them," Ashley said hesitantly. "If this was just about sex, it would be one thing, but if you genuinely care about them, do they need to know the little details?"

"But on the other hand—" Miri started.

Holding up a hand, Nicole silenced them both. "I don't know what I want to do yet, but this definitely isn't helping."

"Would the last mozzarella stick help?" Miri nudged the basket closer to her.

"Only one way to find out."

Nicole swiped the last appetizer and popped it into her mouth. If fried cheese couldn't fill the hole guilt was burning in her stomach, nothing could.

22

NICOLE

Nicole slipped into the kitchen, her takeout box tucked under her arm. Drake sat at the kitchen table with some kind of woodworking project spread in front of him. Sniffing the air, he perked up as she passed by.

"Don't even think about it," she warned.

Fishing through the junk drawer, Nicole pulled out a black marker and scrawled her name across the top of her leftovers. She was all for sharing, but with the way shifters ate, one bite would quickly turn into the whole container. If even one of them touched her chicken, there would be hell to pay.

She tucked the takeout box in the fridge and shot Drake one more stern look.

"If anyone eats my leftover chicken strips, there will be blood," she threatened.

"Yes, ma'am."

"I'm serious, Drake. That is an offense punishable by maiming."

"It's chicken."

Clearly, he did not understand women. "Yes. And it's *my* chicken."

He shook his head, a smile tugging at his lips. He went back to playing with his tools and ignoring her bossy orders. Rude.

And here she had been planning to go curl up in his lap and ask about his day. Now, he could sit and play with his wood all alone.

Nicole grumpily dragged a pint of ice cream from the freezer, grabbing a spoon and flipping the lid off. A giant bite had been taken out of the top.

She sighed. And the were-cat was giving her shit?

Nicole was surrounded by furry food thieves, and no amount of cheeky smiles and six pack abs would make that okay. At what point was she going to have to start trading sexual favors for snack security? Hawthorne might be up for it.

Nicole jumped as a nose poked into the nook behind her ear and sniffed.

Damn shifters. Would it kill them to make some kind of noise when they walked? If they didn't stop sneaking up on her and trying to give her a heart attack, she was going to have to start carrying around a spray bottle.

A couple good spritzes on the nose, and they would learn their lesson. It had worked for her mom's beagle—why not a werewolf?

A flash of a frowning Wes dripping all over her nearly had Nicole choking on her ice cream.

"Mmmmm," Wes rumbled behind her.

Whirling around, she brandished her spoon like a sword. "Back, fiend. No sniffing before dinner."

"What about after dinner?" The werewolf wriggled his eyebrows. "We can ditch the guys and go for a picnic... just the two of us."

"Gee, thanks," Drake snorted.

Wes looped his thick arm around her waist and dragged her closer. A strong hand gave her ass a squeeze as he chuckled in her ear. Fire ignited in her cheeks.

Would she ever not blush when her monsters got handsy? Probably not.

"You smell perfectly edible," he whispered.

He'd certainly thought so yesterday. Wes' eyes had practically rolled back into his head as he'd licked his fingers clean of her.

Nicole blushed harder. She definitely hadn't been thinking of that moment in his garage over and over again last night... and this morning... and in the shower. Definitely not.

The werewolf sniffed her neck and groaned, the sound filling the quiet kitchen.

"What is with you and sniffing me? Is it a wolf thing?" It had to be. None of her other monsters tried to inhale every bit of her flesh every time they passed in the hall. Not even Drake, though he'd come close once or twice.

"No reason." His hand gave her ass another squeeze. "Now, about that picnic—"

His tongue swiped her collarbone and she shivered. Then again... maybe they could sneak away for a bit. Nicole would finally get a chance to strip him naked and see if he really could give her something to howl about.

"You're ovulating," Drake interrupted her lusty thoughts.

The arousal curling in her belly was doused in a heartbeat. "Excuse me?"

Gesturing with his screwdriver, he waved at the werewolf glaring at him over Nicole's shoulder. "He can smell the change in your hormones and it's making him horny."

"Please tell me you're joking?"

"Nope. His nose is telling his pea-sized wolf brain that you're breedable."

Breedable? *Breedable?*

Nicole whirled around and shoved the werewolf away from her. Absolutely the hell not. The last thing her chaotic life needed was a furry baby who spent its bedtime howling at the moon and growing fangs.

Her house was already full of monsters. She didn't need a mini one.

Wes raised his hands and backed away, his handsome face twisted into a mask of contrition that utterly failed to hide his cheeky grin. Sly bastard.

"Are you fucking kidding me right now?"

"It's not my fault!" he insisted. His hand snapped out and caught her fingers. Raising her hand, Wes pressed a light kiss against her knuckles. "You're the one who smells so damn tempting."

"And yet, I'm over here, keeping my hands to myself." Drake rolled his eyes. Balling up a greasy rag, he tossed it at the werewolf's head. "Down, dog!"

Nicole shook her hand free. Clearly, someone was not in his right mind. She didn't know if one could smack sense into a lust drunk werewolf, but she was certainly willing to try.

"You would look gorgeous round with my pups."

Nope, nope, nope. She pushed away the sneaky hand inching for her waistband. Smiling sweetly, she pressed his hand back toward him.

"First off, I'm on the pill, so that's *definitely* not happening." Her smile widened at Wes' pout. If he thought that was bad... "Secondly, if you keep trying to get your hands in my pants, I'm going to have Drake rip your clothes off and hold you down while Hawthorne sprays you with the garden hose."

The lovesick pout vanished off his face. Like a bucket of water washing over him, Wes gave his head a hard shake. If that didn't sober him up, nothing would.

"I need to go for a walk," he grumbled. Jamming his hands into his pockets, he headed for the door.

"More like going to jerk off in the backyard," Drake laughed.

"I swear to Gaia, if you come on the rose bushes I just planted, I'm going to turn your dick into a mushroom!" Hawthorne shouted at his back as he came strolling into the kitchen.

"I'm going for a *walk*," Wes growled, and the back door slammed shut behind him.

Nicole pinched the bridge of her nose. All she had wanted was a cute monster to help pay off her student loans —now, she was listening to overgrown man children fight about jizzing on the landscaping.

"I should've gone to trade school," she muttered under her breath.

Jamming another spoonful of ice cream into her mouth, she ignored the smirking were-cougar and the fae giving her concerned looks. If even one of them said a word about Wes the Ovary-Sniffing Canine, they were going to end up wearing her container of melting ice cream as a hat.

Nicole licked her spoon clean and tossed it in the sink. Somehow, they had managed to ruin her pre-dinner treat. Unbelievable.

She shoved the pint back into the freezer and glared at them both. They might not have been the horny beast trying to put baby monsters in her, but they were guilty by association, at least for today.

The sound of glass shattering cut the tense silence, and everyone's head shot up as an engine revved in the driveway and screeched away. Leaping out of his chair, Drake cleared the kitchen in a single bound and burst out the back door.

"What the hell just happened?"

Hawthorne took a step toward her as wolf howls and cougar shrieks filled the afternoon air. His usual shy smile vanished and hardened into a watchful mask as he carefully gripped her elbow.

Nicole moved closer to him. Something was very wrong. The sweet fae looked like he was about to attend a funeral, and Drake and Wes were nowhere to be seen.

"The glass," she said, looking up at his sharp frown. "Was it a window? It sounded like it came from upstairs."

"Let's go check."

Hawthorne led her out of the kitchen, his grip tight around her hand. Worry clawed at her stomach. What if something happened to Drake and Wes? How would they even know?

They climbed the stairs, each step filling her with dread.

His nose scrunched. "Do you smell that?"

Nicole sniffed the air. The sharp tang of smoke ticked her nose. "Is something burning?"

Weaving their way through the house, Hawthorne and Nicole followed the growing scent. The fae stumbled to a stop. She leaned around him and spotted the door leading to the attic.

Oh, no. They'd forgotten about Jasper and Atticus.

Shoving past Hawthorne, Nicole ripped open the door and charged up the stairs.

"Wait!" the fae hissed behind her.

She ignored him. It was Jasper and Atticus. How could he possibly expect her to wait patiently at the bottom of the stairs?

Nicole burst through the attic door and skidded to a stop as her brain caught up with what her eyes were seeing. It was the first time she'd been up there since the vampires had claimed the space as their own. Gone were the crumbling floorboards, replaced with polished wood. The walls had been draped with swathes of pale gray velvet. Two plush beds covered in throw pillows and cushions rested against opposite walls.

Somehow, they had transformed the attic into a soft and airy suite while the rest of the house slept.

"The sun!" Hawthorne shoved past her to the window.

Her stomach dropped. The shock of the attic's makeover had completely eclipsed the fact that sunlight was pouring in through the uncovered window. Ripping a blanket off the nearest bed, she hurried to the fae's side.

"Be careful of the glass." Hawthorne nodded at the shards scattered around their feet and took the blanket from her. He tied the corners to the curtain rod and tucked in all the edges until the room was shrouded in shadow.

Nicole turned slowly, studying every corner of the dark room. Her heart pounded in her chest. She wasn't exactly the type to pray, but in that moment, she wished she was.

Please be okay.

"Atticus? Jasper?"

23

JASPER

Fuck. Jasper had told Atticus they needed shutters on the window, but *noooo* that would ruin his precious aesthetic. Tinted glass would be just *fiiiine*.

You know what else ruined an aesthetic? Looking like you took a bath in lava.

The vampire slumped in the corner. Waves of unrelenting agony rolled over him, one after another. Burns covered his arms and chest, but at least he'd escaped the worst of it. Atticus hadn't been so lucky. His old friend had been closer to the window when the brick came crashing through the tinted glass, and he looked like he'd gone for a swim in a volcano.

"Jasper? Atticus?" Nicole called again. "Please say something so I know you're okay!"

Sure. As soon as he remembered how to use his vocal cords.

Atticus shifted beside him, and red eyes burned like coals in the darkness. Hands curling into claws, he started to drag himself toward the sound of her voice.

Jasper raised his head. What was he—? Oh, fuck.

He saw the exact moment the other vampire snapped

and lunged forward with preternatural desperation. Shoving his own agony aside, Jasper tackled him, though Atticus fought against him like a man possessed. There was nothing in his gaze but feral hunger as he clawed at the floor to get closer to their precious human.

"Fucking stop!" Jasper hissed. Clamping his arms and legs around the monster, his muscles strained to pin him to the floor. "You're going to hate yourself for this later!"

Flames ignited in the darkness, and he caught a glimpse of Nicole's pale face before Hawthorne shoved her behind him. A ball of fire glowed in his hand, burning just as bright as the glyphs lining his arms. If Jasper lost his grip on Atticus, he had no doubt that the fae would turn them both to ash.

As he should. If Atticus touched a single hair on her head, Jasper would kill him himself. He might be his oldest friend, but he knew Atticus would do the same for him if the situation was reversed.

His arms strained to hold the struggling vampire in place. "Get her out of here!"

"No!" Nicole shoved Hawthorne sideways and crouched out of the vampires' reach. "Tell me how to help."

"Blood," Jasper growled, his arms tightening around the hissing monster he was clutching tight. "Refrigerator in the corner."

She nodded, her eyes wide. He could smell the fear on her from across the room. The sweet human was doing her best not to show it, but it was rolling off of her in devastating waves.

Nicole took a step toward the blood storage, and Atticus doubled his efforts in Jasper's arms.

"No!" he said quickly. "Don't move, pet. It's only making him more desperate."

Jasper sighed in relief when the fae gripped her wrist,

ready to drag her out of the room if the time came. Hawthorne edged around her to get to the mini fridge. Eyes never leaving the vampires, he fumbled for two bags of blood.

"Him first." Jasper jerked his head toward Atticus.

"How?"

Fuck, this was going to hurt.

He moved in a blur. Burns screaming in brain-melting agony, Jasper grabbed Atticus by the jaw. His legs quickly pinned his arms to the floor before he could scramble away. Hooking his fingers in his mouth, he ignored the fangs pricking his fingertips and pried the vampire's jaw open.

"Put the bag in his mouth!" he growled as sweat beaded on his brow. Arms shaking, Jasper struggled to keep his gnashing mouth still for the fae.

Hawthorne jammed the bag in his mouth and jumped back. Clamping down on the blood, Atticus's thrashing stilled. His teeth punctured the thin plastic, and blood spilled down his chin.

Jasper gave him one last worried look and rose to his feet.

"What are you—?" The fae stepped in front of Nicole to shield her, flames bursting to life in his hand once again.

"He should be fine now," Jasper sighed. Every last inch of his body ached. "The blood will take the edge off his survival instinct, and he'll start acting like his usual bossy bastard self."

Eyeing the feral vampire uneasily, Hawthorne tossed him the second bag of blood. Jasper caught it, ripping the corner with his fangs and letting the nectar fill his mouth.

Nirvana. Cool blood ran down his throat, dousing the flames still burning under his skin.

Maybe sucking on a bag of blood like a juice box was unsightly, but in that moment, Jasper couldn't care less. As much as he was falling for Nicole, the sweet relief as his burns began to heal was worth looking like a hot mess in front of her.

Besides, he thought she was beautiful with messy hair and stained pajama pants. Turnabout was fair play.

"What happened?" he muttered around the plastic in his mouth. If the wolf had thrown bricks through their windows for kicks, Jasper was going to twist his head right off his shoulders.

"We heard the glass shatter and an engine rev. The shifters went after the car while we went to check all the windows."

"We could smell you... burning," Nicole whispered. Fat tears rolled down her cheeks as she looked at Atticus.

"Don't cry, pet," Jasper shushed her. Wasn't he in enough pain already? Did she really want to make his chest hurt with her tears? "It's not our first time with a little sunburn."

"A little sunburn?" Her sadness turned fiery. Raising her sleeve, she dashed away the tears on her cheeks. "This is not a *little sunburn!* You look like someone lit you on fire!"

"I mean, technically, Atticus was a little bit on fire."

Of course, he'd put out the flames, but yes, whoever threw the bricks and shattered their window had effectively lit them on fire.

"It's not that big of a deal," he lied smoothly. It was a very big deal.

When Atticus was back to full strength, Jasper had no doubt he would make it his mission to find out who had done this. He wouldn't sleep peacefully again until they knew who had endangered Nicole. If Jasper hadn't been there...

He shuddered. Atticus would have drained her dry and not realized what was happening until Nicole was dead at his feet.

"Is he going to be okay?" Nicole whispered.

Jasper followed her sad gaze. Half of Atticus' flesh was burnt and ruined. He cringed. Even in the shadowed light of the room, they could all see it. It would have looked a thousand times worse if anyone were daring enough to reach for a lamp.

"He'll be okay," Jasper promised—and not just for her. He needed to hear himself say it too. "Atticus will be okay. Just give him a little time to feel like himself again."

Closing the distance, Nicole rested her hand on his cheek. "Are *you* okay?"

She looked him up and down, her eyes lingering on the burns lining his arms. The soft palm resting on his face was like a balm, and Jasper let his eyes flutter closed as he leaned in to the gentle touch.

What he wouldn't give to curl up for a few days with nothing but her soft caresses as he healed.

"I'll be fine." Turning his face, he pressed a light kiss against her palm. "It will take a few days to fully heal with bagged blood, but I'll be pretty for you again, pet."

Ignoring his teasing tone, Nicole's nose wrinkled at his words. "Bagged blood?" she asked delicately.

Jasper laughed. She had no problem with her two vampire beaus looking like barbecue, but medical grade bagged blood made her squirm?

"We get it delivered weekly." He shrugged and crossed to the small fridge. Snagging another bag, he replaced the empty one Atticus was sucking on. "It's not nearly as powerful as live blood, but it will do just fine. We'll have to order more this week, because he's going to burn through most of what we have."

Not ideal, but if it helped stop Nicole from bursting into tears every time she looked at him, Jasper would buy a truckload.

Heavy footsteps shook the attic as someone charged up the stairs. Drake and Wes burst into the room, the door banging wide open. They looked around, eyes wild as they took in the scene in front of them.

Two extra crispy vampires, one fae still holding a handful of flames and shining like a glow stick, and their favorite human with tear-stained cheeks.

Yep. They were definitely going to kill them.

"What did you do?" Wes growled.

He lunged forward... and landed on his ass. Jasper raised his brows at the handful of the wolf's t-shirt clutched in Drake's hand.

The cougar nodded at the glass scattered across the floor. "What did they throw?"

"Bricks," Jasper sighed. "Atticus shoved me out of the way before the second one took out the rest of the window. Did you get the prick?"

He shook his head. "They peeled out of the driveway before we could get to them."

Pity. He wouldn't have minded a snack.

"Will someone help me get Atticus off the floor?" Jasper sighed. His body was burning through the blood he'd consumed faster than he'd liked, his hands already starting to shake.

Drake dropped his grip on the wolf and gripped the burnt husk that was Atticus under the armpits. Moving as gently as they could, Jasper helped him lay Atticus on the bed. A burnt hand patted his arm when he started to straighten.

"Oh, good. Feeling less murderous?"

The familiar red eyes narrowed. Right, definitely not ready to joke about it yet.

"Fuck," Wes cursed under his breath. Avoiding looking

at the crispy vampire, he studied the ruined window. "Do we have enough wood to cover it?"

"I think I have some plywood in my truck." Drake turned and took off down the stairs.

The werewolf shot them an apologetic look. "We'll have to cover you while we get the window sealed up."

By the time the cougar came back with a sheet of wood and a nail gun, Jasper was feeling more like a burrito than a vampire. Swathed in thick blankets, the sun had a better chance of reaching the core of the Earth than it did him.

Nicole stood next to him, her hand resting on his blanket-covered head while they worked. She tapped her fingers gently when the last nail hammered home.

"Okay, you should be good now," she said softly.

Jasper shook off the pile of blankets and tossed them aside. Ignoring the discussion of sourcing stronger glass for the window, he glanced down at Nicole and followed her frown to the aching burns on his arms.

She bit her lip. Hand raising tentatively, her fingers hovered over the ruined flesh.

"You said live blood is more powerful... Would you heal faster if you had it?"

"Yes..." Jasper said, already having a bad feeling where she was going with this. "In minutes."

She nodded, her nose crinkled in thought. What he wouldn't pay to know what was going through her pretty head right then. What was the point of being an immortal with stock options older than some countries if you couldn't buy what you wanted?

Steeling her spine, Nicole raised her head and met his eyes with a ferocity that almost had him taking a step back.

"Then drink from me."

24

NICOLE

A beat of silence blanketed the attic as everyone sucked in their breath. Nicole counted the seconds. It wouldn't be long before—

"Absolutely the fuck not!"

"You can't seriously—"

"Nicole, I really think—"

Yep, there it was. Crossing the room, she threw open the door and pointed them down the stairs.

"If you're not a vampire, get out," she ordered.

Another round of arguments sounded from across the room, and Nicole rolled her eyes. Could they not see that this was completely necessary? Atticus and Jasper could be confused for lumps of coal, and that wasn't going to get better any time soon unless someone took drastic measures.

Since it seemed she was the only sane one, it was going to have to be her. Not that she particularly wanted to be a human juice box after seeing the devastating burns on their bodies—but when a girl was dating vampires, a little blood donation should come with the arrangement.

"This is between me and them." Nicole calmly looked them each in the eye. "Go."

"But—" Hawthorne's eyes flicked to the crispy vampire slumped on the far bed.

"Out. Right now," she snapped.

What did he really think Atticus was going to do? Groan at her?

Jasper would put the bossy vampire in a headlock if he so much as blinked in Nicole's direction with anything less than loving intentions. She wasn't worried... much.

Wes stomped past her and down the stars, Drake close behind him. The cougar shot her a silent, concerned frown as he passed. Hawthorne paused beside her and gave her fingers a quick squeeze.

"If you need anything, call out," he whispered. "We'll hear you."

The door clicked shut, and suddenly, she was very aware of the fact that she was standing alone in a room with two hungry, injured vampires. As snap decisions went, this wasn't one of her best.

"So." Nicole rubbed her hands nervously. "The snack bar is open for business!"

Even she could hear the faint tremble in her voice. The joke fell flat as Jasper and Atticus stared at her. She gritted her teeth. It was really hard to hold their gaze when all she could think about were the agonizing burns covering their perfect skin.

Nicole shrieked if she so much as grazed herself with her curling iron; she couldn't imagine the agony they were both suffering so calmly.

"Does that hurt?" she blurted out.

Atticus barked a sharp laugh. Jumping at the gravelly sound, she took an instinctive step back. So much for her confident bravado.

"You don't know what you're offering, pet," Jasper interrupted her silent panic. "It's okay to back out if you've changed your mind. We wouldn't blame you at all."

Maybe not, but she would blame herself if they had to spend even a minute longer in pain when she could have helped.

"Explain it to me." Ignoring the lizard part of her brain screaming that she was prey, Nicole forced herself to sit on the edge of the bed beside Atticus. "What does feeding from me entail?"

Two sets of red eyes watched her intently. She looked at Atticus and tried not to openly wince. He was covered in twice as many burns as Jasper, all of them blackened and charred.

Moving slowly, Nicole stroked his uninjured arm with her fingertips. He had to be in so much pain, and he was bearing it in total silence. Her arms itched to hug him tight, but even breathing had to be agony right now. The last thing Atticus would want was a hug.

"Tell me," she whispered.

Nicole had to help them. She couldn't walk away, not even if they asked her to.

"It's not a simple thing, Nicole. It's not like we're popping open a can of soda." Jasper thrust his fingers through his hair, half sleep rumpled, half crisped from the sunlight, and she couldn't help but think he looked like he'd stuck his finger in a light socket. "You're a person. Drinking from a living person is... intimate."

A pang of hurt stabbed her heart. Jasper was never the responsible one. He was light and carefree to Atticus' strong, bossy presence. He never hesitated to wrap his arms around her and whisper dirty things in her ear, but suddenly, he was keeping her at arms' length.

Had he really expected that this moment would never

come? Was Jasper having second thoughts about her now that their arrangement was becoming too real?

"Do you not... want... to?"

"I didn't say that," he said quickly. "It's just—"

"You need to heal, and I'm offering to help," Nicole cut him off.

Did he want to spend the rest of the week looking like burnt steak? Not to be vain, but that was kind of a deal breaker for her. Ignoring the sting in her chest, she steeled her spine.

"If you don't want to feed from me, just say so."

"He's dancing around your human sensibilities," Atticus rasped beside her.

His first words since she'd raced up the stairs, and they were filled with pain. Mindful of his burns, Nicole carefully took his familiar hand in hers. He squeezed her fingers, his rings gleaming against his ruined flesh, the polished gold shining in the soft light.

"What do you mean?" she asked quietly, terrified that even her words could do him harm in his state.

"If we do this, we're going to end up fucking you," Jasper sighed. "You're not ready for that, pet."

Nicole blinked. Well... she certainly hadn't been expecting *that*.

Not that she hadn't thought about it. Like a lot. A woman couldn't live in a house with five smoking hot monsters who walked around half naked without thinking about jumping their bones at least a dozen times a day, but none of them had taken that step yet.

And they certainly hadn't taken that step while looking like a burnt quesadilla.

Atticus leaned past her to glare at his old friend. "Has the sunlight completely burned away your manners?"

"I'll be polite when I stop feeling like—" Jasper raised

his arms and did a slow turn to show off his burns— "I took a nap on the surface of the fucking sun!"

Atticus rolled his eyes.

"Just because you're—"

"Okay."

The word burst out of Nicole before she could think too hard about it. She'd done enough thinking about it. Alone in her bed. In the shower. Every time Jasper sent her a kinky text on her lunch break.

She was done thinking about it.

The two vampires turned slowly to stare at her. "What?"

"I said okay." Nicole rose from the bed and peeled her t-shirt over her head, dropping it on the floor between them.

If they stared any harder, it was going to be her turn to spontaneously combust.

Her hands slid under her waistband and pushed her leggings down to her ankles. She wasn't going to lie to herself and say she wasn't nervous, but they needed this... and it's not like she could hide the fact that the idea of banging them both was turning her on. Their damned monster senses were probably already picking it up.

Though, maybe, it could wait until after they'd lost a bit of their crispy exterior. Nicole might be feeling adventurous, but no one was *that* adventurous.

Standing there half-naked, she raised her eyebrows. "Are you two going to get with the program, or do I need to keep stripping?"

For once, bossy Atticus was at a loss for words as he gaped at her, and a slow grin spread across Jasper's face.

"Don't let us stop you, pet."

She reached up to unhook her bra, but a gentle hand caught her wrist and tugged her fingers free.

"Not yet," Atticus murmured. "Jasper, help me up."

Nicole stood back as the vampires maneuvered Atticus

up the bed to rest against the headboard. He hissed with each sharp move but never said a word.

"Grab him another bag of blood, please."

She hurried over the mini fridge and blinked at the neat rows of bagged blood inside. The two vampires might barely be able to work a smart phone, but they certainly were organized.

Swiping a bag, she hurried back. Jasper took the blood from her and jammed the bag into Atticus's mouth.

"One more. Just to be safe." He turned back to her, his fiery red eyes looking her up and down with poorly disguised hunger—though what kind of hunger, she wasn't quite sure yet. "Sit between his legs, your back against his chest."

Nicole crawled up the bed, and her cheeks flushed red as she felt Jasper's eyes on her lacy panties. Thank God Hawthorne had done her laundry yesterday. She seriously doubted her faded granny panties would be getting such focused attention from the dirty-minded monster behind her.

Moving slowly, she settled between Atticus' legs and leaned back against him. A low breath hissed from between his fangs.

"Sorry—" Nicole cringed away from his burnt body. There was no way to do this in a way that wouldn't hurt him.

A strong arm wrapped around her chest and tugged her back. Atticus tossed the empty blood bag aside and hugged her tight.

"It's okay," he promised. "You're worth more than a little twinge, love."

His warm breath curled over her shoulder, dragging shivers down her spine. This was really happening. A couple bites, and it was go time... finally.

Jasper climbed up the bed, his bright eyes still locked on

her. Nudging her knees apart, he lay down between her legs, and cool hands slid up her thighs. Nicole's heart hammered in her chest as she looked down at the handsome vampire resting his cheek against her inner thigh.

"I'm going to bite you right here." A fingertip stroked over tender flesh. "Atticus will bite your neck."

Hands smoothed down her arms even as lips pressed against her throat.

"It will only hurt for a second," Atticus rasped softly.

At that point, Nicole didn't care how long it hurt. As long as Jasper kept petting her thighs like that, it would take an act of God to get her out of their bed.

"And then?" she managed to gasp.

Jasper placed a light kiss over her lacy panties. "And then, pain will be the last thing on your mind, pet."

25

NICOLE

Fangs sank into Nicole's flesh, and a gasp tore from her throat, pain stabbing at her nerve endings. The feeling faded in an instant. Waves of bliss quickly drowned the flash of agony, washing over her again and again.

Leaning back against Atticus' chest, she felt like she was floating. Somewhere in her mind, Nicole was aware that the two vampires were drinking her blood but with liquid pleasure spreading under her skin, it didn't seem so important.

She'd been afraid of this? If she'd known it would feel this damn good, she would have begged them to take a sip on that first fateful drive home.

Hands stroked over her body, and Jasper's thumbs brushed over her panties as he sucked on the inside of her thigh. She arched back at the bolt of pleasure spiking through her body. Atticus wrapped an arm around her chest and hugged her tight, his fingertips stroking the length of her throat.

She moaned. Head flopping back against the vampire behind her, she struggled to keep her legs open as she ached to squeeze her thighs together. If it weren't for the hands holding her legs still, she would be squirming on the bed.

They weren't even fucking her, but already, they were driving her out of her mind.

Atticus shifted behind her, his hard erection pressed against her back. She didn't need to slide her fingers into her panties to know her pussy was just as ready. As if sensing her thoughts, Jasper's thumbs changed direction and brushed over her clit.

"Fuck!" she gasped.

Hands clutching desperately at the arm wrapped around her chest, Nicole arched off the bed, but strong hands pushed her back down. Drowning in pleasure, she almost missed Atticus' flesh smoothing under her touch.

Her blood was working. Some part of her was glad, but another, much louder part was already mourning the fact that it was almost over.

Jasper lifted his head. Nicole stared at his clear face. His burns had melted back into his skin, leaving nothing behind but tiny red marks. His gleaming gaze met hers, and looking her in the eye, he trailed kisses along her inner thighs.

"Sweeter than I ever could have imagined," he groaned against the sensitive flesh.

The pained hunger in his red eyes had been replaced by a feral light—a light that promised to consume her in more ways than one. At least, if she could survive it.

Nicole wasn't so sure she would, but she was willing to try. Any woman would agree; it was better to die mid-orgasm than any other way. Damn it, she was going to die a hero.

Atticus' tongue licked the length of her throat, skimming the edge of the tingling bite. Nicole couldn't help but moan as he teased the mark.

Laughing, he dragged his fangs over the bite. His tongue

swept over her skin, leaving the tiniest flash of pain before the bite healed itself.

"All better," he murmured against her throat.

Just like that? One swipe of his tongue, and the ache in her neck was gone.

Where the hell had he been all her life?

Between her legs, Jasper rubbed his thumbs over his bite. Streaks of red smeared across her thigh as his fingers danced over her flesh, painting tiny marks that he licked clean.

"Jasper," Atticus warned. "She's lost enough blood. You can play next time."

"But—" He sighed at the vampire's sharp look. "Fine."

He dipped his head and licked the bite. Jasper was already kissing his way up her thighs in the seconds it took for the mark to heal, pleasure burning hot in his wake. His mouth pressed a final kiss over her panties before he raised his head to look her in the eye.

Nicole was panting in anticipation as his fingers hooked under her waistband and dragged her underwear down her legs. Jasper wasted no time in replacing the thin lace with his mouth.

The air burst from her lungs in a rush. Pleasure built in her belly with each swipe of the vampire's tongue. Clearly, someone had spent their immortal life honing their skills.

The tip of his tongue teased her clit. Nicole only had a brief second to bask in the glowing pleasure before she felt the prick of his fangs. Pleasure spiked through her like a sunburst, hot, desperate bliss starting from her pussy and spreading outward in burning waves.

A gasp ripped from her lips as Jasper licked the pinpricks and went back to devouring her with his tongue. Thick fingers teased her. One after the other, they dipped inside her and soothed the needy ache.

Nicole panted, the air sawing in and out of her lungs. Just as she felt like the world had turned right side up, the sneaky vampire did it again. Her back arched off the bed, and she was so busy drowning in wave after wave of ecstasy that she didn't notice her bra had disappeared until strong fingers were teasing her nipples.

As Atticus pressed wet, tantalizing kisses along her throat and stroked her breasts, Nicole couldn't help but think of Ashley's words the morning after their tequila nightmare.

Every woman should have a threesome at least once in her life.

She had a half a second to remind herself to send her friend a fruit basket before her orgasm hit her like a battering ram. Nicole's whimpers filled the quiet attic.

She was dying—that was the only explanation. The two vampires had drained her dry and her mind was protecting her from the pain of death with pleasant hallucinations.

As if sensing her thoughts, Jasper raised his head and licked his smirking lips.

"I think she's ready now."

Ready? *Ready*? Nicole's nerve-endings were greedy sluts drowning in pleasure. The only thing she was "ready" for was a very long nap.

The two vampires were far from done with her. Nudging her limp body forward, Atticus arranged her on her knees, her ass in the air. Nicole dragged herself up onto her elbows. If she weren't already flushed from her orgasm, the intimate pose would have had her cheeks scorching red.

Cool fingertips cupped her dripping cunt. Burying her face in the sheets, she moaned into the mattress. Jasper's smoky laugh had her raising her head to glare. The smug bastard knew exactly what they were doing to her, and he was reveling in every second of it.

He kissed her hard. Tongue dipping into her mouth, he tasted her moans. "Ready, love?"

Atticus didn't bother waiting for the answer that would never come. He pressed the tip of his cock into her opening and, inch by agonizingly slow inch, he pushed inside of her. The tight stretch burned as he sank deeper and deeper, and Jasper swallowed her groan. She wasn't sure where the pleasure ended and she began anymore.

She was wrong. *This* would be the death of her.

Strong hands curved over her hips, the cold metal of Atticus's rings biting into her skin with the tightening of his grip. The first slam of his hips nearly took her out. Blackness crowded the corners of her vision, teasing oblivion as the slide of his cock rammed her with pleasure.

Blood-red eyes watched her with glee as Jasper palmed his dick and stroked the length. He eyed the snap of Atticus' hips as he pounded her pussy with abandon, a dark smile curving his lips.

"Look at you. So needy." He stroked her jaw and raised her face to look him in the eye. "You've been aching for his cock for a while, haven't you, pet?"

Nicole opened and closed her mouth. Was he really expecting an answer? The only sounds she was capable of in that moment were desperate whimpers as she danced along the edge of an orgasm that would surely be her undoing.

"That's it. Keep moaning, sweetheart." Jasper kissed her, his tongue dipping into her gaping mouth to tease hers. "Show him how much you like that dick."

A sharp slap across her ass cheek had her legs shaking. Atticus spanked her again, his rings bruising her flesh. Nicole fisted her hands in the sheets as they took turns driving her over the edge.

"I'm go—gonna—come!" she groaned.

Jasper grinned. "What was that, pet? You want this dick too?"

He stroked his hard cock, his thumb teasing the weeping tip with each pass. Nicole couldn't tear her eyes away. She wanted it. She wanted every bit they had to offer.

Clearly, they were aiming to kill her tonight, and she wanted to do the thing properly.

Atticus leaned over her, his chest pressing her deeper into the bed. Fingers wrapping around her throat, he held her tightly in place even as his hips pounded forward.

"He asked you a question." A sharp fang nipped her ear with his growl. "Answer him, Nicole."

The vampire ground his hips in a tight circle, stroking every secret button she didn't know she had.

"Yes!" she gasped. "Both. I want you both!"

Atticus straightened up, his hand dropping away only to be replaced by Jasper's.

"Open up for me."

The strong hand on her jaw opened her mouth wide. On his knees in front of her, Jasper fed the first couple inches of his cock into her waiting mouth. Her tongue swiped the first beads of cum from his swollen tip, and for once, his moans matched hers.

"You want more, don't you, pet?"

Fingers threaded through her tangled hair as the dirty-tongued vampire pushed deeper into her mouth. Lips ringing his cock, Nicole relaxed her throat. It was the only part of her she had any control over anymore.

The two vampires moved together, fucking her back and forth between them. Soon, the only sounds in the room were her sucking gasps for air and the wet slap of cock driving into her pussy.

"Good girl," Atticus groaned, his hand smoothing over her ass. "Taking us both so perfectly."

Jasper stroked her jaw. "Just like that, pet. Let me fuck that perfect, pretty throat."

Nicole moaned around the fat cock filling her mouth with each additional scrap of praise. She wasn't sure when she started to come, or if she had ever really stopped. Pleasure burned inside her, mounting higher and higher until there was nothing left to do but tremble.

The two vampires continued with their gentle pets and sweet praise, all the while fucking her faster and faster. Spit ran down her chin and breasts even as her pussy dripped down her thighs.

Her legs shook beneath her, threatening to spill her onto the mattress. Nicole wasn't sure how much more her body could handle. There were only so many back-to-back orgasms a girl could take before she descended permanently into madness.

Atticus spanked her handprint-covered ass one more time. "Come again for us, love."

Hands knotting in her hair, Jasper forced her to look him in his feral red eyes.

"Show us how badly you want to be filled with our cum," he growled.

Commanding fingers dipped between her legs and stroked her clit. Nicole managed one whimper before everything went black, though she was vaguely aware of Jasper telling her to open wider as she floated in an ocean euphoria.

Nicole didn't care. Her mouth was his problem now. Her whole body was their problem; she was busy finding heaven.

Jasper thrust balls deep into her mouth, and cum spilled down her throat and dripped from her lips. She swallowed around the thick cock and basked in his satisfied groans.

No reason he couldn't join her in paradise.

The vampire pulled out slowly, and a gasp slipped out of her swollen lips along with his cock. Another sharp slap landed on her abused ass, and then Atticus was slumped over her back, his body shaking as he filled her with his own release.

Free of their strong grip, Nicole collapsed on the bed. Never in her life had she sympathized with a wrung-out towel before... if a wet towel had just had back-to-back orgasms between two vampires with filthy mouths.

The bed dipped. In a herculean feat, she raised her head and frowned at their naked backs. Were they seriously leaving her after that?

Before she could open her mouth to protest, they were slipping back into bed beside her. Gentle hands petted her hair and placed a cookie in her hand.

"Hold still, love." Atticus pressed a light kiss against her temple. "Jasper will clean you up."

A damp towel swiped over her skin, cleaning every bit of their cum away with careful tenderness. Nicole lay back and let the blond vampire take care of her. After all, a good deal of it was a direct result of his dirty words.

Jasper tossed the towel into a hamper and climbed back into bed with a juice box—an actual juice box, thank heavens.

"You need the sugar," he told her confused frown. "Drink up."

Atticus popped the straw into her mouth, and Nicole relaxed as they cuddled her between them, hands stroking over her bare skin.

"Why do you have cookies?" Nicole yawned.

"The blood bank sends them with our bagged blood to encourage using live donors when one is available." Atticus tucked her tangled hair behind her ear. "There's a blood shortage right now."

The two vampires kept her awake until she'd finished the cookie and juice box. Settling into the fluffy mattress, Nicole let her eyes drift shut, the taste of chocolate and sugar still heavy on her tongue.

She couldn't help but wonder—if the Red Cross was handing out earth-shattering orgasms, maybe they'd have more donors. She made a mental note to write a letter and drifted off to sleep.

26

HAWTHORNE

Humming to himself, Hawthorne trudged down the stairs and into the kitchen. He had a to-do list as long as his arm, but he had no intention of starting his day without a good morning kiss from Nicole. Knowing her, she wouldn't be dragging herself out of bed for a while.

Might as well enjoy a cup of tea while he waited.

Hawthorne set the kettle on the stove and grabbed a mug. It wasn't her mug, but it would do. The kitchen was quieter than usual. Drake sat at the table with a bowl of cereal while Wes stared out the window with a grumpy frown on his face.

Someone had woken up on the wrong side of the bed this morning, and it definitely wasn't Hawthorne. It didn't take a mind reader to figure out why.

No one had seen Nicole yet. They hadn't seen her at all since she'd kicked them out of the vampires' suite—they'd certainly heard her, though. For most of the day and part of the night, in fact.

The young werewolf might have had a problem with that, but Hawthorne didn't. He wasn't a jealous elf by any means, and he would be lying if he said he didn't enjoy listening to her pleasurable moans filling the house.

Or that he didn't stroke himself as he lay in his bed and listened.

Wes glared impatiently at his watch. "First solo date, first sleepover," the wolf grumbled. "Damned bloodsuckers."

"Jealousy is an ugly color on you." Hawthorne dropped a tea bag in his cup and filled it to the brim with hot water. He was going to need a lot of herbal stimulation if he was going to have to deal with a sulky werewolf all day.

"Why aren't you annoyed?" Wes growled. "Wouldn't you have rather been up there with Nicole instead of those leeches?"

Hawthorne smiled and sipped his tea. Of course, he would, but he also hadn't been burned to a crisp like Jasper and Atticus.

"He ate her pussy over her morning coffee the other day," Drake said, never once looking up from his massive bowl of cereal.

Wes looked back and forth between them, his jaw dropping. "Am I the only one not getting invited to the house orgies or something? Unbelievable."

"You fingered her in your garage," Drake mumbled around a mouthful. "Stop being a hypocrite."

"Big words for someone in last place."

"He sleeps in Nicole's bed at night," Hawthorne pointed out. Technically, Drake was in his furry form, but he wasn't about to point it out. It was more fun to watch Wes squirm.

"He what?"

"Good morning!" Nicole breezed into the kitchen, her baggy sweatpants swishing around her legs. Her t-shirt sagged over her shoulder, and a dark red bite bruised her throat.

Hawthorne's pale brows soared. There was only one bite

mark on her neck... so where was the other one? He looked her up and down. He knew exactly where he would have put it if he'd had fangs.

Would she tell him if he asked? Or would she just blush? Hell, he would probably blush if he managed to ask.

Nicole gave them each a quick kiss on the cheek before beelining for the coffee maker. Stepping out of her way, Hawthorne knew better than to get between her and caffeine by now.

She opened the cupboard and frowned. "Where's my lucky mug?"

"The sink," Wes grumbled.

Bending over the sink, she pulled the dirty mug out of the mess and turned to frown at the monsters in the room.

"All right. Who used my mug?"

Hawthorne shrugged innocently. Hopefully, she didn't look too closely at yesterday's tea ring in the bottom of the mug. In his defense... he'd thought the dishes would be done by now.

"The vampires were supposed to do the dishes last night." Wes looked pointedly at her. He sniffed and took a sip of his own coffee. "They were doing something—excuse me—*someone* else."

The fae's eyes widened. Pushing an uncaffeinated Nicole was dangerous. Was the werewolf trying to get himself throttled before lunch?

"You really want to start with me this morning, Wes?" she growled.

"I don't know. Maybe." He shrugged his broad shoulders. "You won't go on a picnic with me but the bloodsuckers want some nookie—"

"Finish that sentence and see how it goes for you."

"I'm just saying—"

Hawthorne looked past the furious human and caught

Drake's eye. This was going to end badly if one of them didn't intervene. The cougar shrugged and kept eating his cereal.

Seriously? He was content to watch breakfast descend into chaos? Typical cat.

Rolling his eyes, Hawthorne slipped into the laundry room and rifled through the clean laundry. He grabbed a pair of Nicole's leggings and a random sweatshirt, probably Wes' based on the grease stains permanently ingrained into the fabric.

He hurried back to the kitchen and thrust them into her arms.

"Enough!" the fae snapped. They fell silent, their argument cutting off as they both turned to glare at him. "You have the day off from work, so you're coming with me to run errands."

"What?"

Clearly, he was going to have to simplify this for her pre-coffee brain cells. Hawthorne pointed at the bundle of clothes in her arms.

"Clothes, on. Your butt, in the truck. Let's go."

Mouth dropping open in a silent "o", her eyes widened at his snappy tone.

"You're bossy in the morning."

"If you get moving, I'll buy you coffee."

The clothes landed on the table, and Nicole peeled her t-shirt over her head. He blinked at her haste. Were those the magic words? Did he just unlock some secret Nicole level he'd been unaware of?

"You should have led with that, hon."

She kicked off her sweats. Watching her stand in the kitchen in nothing but a bra and panties, it was the best morning Hawthorne could have asked for.

Drake's spoon clinked into his cereal bowl as he finally

gave them his full attention. Wes watched her with wide eyes, his frustration forgotten. The fae rolled his eyes.

Sure, *now* they were behaving. All it took was a look at her underwear.

He bit back a laugh as he caught sight of the werewolf's dumbstruck expression. Nicole was definitely punishing him for his pouty attitude... of course, the striptease was somewhat less sexy than it should have been as she hopped around on one foot trying to get her leggings over her feet.

Hawthorne grinned at the immaculate view of her ass. The green panties hugging her curves might just be his new favorite. The fae had been silently rating her undergarments every time he did a load of laundry.

The current winner was a blue thong with little white flowers.

Unlike the wolf, he was patience incarnate. Hawthorne had no doubt he would see the sweet human in every pair of those tiny panties at some point—he was just biding his time.

Nicole dragged the sweatshirt over her head before flipping her head over and tying her hair in a ponytail. She straightened and shot him a thumbs up.

"Coffee time!"

Shaking his head, he nudged her toward the shoes waiting by the back door. Wes shoved back his chair and stepped in front of her, a tower of growling muscle. The werewolf gripped her chin and kissed her hard before giving them his back and stomping out of the kitchen.

Hawthorne looked pointedly at the cat still sitting at the table. "He's your problem today. Try to fix him before we get back."

He grabbed Nicole's hand and dragged her toward the door. By the frown on her face, Hawthorne was pretty sure she was debating going after the grumpy wolf and giving him a piece of her mind—or punching him in the head.

His money was on the latter.

"Stop trying to start a fight and I'll buy you a snack too," he urged.

"It had better be a big snack," Nicole grumbled. She shoved her feet into her sandals and stomped out the door.

Hawthorne sighed. If he didn't get some sugar and caffeine into her soon, his errands were going to turn into a nightmare.

By the time he pulled the truck to a stop, Nicole was only a fraction less irritated. Her favorite coffee shop being out of a cinnamon syrup had just been another hit to her morning.

The fae patted her knee and climbed out of the truck. Hopefully, the serenity of his workspace would be enough to draw his normally sweet human out of her funk.

Sliding the key into the lock, he took a deep breath. A small part of him was worried she wouldn't like it. His greenhouse was almost like an extension of his soul and suddenly... he really needed her to like it.

Hawthorne stepped back and waved her inside. Nicole paused in the doorway, her eyes rounding at the view. Greenery dripped from every surface, giving the illusion that they had just walked into a tunnel of leaves. Vibrant flowers bloomed in sprays, perfuming the air around them. A butterfly floated past to land on a flower bigger than her face.

"It's like a fairy tale," Nicole gasped.

"I *am* fae," he laughed.

Hawthorne wasn't about to say it aloud, but he was proud of his greenhouses. They were his quiet sanctuary away from the noise and chaos of the rest of the world. He wasn't good at a lot of thing, but plants? There was no one better.

And now, Nicole was seeing it firsthand.

He slipped past her and flipped over an empty crate. Waving for his awed human to take a seat, he turned away so she wouldn't see the fire burning in his pointy ears. The fae pulled on his favorite gardening gloves and got to work.

Nicole sat quietly on her crate, coffee in one hand and a giant cherry danish in the other. Every now and then, he would catch her contented noises as she chewed. He smiled to himself.

Hawthorne could spend every day of his life up to his elbows in dirt and leaves, listening to his favorite human's quiet gasps as she discovered another treasure in his greenhouse without a single complaint. He worked in silence and waited for her to finish waking up.

"You're not going to get all jealous on me too, are you?" she finally sighed.

"No. I'm not a wolf."

"What does that have to do with anything?"

Everything. It had everything to do with it.

"It's close to the full moon," Hawthorne explained. "Wolves always get a little possessive—or, in Wes's case, a lot possessive—of their mates around that part of the lunar cycle."

Nicole choked on a sip of iced coffee. Bending over, she coughed as it went down the wrong way. Hawthorne tugged off his dirt-caked glove and patted her on the back.

Sure, she had spent the night with two injured and starving vampires, but he was going to be the one to kill her with a caramel macchiato.

"Mate?" she finally gasped out.

He shrugged. "Girlfriend, significant other, main squeeze, whatever verbiage you prefer."

Nicole sat up. Brushing his knuckles over her pink cheeks, he turned back to the order he was filling.

"So, the moon is actually making him crazy?"

"That... and you're ovulating, apparently." Hawthorne grinned at her over his shoulder. "He got double whammied this month."

Nicole groaned. Hiding her face in her hands, she flushed bright red. He laughed. She could hide all she wanted, but everyone in the house knew the wolf was going out of his mind with lust. It wasn't exactly a secret what was causing it.

Frankly, they were all surprised they hadn't walked in on the two of them going at it on the kitchen table already.

"It's not funny!"

He chuckled at her fiery face. "It's a little funny."

Swiping a pebble off the ground, she tossed it at his back. It thumped gently against his shoulder and fell away.

"Keep talking about my ovaries, and you'll get even further from sex than the werewolf."

"Have I mentioned how beautiful you look today?" he teased. "Truly effervescent."

She could put him last, and he still wouldn't mind. That Hawthorne was even included in the running was enough for him. Once a month, every day—it didn't matter to him. As long as he had a little piece of Nicole, he was content.

But hey, if she wanted to bump the werewolf to the back of the line, who was he to argue?

Nicole shook her head and jammed another piece of danish into her mouth. Grumbling around her bite, she ignored his unapologetic grin.

Hawthorne nudged her knee with the toe of his shoe. "I would like it noted that I was not being a jealous, moon sick brat this morning... unlike Wes... who should clearly be lower in the sex ranking... just saying."

"I'll make sure to pencil it into my journal later."

"See that you do."

Hawthorne started to turn back to his work but paused as he caught a flash of hunger in her eyes. He frowned. Had he not fed her enough? There were probably granola bars in his truck. Her dark eyes looked him up and down, lingering on the blue elvish runes lining his arms.

Oh... it wasn't that kind of hunger.

Hawthorne took the coffee from her hands and set it on the ground. Gripping her hand, he tugged her to her feet. Nicole stepped close, her chest pressed against his and her big brown eyes looked up at him.

Her gaze dropped to his lips. For the thousandth time since the fae had met her, he felt the tips of his ear burn as she studied him. For once, he didn't spare it a thought.

Standing on her tiptoes, Nicole wrapped her arms around his neck and dragged him down to kiss her. Her lips parted, and her tongue teased his, each brush of her hot mouth was a bolt of pleasure through his body.

Did she have any idea what she did to him? What she did to any of them?

Hands sliding down her back, Hawthorne cupped her ass. He lifted her up and turned to balance his precious human on the table. Her legs tightened around his hips.

Leggings had been the right choice. Sure, they covered everything, but the thin fabric left nothing to his imagination as he stroked his hands down her soft thighs. What he wouldn't give to strip them off her.

The thought of Nicole standing in his beloved greenhouse in nothing but her tanned curves was enough to make his already aching cock swell. Nicole jerked back a fraction of an inch as he ground against her. He broke away from her kiss swollen lips and leaned back to meet her eyes.

"Sorry." Her flushed cheeks darkened. "I guess I'm a little sore from last night."

"Don't apologize."

A mischievous grin curved her lips. "I have a better idea anyway."

Nicole gave him a quick peck and pushed him back. She jumped down from the table and turned him around to switch places. Nudging him back until there was nowhere left to go, she grinned wickedly.

Sliding down his body, the sweet human dropped to her knees and reached for his zipper. His eyes widened. Was she going to—yes, yes she was.

Hawthorne sucked in a breath as she dragged his jeans down his hips and slipped her fingers under his waistband. His erection springing free, his boxers joined the pants bunching at his thighs.

Nicole looked at up him with gleaming, hungry eyes as her fingers encircled his cock. Her free hand rose to trace the blue glyphs tattooed on his hips, and Hawthorne groaned.

"I wondered how far down these went," she murmured. The fae bit his lip. She could wonder all she wanted, just as long as she didn't stop touching him. "I guess now I know."

Lowering her head, Nicole licked the tip of his cock. Her tongue traced him from root to tip, and Hawthorne's desperate moan echoed through the cavernous greenhouse.

"Nicole—"

His words choked off as she sucked him deep into her mouth. Any chance Hawthorne might have had to string together a full sentence vanished as she took every inch of his aching dick into her sweet mouth.

Nicole's head bobbed up and down, her dark ponytail swinging. Burying his hands in her soft hair, he held on for dear life as pleasure danced like lightning up his spine. Fingertips teased the edges of his magical tattoos.

Did she have any idea how sensitive the blue marks on his flesh were, or was she as fascinated by them as he was by the sight of her pink lips ringing his cock?

As Hawthorne stood in his green sanctuary, with the human he cherished worshipping every inch of him, he couldn't help but think how lucky he was... and how stupid a certain werewolf was.

"Fuck!" the shy fae moaned.

Nicole pulled back, her lips wet and swollen. Her soft hands stroked the hard length as she grinned up at him.

"You'd better hold on to something," she teased. "I'm just getting started."

Hawthorne gaped at her, her head dipping down to take him in her mouth again. He was one lucky, lucky fae.

27

WES

Wes slammed his bedroom door. He knew he was being a possessive, jealous prick, but he just couldn't seem to pull it together. Not even a run in the woods had helped. It hadn't mattered how long he had run, how long his paws had beat against the hard ground; he couldn't get comfortable inside himself.

Grumbling under his breath, he flopped onto the mattress on the floor. As his feet hung off the edge, the werewolf made a mental note to buy a bed frame, and maybe a throw rug.

He gritted his teeth at the wolf gnawing for freedom inside him. The moon was almost full, and he was crawling out of his skin. The need to turn himself furry again and claw at something was almost overpowering. At that point, he was ready to claw his way through the floor and go live in the woods.

Wes fisted his fingers in his hair. Why did he have to wake up and make a mess of things? Now Nicole was mad at him, and she smelled so fucking tempting. It didn't matter that she had glared at him and challenged his dickish behavior, all he wanted to do was strip her naked and tie her to his bed for a few days until the moon was waning in the sky.

But instead, he had to stand back while she fucked vampires and ran off with socially awkward elves.

Flexing his hands, he let his claws extend and jammed them into his palms. The small bite of pain was enough to give him a tiny moment of clarity. He needed to turn his brain off before the moon drove him to do something really stupid.

Wes rose from the bed, peeling his t-shirt over his head and dropped it on the messy floor. Ripping the zipper down, he kicked off his pants. He stood naked in the middle of the bedroom and forced himself to take a deep breath.

"Just do it," he growled at himself.

Bones cracked and stretched. Wes let his body twist and fur to sprout from his skin before dropped to his hands and knees and let the rest of the shift take him. It always hurt more during the full moon, a fact that never ceased to piss off werewolves everywhere. It wasn't enough that they were forced to change during the full moon; it had to hurt more? Total bullshit.

Standing on four paws, Wes shook himself. His fur puffed up, and his screaming nerve endings finally settled down. A fresh wave of Nicole's scent tickled his sensitive nose. He growled.

At least she had left with Hawthorne. If the sweet human were still in the house, his wolf would be sitting in her lap, licking every inch of bare skin it could find.

Did she really have to ovulate *this* week? She couldn't turn that shit off or something?

He shook his head at the ridiculous notion and jumped up on the bed. Turning in a circle, Wes laid down on the mattress and closed his eyes. It was a little easier in his furry form. Thoughts were simpler, and it was less of a challenge to stay still.

Plus, it was really hard to work a doorknob when you didn't have thumbs.

Burying his head in the pillows, Wes pretended the world didn't exist. As if finally sensing his zen, the door swung open. He raised his head and growled. Either someone was an idiot, or they wanted to get their leg chewed off.

The cat strolled into the room, the door hanging open in his wake. Wes' hackles rose. Of course, it was the fucking cat. The condescending prick never knew when to leave well enough alone.

Drake crossed the room and flopped onto the mattress beside him as Nicole's luscious scent pounded his senses. Wes looked around, expecting to find the tempting human peeking in the doorway or hiding in the shadowed corners of the room.

The cougar held up the pajamas she had stripped off in the kitchen. Oh... that made more sense.

Tucking her sweatpants around a pillow, Drake offered up the sweet-scented clothes for him to nuzzle, and Wes buried his furry face into the fabric. Her soothing scent washed over him, the usual candied floral fragrance spiked with the teasing ribbon of her hormones. Somehow, it was both a balm to his over-anxious mind and a shot of adrenaline.

Still, it was better than nothing. Too bad he hadn't thought of it himself.

"You're being a dick," the cat finally interrupted the silence.

Wes raised his furry head and glared at him. Seriously? He was going to walk into *his* bedroom, climb all over *his* bed, and insult him? In his time of need?

What a prick.

Drake shrugged. "I'm not going to lie to you, furball. You were a colossal dick this morning."

Baring his teeth, Wes nipped his elbow. The were-cat spun and caught his snout between his strong hands. Dragging him up to look him in his steely-gray eyes, Drake glared into his face.

"Bite me again, and you'll regret it."

Wes growled. They stared at each other, daring one another to move first. Drake's eyes softened first. Releasing his grip on the wolf's head, he lay back on the bed and stroked his fingers over his furry ears instead.

He lay down, resting his head on his paws. His eyes dropped shut as the gentle touches calmed him. Fucking cat.

"You know you have to rein in the jealousy," Drake said quietly. "You're going to drive her away if you keep that shit up."

No, even if Nicole was angry, she still cared about him, and he would apologize later and explain about the full moon. Wes wasn't a complete idiot.

"Lots of monsters are in some kind of polyamorous bonded group, so it's not like this is something new or unexpected," he continued. "If you aren't ready for the reality of what that entails, you need to communicate that. We can't make adjustments to the dynamic if you don't actually voice your needs like an adult. If you'd prefer to be a jealous wank, then that's fine too. This house will function just fine with five people as it will with six..."

Wes harrumphed. It's not like he was trying to be a jealous dick. It was the moon—

"Don't even try to blame it on the moon," the cat interrupted his thoughts. Stupid mind-reading pussycat. "The moon might be full, and Nicole is more tempting than usual right now, but that's no excuse to act like a horny, tantrum-throwing teenager."

The wolf's head jerked up. He was *not* throwing a... Oh, for fuck's sake.

Giving in to the frustration boiling under his fur, Wes shifted back. He sat on the bed beside the sprawling cat, naked and pissed off.

"I was not throwing a tantrum!" he growled.

Drake snorted and propped his head under his arm. "Says the full-grown wolf throwing a tantrum."

"I am not!" Okay, this really wasn't helping him make his point.

Wes shook his head hard. Why was the cat in his room anyway? It's not like they were friends. They were barely acquaintances. Fellow boyfriends? He really wasn't sure what the term was.

"Go away," he grumbled.

"No."

"Get out, Drake," Wes snapped. "I don't want to deal with you right now. The moon—"

Rolling his eyes, the were-cougar shoved himself upright. "Will you stop with the damned moon already? Take some responsibility for your actions!"

"Why are you interfering anyway? Your life would be so much easier without me in it anyway. One less person to compete with for Nicole's attention—"

"Oh my God. Shut up, you giant, whining man child!"

Grabbing his face, Drake kissed him hard, and his brain stopped growling. Okay, that wasn't too bad. His mouth slanted over Wes'; As hard as the cat kissed him, his lips were surprisingly soft.

Wait, a minute. Wes shoved him back. "I am not a man child!"

Gray eyes rolled. Stupid cat.

The werewolf wrapped a hand around the back of his neck and dragged the were-cat back to him. Drake's stubbled jaw bit into his palm as their tongues danced, teasing and exploring until they were both panting on his pathetic mattress.

Drake pulled away. "You're still an idiot."

"And you're a pussycat who can't stop meddling in everyone's business."

"Shut up."

"You first."

They kissed again. It wasn't gentle or particularly kind, but it soothed the savage heat toying with them both. Neither of them was the human who stood at the center of their universe, but for a brief moment, it felt a little less lonely waiting for her to come home.

Someone cleared their throat in the doorway, and they broke apart, heads shooting up to glare at whoever was intruding on their comforting moment. Nicole leaned against the doorframe, her dark brows soaring.

"I was going to see if Wes was okay after this morning." She looked over at Drake. "But you two look a bit more than okay."

Wes' cheeks burned. Was she mad?

Pretty much every shifter he'd ever met was pansexual. It was just part of being a shifter. When you didn't always look like yourself, it was easier to disregard the importance of appearances.

But did Nicole know that?

The wolf opened and closed his mouth, looking for the words to explain what she had just walked into. What was he supposed to say? How did he make this right?

Drake didn't look remotely worried. He raised a hand and waved her closer. Nicole crossed the room and let the cat thread his fingers through hers. He gave a tug, and their sweet human landed between them on the mattress.

Cupping her jaw, the cougar kissed her. Wes watched his tongue slick over her lips exactly the way it had just been teasing his, and then Drake was turning her face to him. The wolf kissed his human, pouring all his devotion into the meeting of their lips.

They went back and forth, kissing and petting the curvy creature tucked between their hard bodies. Nicole yawned, her kiss-swollen lips flashing.

Wes nuzzled her shoulder, the red bruise on her shoulder stark against her soft skin. She probably hadn't gotten much sleep last night and then his bullshit had had her running off with Hawthorne all day.

Tucking her against his naked chest, Wes lay back on the bed. The three of them wiggled until they were all comfortable on the sagging mattress. The wolf rested his head on her stomach, and gentle fingers teased his hair, stroking and petting the messy locks.

Her scent wafted over him. Gently pressing his lips against a sliver of exposed belly, Wes closed his eyes and hugged her tightly.

Drake's legs weaved through his as he curled against Nicole's other side. For a brief moment, the werewolf considered raising his head and glaring at the cat, but he decided against it. Sharing wasn't so bad after all.

28

ATTICUS

Atticus straightened his tie, frowning at his reflection in the mirror. He brushed a piece of lint off the sleeve of his shirt. All his burns had healed in the ensuing hours after Nicole had fed the vampires, but he still looked far paler than he would like.

Getting turned into a piece of firewood was never good for the complexion.

He adjusted the drape of his suit. The bespoke fit was off, hanging loose on his thin body. Healing himself had taken more energy than he had predicted. It would be another week at least before he was back to his usual physique.

Another taste of sweet Nicole could cut that down to a day, two at most. His mouth watered at the thought. Her tantalizing blood had been like honeyed wine as it ran down his throat. Even in his weakened and burned state, Atticus had recognized the rare indulgence on his tongue.

Nicole was special. She might appear an ordinary human, but her blood was the most exquisite he had ever sampled. Maybe another vampire might feel differently, but for Atticus and Jasper, she was incomparable.

He took a deep breath and adjusted his suit one last time. He would wait for the bagged blood to do its job. His precious Nicole had done enough for them already, and taking her blood again so soon could be detrimental to her health.

And that was something he would never risk.

Shaking off his worry, Atticus descended the stairs. He could just hear the rest of the household sitting down to dinner as he stepped off the staircase. Following the sounds of laughter and clinking forks, the vampire found his way to his favorite human. His eyes landed on her bright smile. Perfection.

Eyes flicked in his direction as he glided into the room, but they turned back to the conversation without a second glance. Only in a house full of monsters would a vampire descending from his lair be considered happenstance.

There was something to be said about modern times. He certainly didn't miss the terrified screams and torches that used to follow if anyone caught a glimpse of his fangs. There were only so many times a man could pick up and rebuild his life under a new identity.

Nicole smiled as he walked around to her side of the table. She looked up at him with gleaming eyes, and his dead heart leapt in his chest. Despite feeling unsettled after the unfortunate sunlight incident, being around sweet Nicole was like a balm to his healing soul.

Atticus gripped her elbows, and a tiny squeak fell from her lips as she hovered above her chair. He took her seat and ignored the rolled eyes from the rest of the table. The vampire settled her into his lap, savoring the feel of her melting against him.

Leaning back, Nicole smiled and cupped his chin in her soft hand. "How are you feeling?"

"Better." He kissed her sweet lips. "Much better, love."

Her fingers stroked over his jaw before she turned back to her dinner. Arms folded around her waist, Atticus ignored the bantering shifters and fae and focused on the delicate creature in his arms. Her soft hair was twisted up into a clip, exposing the lines of her throat. He pressed his nose into her shoulder and inhaled her heady scent.

She was too tempting. Even now, mere days after he and Jasper had sunk their fangs into her luscious flesh, his mouth watered at the thought of doing it again. He placed a gentle kiss on her shoulder and reined in his instincts.

Nicole still needed time to recover. Small purple bruises dotted her tanned flesh—bruises *he* had made. His fingertips stroked over one of the fading bruises and she shivered in his lap. The corner of his mouth curved into a smile.

Clearly, they didn't bother her, and that little quiver of hers? If Nicole wasn't careful, he'd be bending her over the dining room table and making her shake for real.

Atticus slipped his phone from his pocket and typed in the web address of his favorite boutique. Flipping through the options, he selected a silk scarf and had it express shipped. It would be perfect for covering the marks—and any future ones—but he could still tug it off and lick the tiny claims whenever he wanted.

Plus, it would be perfect to tie her hands with the next time she tried to argue.

"I just don't see why they couldn't have done a paternity test!" Nicole argued. Atticus dodged her waving hands. "Obviously, Bill was her father, but that doesn't mean they couldn't have had a whole song and dance number around opening up the DNA results!"

Atticus had no idea what a "mamma mia" was, or who this Meryl Streep woman was, but his precious human clearly had strong opinions about her choices. Leaning around Nicole's gesturing hands, the vampire checked her plate and shook his head. Whatever point she was trying to make was distracting her from her food.

Snatching the fork from her hand, Atticus scooped a bite of mashed potatoes onto the tines. He raised it to her mouth and slipped it between her lips before she could argue. If she wasn't going to take care of herself, then he would happily do it.

Mouth full of potato, she looked over her shoulder at him and narrowed her eyes. He met her annoyed glare with his own. If the stubborn human wanted to have a staring contest with a vampire, she was going to lose.

Nicole took one look at his stern face and rolled her eyes. Wisely opting not to argue, she turned back to the conversation and tapped his hand for another bite. Atticus smirked.

His smug victory vanished as she leaned forward, her ass wiggling in his lap. Clever little minx. Every time Atticus raised the fork to feed Nicole another bite, she rubbed herself against him.

He dragged his fangs gently over her shoulder. The silly creature was only going to get his cock hard if she kept it up. Did she realize it was a win-win for him? Atticus would get to savor the sight of her tongue flicking over the fork as he fed her AND he would have the joy of feeling her ass grind in his lap.

If anything, Nicole was only urging him to keep going, a demand he would happily meet.

The front door rattled under a rapid knock as he lifted the fork to her lips.

"I've got it!" Jasper called from the stairs.

Atticus ignored him. Jasper was expecting some kind of shipment. He hadn't asked for the details, but he had already seen the charge on the credit card statement. From the discrete company name on the bill, he was fairly certain it was a package full of sex toys.

Was it an obscene amount to spend on toys when they both had perfectly good cocks? Yes. But watching his old friend use them on Nicole would be well worth the money.

The werewolf stopped whatever grandiose statement he was making about the musical talents of someone named "Colin Firth" as Jasper led a stranger into the room. Atticus raised his eyebrows. It must be serious if his friend was willing to disturb dinner.

A short man in a courier's shirt stood awkwardly in the doorway, the kitchen lights reflecting off his bald head. Shifting from foot to foot, he hugged a large yellow envelope to his stomach and looked nervously back and forth between the two vampires.

"This gentleman is looking for you, pet." Jasper waved at the little man.

He quickly stepped forward and thrust the envelope into her hands. Nicole reared back, her eyes widening as Atticus bit back a hiss. He didn't like the way the weaselly little man was eyeing the monsters in the room. The vampire could hear his heart hammering in his chest as he looked for the nearest exit, his blood rushing through his veins.

"You've been served," he announced nervously. Turning quickly, the courier hightailed it for the front door.

Nicole stared at the envelope in her hands. "What the fuck?"

She ripped into the envelope and tugged out a sheaf of neatly typed paperwork. The room fell silent as they waited for her to share. Atticus felt the precise moment Nicole comprehended what she was looking at. Every muscle in her body tensed in his lap.

Hands shaking, she gaped at the papers in her hands.

Peering over her shoulder, Atticus read the first page of the document.

"She's being sued for ownership of the house."

"By whom?" Wes growled.

"My cousin," she snapped.

Atticus just managed to move her mug of wine out of the way as the furious human slammed the papers down on the table. It had taken Jasper over an hour of scrubbing before she would touch her pickle mug again after his foolish decision to fill it with blood.

That would undoubtedly be the last time the impulsive vampire decided to drink blood from anything but the bag it came in.

He cradled the ceramic cup in his hand. The last thing they needed right now was for her to smash the precious thing and dissolve into a full-on mental breakdown.

Hawthorne inched his plate aside and reached across the table to grip her hand. Atticus winced; he could feel how tense Nicole was in his lap. She wasn't upset; she was furious. The elf would be lucky if she didn't pick up her knife and jam it through his calming hand.

Hawthorne jumped back as she lifted the court documents to hurl across the table. His pale eyes widened. Jasper took two steps and snatched the stack of paperwork out of her hand before it could launch into the air. The last thing they needed was to clean up a flurry of complicated legal paperwork and reorganize it into the proper order.

"I'll just take those," he said, catching Atticus's eye and flipping through the documents.

Not for the first time in his long lifetime, he was glad he had his law degree. Her cousin thought he could expel her from her own home? That he could swoop in and take the house their precious Nicole coveted? He thought wrong.

Atticus pressed a kiss against her throat and lifted her off his lap.

"Leave it to us, love."

29

NICOLE

Nicole paced circles around her kitchen. She couldn't stop thinking about the papers Jasper had snatched from her hand. No matter how she turned it in her mind, she couldn't figure out how her cousin thought he was justified in suing her.

Fucking Tyler.

She hadn't seen the greedy prick in well over a decade. Even as a kid, Nicole couldn't stand him. He was a greasy little rat of a human being who was always crying victim.

Even when they were small, he'd been the type of jerk who would steal her candy right out of her hands and gobble it down. Then he would go crying to anyone who would listen that she had stolen his treat. It wasn't fun for him unless someone else got in trouble.

Usually, her.

The last time Nicole had seen him, she'd broken his nose for calling her a slut. All because she was wearing cutoff shorts. What she wouldn't give to slug him again.

Hissing under her breath, she ripped open the freezer and grabbed the secret pint of fudge ripple she had stashed in the very back. There's no way the shifters would have found it under the bags of frozen peas.

Grabbing a spoon, she resumed her nervous pacing.

"You're going to wear a hole in the floor."

Her eyes lifted from the fudge goodness in her hands to the werewolf leaning against the doorframe.

"The tile is getting replaced anyway," she grumbled.

Crossing the room, Wes caught her hips and boosted her onto the counter. He swiped her spoon and dipped it into the pint. He jammed the ice cream into his mouth before she had time to protest—damned shifter.

Callused fingers caught her chin and tilted her face up to meet his. His lips pressed against hers, and the sweet taste of chocolate rolled over her tongue, drawing her in closer. Nicole licked the fudge of his lower lip. It was only fair. It was *her* ice cream after all.

And he was her werewolf.

She wrapped her legs around his trim hips and pulled him closer. If she couldn't keep her mind off her asshole cousin, maybe Wes could.

He slid the pint of ice cream onto the counter next to her abandoned wine and threaded his fingers into her messy hair. Soft lips trailed along her jaw as Wes kissed his way down her throat to the edge of her thin t-shirt.

He looked up at her with gleaming golden eyes, silently asking for permission.

"Rip it," she panted.

His fingers had just brushed her shirt when Hawthorne came stomping into the kitchen. She sighed. Drake had been right... the fae really did have terrible timing.

"Why the hell is there no water?"

Leaning around Wes, Nicole raised her eyebrows at the fae. Suds covered his long silver hair, and a towel wrapped around his hips, leaving almost nothing to the imagination as he dripped all over her kitchen floor.

She looked him and down. Gardening had been kind to his physique. Carved muscle tensed as he glowered at them both. And those tattoos...

Nicole bit her lip. She had seen the glyphs on his arms... and thighs... but it was the first time she'd seen the marks swirling over his chest and stomach.

"The water?" he asked again.

Wes shrugged. "No idea."

Hawthorne frowned, suspicion coloring his normally serene face. He flicked a soap bubble in their direction and stormed out as Wes smirked in the empty kitchen.

"The cat was messing with the plumbing," he admitted. "He turned the water off ten minutes ago."

She giggled. It wasn't very nice of them to torment poor Hawthorne, but after that dinner, she could use a laugh.

"The cat?" Nicole teased. "The same cat who had his tongue in your—"

Red flooded his cheeks, and Wes look away, glancing around for a distraction. He grabbed her mug of wine off the counter and took a silent sip.

"So... about that..." She twined her arms around his neck before he could run away. "Is that a you thing or a shifter thing?"

Not that it really mattered. Watching the two monsters make out had been surprisingly hot. Still, Nicole wouldn't have minded a head's up if they were thinking about dabbling in a relationship outside of... well... her.

"It's a shifter thing."

"Mm-hmm." Was she going to have to pry the information out of him? Maybe she should start peeling off an article of clothing for every answer he volunteered... though

Nicole had a feeling that would only distract them both. "Have you been with other shifters before?"

The werewolf arched an eyebrow. "You mean have I been with men before?"

"Yes."

"Yes."

"So... Drake?"

Now that she thought about it, Jasper had alluded to the fact that their tiff at the barbecue could have ended in bloodshed or kissing. Maybe she shouldn't have been so surprised to find them wrapped around each other.

Wes studied her face for a moment before his hands slid up her sides and pulled her closer to his chest. Thumbs making little circles on her ribs, he met her questioning gaze.

"Let me put it this way. You make my wolf howl. He makes the wolf growl. Playfully, but still... I don't howl for him, and he doesn't for me." His mouth slanted over hers, his teeth teasing her lip. "You're the only one who makes my wolf howl, Nicole, and the only one who ever will."

That was kind of sweet... in a feral way.

Wes pulled back to study her reaction. "Do you have a problem with that? Drake and I can avoid each other if that's what you need."

"No." Nicole kissed him again, her hands smoothing down his chest. "I thought it was kind of hot. As long as I don't catch you with someone we haven't talked about, I don't have a problem."

It was only fair. She was involved with five monsters. As much as Nicole wanted to keep them all for herself, she wasn't going to be greedy.

Besides, the werewolf howled only for her and the moon. That wasn't something she was about to give up lightly.

"These lips won't touch anyone but you... and the monsters who belong to you," Wes promised.

Well, that certainly limited his dating pool. Her, Drake... and maybe Jasper?

Now that was an image. If she had to listen to both Wes and Jasper whispering dirty things in her ears, Nicole was pretty sure her vagina would spontaneously combust.

Wes leaned forward to steal another kiss. Lifting her mug, Nicole took a sip before his lips could land. He jerked back and laughed.

"Tease."

The wolf grabbed her cup and drained the rest of it.

"That was mine!"

He smirked. "I was thirsty."

"There's half a bottle right over there!"

"I like this cup better." Wes wiggled his eyebrows and licked the rim clean.

Her nose wrinkled. "Do monsters have some kind of aversion to using their own coffee cups?"

"No."

"I bought five brand new ones, and yet you all insist on using mine."

Wes smiled at the chipped pickle mug. "It smells like you."

It did not. Nicole snatched her mug back. Poking her nose inside, she gave it a deep sniff. "You liar. It smells like cheap wine and dish soap."

"And you," he argued. "It doesn't matter what's in it. It always smells perfect. Like you."

Damn it. Why did he make it so difficult to be annoyed?

"If I cuddle with all of your mugs, will you give mine back?" Nicole sighed. It was turning into a daily war to hunt down whoever had stolen her favorite cup.

She still hadn't fully forgiven Jasper for his blood cocktail.

"How about you bathe with them instead?"

Ew. Nicole tapped the perverted wolf on the nose. "Don't be creepy, furball."

A laugh burst from his chest, warming the quiet kitchen. Her lips curved into a smile. How could he possibly think she would ask him to give up something that made him happy, especially when his laugh sounded like that?

Drake slunk into the kitchen, a tool belt wrapped around his waist, and Nicole nearly snapped her neck craning for a look. The cat raised his eyebrows and changed course. Leaning around Wes, he kissed her on his favorite spot under her jaw.

She shivered. How did he always do that?

Drake swiped her empty mug from her hands. Grabbing the bottle of wine, he filled her cup and took a sip. She snatched the mug back before he could try walking away with it.

If Nicole had to put a tracker on her lucky mug, she would, damn it.

She sipped at her wine and groaned. It was perfect. Drake hadn't even done anything to it, but somehow, it was better. It was the same wine bottle Nicole had poured from, yet it tasted even better when he poured it. It always did.

Stupid cat magic.

The tricky cougar leaned against the counter and wiped his damp hands on a towel. Hopefully, he had fixed whatever problem was plaguing the plumbing.

Yawning, she rested her head on Drake's shoulder. A heavy hand landed on her lower back, warming her through. She could stay like this forever.

"You caught Thorne in the shower," Nicole murmured.

Drake laughed, grinning at the werewolf still massaging little circles on her sides.

"I told you to warn him."

"It must have slipped my mind," he said innocently, but an evil grin stretched his lips, giving him away. "Maybe we can get Jasper with it later.

Nicole rolled her eyes at the laughing shifters. "Men."

The sharp click of expensive loafers had them sobered up in an instant as Jasper and Atticus strolled into the kitchen. The looks on their faces were just as dark and crisp as the luxurious suits they wore.

She shivered and made a mental note to never stand against them in a courtroom.

"What did you find out?" Drake asked, breaking the tense silence.

"Nicole's cousin is challenging her great aunt's will," Atticus said sharply.

"How?" She looked back and forth between the storm clouds on the vampires' faces. "She very clearly left the house to me in her estate."

"He says there's a clause." Jasper opened his briefcase and pulled out a stack of papers. "It says if the house isn't kept up to a livable standard by the end of the first year, ownership reverts to him."

"That's bullshit!" Wes' hands on her sides were the only thing keeping Nicole from falling off the counter. "I have a copy of the will, and that is definitely not in it!"

"I'm sure it's not, pet." Jasper looked downright murderous as he glared at the copy of the false will.

"We'll review your copy and take care of this," Atticus promised.

Nicole clenched her fists. She wanted to throw something, but the only thing she had on hand was her prized mug and that definitely was not happening.

"The explains the sabotage," Drake growled.

"What?"

"Cutting the power. Poisoning the lawn. Junking the cars. Breaking the waterlines." The were-cat hissed as he counted off on his fingers. "He's trying to make the house look like a dump and drive us out so we don't help you."

That motherfucker.

Wait a minute. "Breaking the waterlines? Poisoning the lawn? When did all that happen?"

"I was out fixing the waterline today. That was the most recent sabotage." Wincing, Drake scratched at his sandy stubble. "The lawn was poisoned the day Hawthorne moved in. He saved most of it; there was only a small dead patch left. That's where we put the gazebo."

Nicole gaped at him. Was she really that oblivious, or were they actively teaming to keep things from her?

"Is there anything else you're keeping from me?" She glared at each monster in turn.

Hawthorne had better count his lucky stars he wasn't in the room, or else she would have glared a hole right though his head. Poisoned grass? Seriously?

"Your car is leaking oil, and Drake keeps scratching up the woodwork with his claws," Atticus recited tonelessly. "The fae broke an antique vase in the living room, and Jasper and I re-homed the squirrels to the shed out back."

Nicole stared. Un-fucking-believable.

"I'm going to bed."

30

NICOLE

Nicole glared at the ceiling. So much for willing herself to go to sleep.

Hours had passed, and no matter how hard she tried, her whirling brain just wouldn't turn off. It kept going over that sham of a lawsuit and plotting how best to kill her cousin.

Of course, then she had to remind herself that she could barely chop carrots without nicking herself. The odds of her successfully murdering her bully of a cousin were slim to none.

Dragging herself out of bed, Nicole kicked away her blankets. She couldn't lay there anymore, not when she felt like ants made of pure anxiety were crawling around her skin.

She trudged into the hall and down the stairs. The light of the television glowed from the living room. Following it like a moth, she peered through the doorway.

Wes was sprawled on the couch, his mouth hanging open as he snored. Infomercials played on the screen to an audience of none. She didn't need a milk carton spigot, but Nicole could appreciate the creativity.

She looked down at the werewolf, and warmth heated her heart. From that angle, he looked almost innocent. No cheeky smirk, no mischievous laughter, no naughty looks that promised an evening of screaming his name.

Nicole gently shook his shoulder, and golden eyes cracked open and blinked at her.

"Mmm?" Wes grunted.

"You fell asleep on the couch. Go on up to bed."

His eyes started to drift closed again, and Nicole nudged him harder.

"I'm up," he yawned. "I'm up."

Shoving himself upright, Wes stomped to his feet. He swayed in place, and Nicole placed a hand on his side, doing her best to steady the wolf towering over her. Not that it would do any good. If he decided to pass out, odds were, he was taking them both out.

"Go to bed," she urged.

Ignoring her soft words, Wes nuzzled the top of her head. The spicy scent of pine needles and motor oil washed over her as she pressed her nose into his shoulder.

Then again... maybe she had a better idea.

Nicole hooked her fingers into his belt and dragged the werewolf close. When she looked up at him, his golden eyes were alert, all lingering dregs of sleep vanished in an instant.

Standing on her tiptoes, Nicole closed the distance and kissed him. Wes wasted no time, slanting his lips over hers and drawing her deeper into a kiss with no escape. Muscled arms wrapped around her waist.

Her body pressed against his, sparking heat under her skin. Wes was so different from the vampires. Even as they sank their fangs into her throat, she hadn't felt nearly as devoured as she did when the werewolf pillaged her mouth. His tongue swept over hers, teasing and tempting her into sin with him.

His hands roamed over her body, the only barrier between her flesh and his rough hands was the thin fabric of her t-shirt and panties—and they didn't stand a chance against a lusty werewolf.

Wes pulled back a fraction of an inch, their lips parting with a wet smack.

"You sure about this, babe?" His bright eyes glowed with preternatural light. If a gaze could burn, Nicole was positive that golden glow would be scorching her.

"The only thing stopping me from jumping on you is the fact that I'm still dressed," she teased. "Do something about it, Wes."

A feral grin stretched his soft lips as strong hands caught the collar of her shirt, claws tipping his fingertips. He looked her in the eye and ripped it right down the middle. The cool air tickled her bare belly as the wolf peeled it down her arms and tossed it aside.

Wes looked down at her breasts. Licking his lips, he reached for her panties. Careful of her soft skin, he hooked his razor-sharp claws under the edge of her panties and shredded the fabric until her ruined underwear fell away.

Red-hot hunger filled his wolfish eyes.

"Last chance," he warned.

What was with this wolf? He'd been trying to get in her pants since they met, and now he wanted to be a gentlemen?

Grabbing him by the front of his shirt, Nicole dragged him down to look her in the eye. He met her gaze, the feral edge sharpening his handsome face.

"If I have to ask you fuck me again, I'll cut my losses and go knock on someone else's door," she growled. "Maybe Hawthorne's... or Drake's."

She didn't know if it was the threat to walk away or the fact she'd uttered another shifter's name while standing naked in front of him, but the werewolf didn't hesitate.

Hand wrapping around her throat, Wes pushed her backward until the arm of the couch hit her ass. He curled an arm around her waist and lifted her to sit on the edge.

"You want me to fuck you, baby?" he growled in her face. "I can do that."

The edge of his teeth scraped her jaw as the hand collaring her throat held her still. He nipped at her earlobe, the sharp bite of pain was a bolt of pleasure straight to her core.

"You want me to ruin you right here in this living room? I can do that too."

Nicole panted as his stubbled jaw scraped her cheek, the hand on her back smoothing over her skin to her front. Claws still tipping his fingers, Wes palmed her breast and gave it a tight squeeze. She gasped.

"You want me to bend you over and breed your tight little pussy so the whole house can hear what a greedy slut you are? That's just fine." The wolf pulled back to slick his tongue over her lips. "I tried to be nice, Nicole, but I guess you don't want nice."

"No," she gasped against his lips. "I don't."

"Good."

Wes kissed her—no, he *consumed* her. His mouth pillaged hers, taking what he wanted and leaving her to desperately clutch his arm to stay upright. Hands stroked down her body, palming and squeezing every curve.

Strong fingers pinched her nipples. The wolf teased and tortured until she was a panting, whimpering mess. Nicole wrapped her legs around his waist and drew him closer. Rubbing herself on the hard bulge in his jeans, she relished every one of his rough growls.

His hand slapped her breast, and the sharp sting had her gasping into his bruising kisses. His fingers smoothed over the tender mark, soothing the burn.

Fuck. If she'd known tempting the big bad wolf would be like teasing a force of nature, she would have kissed her sanity goodbye on that very first group date.

A shadow crossed over her as Wes squeezed her ass and ground her body against his erection. Nicole's head rocked back, and she blinked at the gray eyes grinning from the other end of the couch.

"Drake?"

Wes' head shot up to glare at the were-cat. He growled possessively and clutched her naked body tighter against his chest.

"Don't mind me," Drake said casually. "Just admiring the view."

The wolf looked him up and down before pressing his lips against her ear. "I think the cat likes to watch."

Nicole knew for a fact the kinky cougar liked to watch. She'd watched him casually eat orange slices and grin at her while Hawthorne licked her pussy on the kitchen table. He hadn't tried to interfere or take a turn. Drake had stood there, cock tenting his pants as he watched her come.

"Let him," she whispered back.

Wes didn't argue. Instead, he shoved her down onto the couch until her back hit the throw pillows, her hips still resting on the arm of the couch.

"You want him to watch while I breed your pussy?" the werewolf asked, his hands dropping to his fly. "You want him to watch as I stuff you full of cum, baby?"

Wes shoved his pants down his hips and grabbed her thighs. Jerking her hips to him, he rubbed his hard cock between her legs.

"You want the cat to watch you come all over my dick?" he asked again. "Is that what you want?"

The hard length glided through her aching folds, teasing

at her clit. Pleasure burned in her belly, promising a different kind of pleasure altogether.

"Yes!"

The wolf chuckled. "Of course you do."

The tip of his cock pressed into her opening. Nicole looked back at Drake, watching him unzip his pants and palm his thick cock when Wes sheathed himself in her pussy. Her gasp filled the quiet living room.

Holding her thighs in his tight grip, Wes snapped his hips. His cock pounded her pussy mercilessly as Nicole looked up at him and his feral grin. She moaned, and the spark in his eye brightened.

Pleasure swirled through her, a storm that kept building higher and higher with each hard thrust. Every inch of the wolf's cock slamming home pushed her closer and closer to her inevitable orgasm.

"Take it, baby," Wes groaned. "You take my cock so well."

"She does," Drake agreed, his deep rumble filled with glee.

Nicole turned her head back to watch the were-cat stroking himself. His dick gleamed in his tight grip as he dragged his palm back and forth over the length, his gray eyes watching her breasts bounce.

"Come for me," the werewolf ordered. "Show me how bad you want a pussy full of wolf cum."

Was he trying to drive her mad? Chest heaving, Nicole dragged her hands over her breasts and pinched her aching nipples. Wes fucked her faster, his cock hammering between her legs. His hand slapped her ass cheek and she was gone, tumbling headfirst over the edge. Her orgasm slammed into her and Nicole's mouth dropped open in a loud moan.

Thick fingers pressed over his lips. "Shh. This party is for us, kitten."

Legs shaking in the werewolf's grip, Nicole came hard. Wes followed right after, his release flooding her quivering cunt. She was still panting as he pulled out, but he didn't have long to mourn the absence before his fingertips were pressing the cum back into her pussy, a satisfied grin twisting his smug lips.

Drake rose from the couch, his pants low on his hips. His hard cock still stood at attention, and Nicole licked her lips. Was he going to fuck her mouth like Jasper had?

He tossed something to Wes and bent over her. The cougar kissed her, his teeth nipping at her kiss-swollen lips as strong hands dragged her upright and turned her around. The world spun in lazy circles as Drake lifted her off the couch and wrapped her legs around his waist.

The aftershocks of her orgasm were still washing through her as the cougar stroked his hands over her body and kissed her like a drowning man. A hard chest pressed against her back. Sandwiched between the two shifters, Nicole slumped against them and let them have their way.

Why had she ever protested monsters moving into her house? Apparently, she hadn't considered the benefits of their overbearing natures when she was bemoaning their presence.

If Nicole could go back in time and tell past-Nicole to shut up and jump on their dicks sooner, she would hop in the time machine and be on her way already.

Wes nipped at her ear, his hands massaging her ass cheeks. Suspending her between them, they took turns stroking their hard cocks through her dripping folds.

"So this is where you were hiding your tattoo," the wolf chucked in her ear, his fingers smoothing over the tiny red heart on her ass.

"Remind me to kill Miri," Nicole panted. It was Miri's fault she had the drunken stamp on her skin. She'd known the only way to get her under the needle was with copious amounts of tequila and had planned accordingly.

"I like it. It's sweet... like your pussy."

Wes slapped her ass, landing the sharp sting right over the small tattoo. Laughing, Drake positioned her over his cock and teased her with the tip. She wriggled desperately. Taking pity on her, they lowered her slowly down the hard length.

"Fuck!" she moaned.

"Not yet, kitten."

She blinked in confusion. Wes stroked his hands over her ass cheeks, and their plan became apparent as his fingers glided over her back hole. Nicole tensed; was she ready for that? More importantly... was she really going to stop him?

His slick finger teased the pucker before he first finger slipped inside her ass and tore a sharp moan from her throat. The tight sensation sent a crackling bolt of pleasure up her spine.

No. No, she was not. As far as Nicole was concerned, the shifters knew exactly what they were doing. As long as they didn't stop that sharp bliss already teasing her body, she was theirs to fuck as they saw fit.

A second slippery finger joined the first. Soft kisses peppered her shoulder and throat, promising rapture if she was patient enough.

"Relax, baby." Wes' tongue teased the shell of her ear. "Almost there."

The third finger had Nicole's eyes rolling back. She wasn't sure if she could take his cock back there, but if it was anything like being stuffed full of his fingers, she was willing to try.

Wes withdrew his fingers from her ass. She almost

opened her mouth to protest but was reward by the tip of his cock teasing her instead.

Tipping her head forward, Drake caught her lips, and swallowed her whimpers as the werewolf eased into her ass, inch by thick, hard inch. They paused as he stopped, balls deep between her cheeks.

"Catch your breath, kitten," the were-cat ordered. The glint in his eyes promised that it was the last chance she would have, and Nicole believed him. She was full enough to burst.

Wrapping her arms around his muscled shoulders, she kissed his jaw in the same place he always pressed his kisses. She knew this had to be testing his patience as his cock stilled in her pussy. Every inch of Drake's dick pressed more firmly inside of her as Wes filled her ass.

"Fuck me," Nicole demanded.

"So desperate," Wes chuckled in her ear.

The shifters moved together, fucking her between them. Her head rolled back as every hard thrust filled her to the brim, again and again. Her mouth lolled open as she hung limp between them.

"Such a naughty thing, taking me in your tight little ass," Wes groaned.

Drake suckled on her throat, his cock driving into her. "I don't know. I think she wants more."

Nicole whimpered. "Please, please, please—"

The two monsters fucked her faster, pounding into her body. She clutched Drake's shoulder and Wes' arm banding her ribcage, her nails digging in to their flesh. The orgasm hit her hard. It rolled over her like a wave, dragging her under over and over again.

Legs shaking around the cougar, Nicole's moans carried through the house. She couldn't stop coming and the shifters showed no signs of stopping. They hammered inside of her, each slam of their hard cocks spurring her on.

Nicole was vaguely aware of the infomercials still playing on the glowing television. What a sight they must make: naked and hanging on for dear life, two savage monsters ravaging her pussy and her ass while she soaked their thighs with her non-stop orgasms.

Where was a ShamWow when you needed one?

Drake broke first. He burst inside her, his cum flooding her already full cunt. Wes didn't last much longer. Moaning into her shoulder, his cock twitched and filled her ass in a hot rush.

Nicole rested between them, her burning face pressed against Drake's heaving shoulder. She didn't need a mirror to know her face was cherry-red.

As she watched a spokesperson go on and on about his amazing copper skillet, Nicole couldn't stop wondering: how did this become her life? And why the fuck did she love it so damn much?

31

JASPER

Jasper sighed at the rising sun. For the first time in a very long time, he was glad to see the night coming to an end. If he were a more dramatic vampire, he would thrust his hands into his blond hair and tear it out. But for all his charm and mischief, Jasper was not prone to theatrics.

He and Atticus had spent the last few days trying to figure out how to nail Nicole's prick of a cousin. The will was definitely fake, they were sure of it, but trying to prove that the bastard had fabricated it was more difficult than they had anticipated.

With a little more time, the vampires were sure they could tear him apart in court; they just weren't sure how much patience the shifters had left. Wes and Drake were chomping at the bit to get their hands on the man, and if that happened, there would be nothing left but a handful of blood scraps and errant teeth.

As tempting as it was to let them have their way, Jasper wasn't about to risk a murder charge for Nicole.

Trudging up the driveway, he ran through the case in his head. Maybe they could find a witness? Somebody who had witnessed the original will being signed would do perfectly. He made a mental note to double-check the name on the paperwork.

His steps slowed as he spotted an envelope waiting on the doorstep. Jogging up the steps, Jasper swiped the small envelope and flipped it over. His and Atticus' names were scrawled across the back in sloppy black ink.

He passed it to Atticus to handle and turned his attention to unlocking the front door. Correspondence was the other vampire's domain. He was more of an opening and closing arguments man.

Atticus had always said he could sell water to a cactus, whatever the hell that was supposed to mean.

"I'm thinking we should run a background check on the cousin, maybe work on poking holes in his character as well as disproving the validity of the will," Jasper said absently. "What do you think?"

Silence followed him into the house. Jasper glanced over his shoulder and stumbled to a halt as he realized Atticus was still standing in the doorway.

"What's wrong?"

His old friend looked up, his blood-red eyes dark and angry. He held out a slip of paper for Jasper. Snatching it from his hand, he unfolded the note, and his dead heart stopped in his chest.

Are you really sure you want to represent a gold digger?

"What the fuck?"

He looked up at Atticus, hoping his old friend had some idea what the message was supposed to mean. Surely, it couldn't be referring to Nicole. Atticus turned the envelope over and emptied a thumb drive into his palm.

"Does this plug into something?" he asked curiously. The vampire raised the small drive and turned it over in his fingers.

Jasper rolled his eyes. "It plugs into a computer."

Snatching the drive from the other vampire, he laid his briefcase on the coffee table and slipped his laptop out. He plugged in the thumb drive and booted up the laptop.

Jasper crossed his fingers that he wasn't about to download some kind of virus. With their luck, it would be something that would wipe his entire computer. He barely knew how to pull up the internet on a good day; a virus would pretty much cripple them.

Luckily, the file opened automatically, and a video started to play. Atticus and Jasper frowned at the screen as a clip of Nicole with her two friends played out in front of them. They sat at a restaurant chatting and laughing.

Pain arched through his chest as her words registered in his brain.

"Dating monsters to pay off student loans and fix up her house? It's all going according to plan?" His stomach rolled uneasily.

Surely, Jasper wasn't watching what he thought he was watching. It had to be taken out of context. Sweet Nicole? She wouldn't do that to them.

As he sat on the couch, a small voice in the back of his mind pointed out that each of Nicole's monsters had their uses. That's why she'd picked them, he realized. As he rose from the couch, his blood boiled with fury. Every conversation they'd ever had replayed in his mind.

Nicole bemoaning her credit card bills. Her car mysteriously breaking down on their first date. The way she rationed her food like it was made of gold. It was all a ploy to garner their pity.

Throwing back his head, Jasper shouted up the stairs. "Everyone get down here!"

The shifters came thundering down the stairs, their sleepy faces alert and eyeing the shadowy corners for danger. Hawthorne and Nicole stumbled down the stairs last, yawning and scrubbing at their tired eyes.

"Have a seat," he snapped.

Nicole fumbled her way to the couch and slumped down onto the sagging cushion. Jasper had to look away from her; every image of her cute and sleepy was clawing at his heart.

Atticus bent down and turned the computer screen to face them. "Play it."

Wes tapped a key on the laptop, and the terrible video played again. Silence filled the room as the clip came to an end. Drake leaned forward and played it again. They turned, one-by-one, to look at Nicole, but Jasper had seen enough.

The second the video had started, the color had drained from her face. Eyes rounded with horror, their sweet human looked worried.

"It's not what you think—" she started.

"We just watched a video of you admitting you planned to use our money to pay off your debts," Jasper growled.

Nicole looked desperately at the monsters gathered in the room, silently begging even one of them to believe her. Maybe they would have if they weren't all staring at the image of her face plastered on the screen, mid-laugh at something Ashley had just said about being a gold digger.

"Look me in the eye and tell me you didn't choose us because of how it would benefit you," he snapped.

She couldn't. Her mouth opened and closed, but no sound came out. There was nothing Nicole could say that could make this right.

Shaking his head, Jasper backed away. He didn't even want to look at her now. From the expressions of the other monsters in the room, they didn't either. The werewolf looked like a kicked puppy, and the cat was practically hissing. Drake settled his hand on Wes's shoulder, tugging him incrementally closer to himself. Whether consciously or not, the werewolf leaned into the touch. Shy Hawthorne's face was completely blank; he couldn't seem to tear his eyes away from the Nicole on the computer screen.

"Please," she begged. "Just let me explain."

Hawthorne rose from his seat. He turned to look at her, his face devoid of emotion. Walking past her, he took the stairs two at a time and disappeared into his bedroom. The living room was silent as they listened to him pace around his bedroom. Two minutes later, his door opened, and he charged down the stairs with a bag in his hand.

Without a second glance, the fae walked out the front door.

Good for him. Jasper was still reeling, and he'd seen the damn thing three times now. As badly as he wanted to rush out the door on the heels of the elf, he couldn't make himself move. Why did his feet feel like they were cemented to the floor?

The shifters rose from the couch. They beelined for the door, not even bothering to gather their things. Nicole jumped up and started after them as tears streamed down her face, dripping onto her t-shirt.

"Don't," she begged. "Please don't."

The door slammed behind them, and within seconds they could hear the rumble of Wes' motorcycle in the driveway. Silently sobbing into her hands, she turned to the last two monsters in the room.

"It only started out that way, I swear. But it was more than that," Nicole insisted. "*We* were more than that!"

He wanted to believe her. Jasper wanted to cross the room, and take their sweet human in his arms, and kiss her tears away. He wanted to go upstairs and climb into bed with her soft curves wrapped around him and pretend like this had never happened. But he couldn't.

He just couldn't.

"I wish I could believe that," Jasper shook his head as he voiced aloud the part that stung the worst. "Atticus and I would have given you the money if you had just asked."

Turning away before he lost his nerve, Jasper walked out the front door. Breathing in the morning air, he hated the rising sun even more than he had before. Now, he had all day to fill his mind with nightmares of her face.

He knew without a doubt that he was going to see that clip on repeat in his dreams until the sun went down again.

He hurried back to the car and slammed the door. He waited patiently in the passenger seat, doing his best not to scream. Why couldn't he just rewind time? What he wouldn't give to go back even fifteen minutes ago.

Jasper would have snatched up that envelope and tossed it straight in the trashcan. If he had never known, would it even have mattered? Would he have lived the rest of his long life without ever giving Nicole a second of doubt?

Of course, he would. She was *Nicole*. Her bright smiles and chirping laughter had become the sunshine he hadn't seen in nearly two-hundred years, and now, it was gone. All that was left was him and Atticus and eternal night. Again.

Atticus hadn't said much—hell, he hadn't said anything at all. Knowing his old friend, he wasn't even that angry with the devious human. Atticus had been intent on spoiling Nicole from the very beginning, and Jasper had been happy to go along with his plans. He'd been just as obsessed with the luscious human as Atticus.

But now, everything felt tainted. Every kiss. Every touch.

Every soft smile and cheeky wink. Every time he drove his cock into her and heard her sweet whimpers. It was poisoned by the confirmation in her eyes when she saw that video.

Atticus walked calmly out of the house and down the steps, both of their briefcases tucked under his arm. The vampire climbed into the driver's seat and calmly pulled the car out of the driveway. Now, they had to race the rising sun to their penthouse, the one they had just decided to put on the market for good.

Shaking his head, Jasper stared out the window. Nicole's sweet scent still just barely lingered in the back seat of their car. It teased his nose and begged him to turn the car around and run back into her arms.

Gritting his teeth, Jasper rolled down the window and let the breeze wash it from the vehicle for good.

32

NICOLE

Nicole stared at the peanut butter and jelly sandwich. What was the point? Misery didn't pick at its food— misery consumed with devastating hunger, but it sure as hell wasn't consuming peanut butter and jelly sandwiches.

It was too busy eating her alive.

Shoving the food away from her, Nicole stared at the worn wood of the kitchen table. How was she supposed to eat when all she could focus on were the knots in her stomach and the aching of her heart?

For three days, she had dragged herself out of bed and stumbled into work. She did her job and ate instant ramen. She answered emails and, most difficult of all, she pretended like her whole world hadn't crumbled at her feet.

Even going through the motions was becoming painful. Her new coworkers were looking at her with wide-eyed concern, like she was a ghost rattling around her office. How many times had Nicole been asked if she was ill in the last three days? More than she had in her entire life.

Her phone buzzed on the table, and her heart jumped into her throat. Not that there was any point. It would just be

Ashley or Miri again. They'd called and texted dozens of times, desperately checking on her and trying to get her to speak to them. Nicole knew it couldn't last. If her silence went on too long, her friends would storm the house and drag her out, kicking and screaming into the sunlight.

Rising from her seat, Nicole stumbled to the trash can and threw her sandwich away. She turned in a slow circle and studied the painfully silent kitchen. Even just looking at it made her want to curl up in a ball and weep.

Every room in her house made her want to cry now. Every room reminded her of *them*. Wes' laughter, Drake's quiet smirks. Hawthorne and the sweet way he tucked flowers away for her to find. Atticus and Jasper pacing in the attic, the floorboards creaking under their polished shoes. Every room in her house was a reminder of what she'd done and what she'd lost, but Nicole couldn't leave.

The house was all she had left of them.

Her eyes landed on the wilting flowers on the table. Hawthorne's shy smile flashed in her mind, followed by the blank mask he had worn as he walked out of her life without a second glance. She couldn't even sit on her couch anymore because the scent of motor oil and sawdust lingered on the cushions. Drake and West had held her in their arms on that couch. They had loved her right there.... and then they had walked out together, Drake practically snarling as she watched.

Even the empty wine bottles in the recycling bin reminded her of her monsters—the taste of wine on Atticus and Jasper's lips, how they always kissed her the second they laid eyes on her, the way their cool skin warmed against hers as they held her tight. Like they were afraid she was going to vanish at any second. She couldn't stop picturing the disappointment in their eyes when they turned to leave.

Especially Jasper. Poor, charming Jasper. He had stood in front of her with desperation in his eyes and Nicole had been forced to watch the hope and love die between them.

They were gone. All of them, leaving her a shell of a woman in a shell of a house.

Had they thought about her since they had walked out the door, or were they already on to their new conquests? She was too afraid to open up MONSTR and see if she could stumble across their profiles.

The damned monsters had ruined her. They had broken her into tiny pieces and stepped over the remains and out the door, and she had no one but herself to blame.

Her phone buzzed again. She glanced down at the screen and sighed.

"Fuck off, Miri," Nicole grumbled to herself.

It wasn't her friends' fault, not really, but talking to them only reminded her of how this whole mess had started. She never should have agreed to Ashley's plan. She never should have let the tequila win.

Nicole sent the call to voicemail and shoved the phone across the counter. Dragging her lucky mug from the sink, she dropped it on the counter and fished out a half-empty wine bottle. Sloshing wine into the cup, she ignored the tears on her cheeks.

She raised the dill mug and stared at the happy little pickle on the ceramic. Sobs choked her, freezing in her throat. Whirling around angrily, she hurled the mug at the wall, and the shattered pieces fell to the floor in a puddle of moscato.

Sliding down the cupboard, Nicole sat on the floor. Cold tile bit her flesh through her thin leggings.

"How did I mess this up so badly?" she cried.

She'd gone from five wonderful men who adored her to zero in a matter of minutes, all because of one damned video. Nicole knew her cousin was behind it. She didn't know how, and she didn't even care. Not even his lawsuit could ruin her life as thoroughly as she had ruined it herself.

"I should've joined a nunnery."

Nicole should've done a lot of things... like deleting that damned MONSTR app when she'd sobered up. Instead, she'd given her heart to five monsters. Apparently, there was no take-backs when it came to monstrous boyfriends—something that definitely should have been in the fine print.

A knock shook the front door. She ignored it. With her luck, Ashley and Miri had lost patience with her avoidant bullshit and were there to kick the door down and drag her to therapy... or a bar.

The thought of more tequila made her stomach roll. Never again.

Another knock rattled the front door, loud and impatient. Nicole swiped at her tears with her sleeves. She may as well answer it. It's not like ignoring it would avoid the eventual confrontation.

Every time someone knocked on the door—hell, every time a breeze twisted through the old house—a tiny part of her hoped, and every time, it was dashed. The only people she wanted at her door would never knock again.

Nicole dragged herself to her feet and stumbled to the door. She ripped it open to an impatient delivery man.

"I need you to sign for this."

He thrust a digital pad into her hands and tapped his foot while Nicole scribbled across the screen and handed it back. He tossed a small box to her and jogged off the porch, disappearing in the depths of a delivery truck that was already backing out of her driveway.

Closing the door, she looked down at the package in her hands. She hadn't ordered anything. She couldn't afford to order anything. Even if she could, what could she possibly want that would soothe the hurt and frustration inside her?

Tearing through the cardboard, Nicole pulled out a white gift box tied with a black bow. She pulled the ribbon free and tossed it aside. Inside the box lay a pale green scarf with swirling gold embroidered leaves. She raised the silky scarf to her face and breathed in the perfumed scent.

Where the hell did it come from?

Nudging the box on the floor with her foot, she shook out the invoice and snatched it off the ground. A fresh batch of tears welled in her eyes. Atticus had ordered it for her two days after they had fed from her, a scarf for the throat that had brought them back to life.

Nicole hugged the scarf to her chest, careful not to let her tears drip onto the expensive silk. Did he know it had been delivered? Would he even care?

Hurrying back into the kitchen, she grabbed her phone. Nicole typed out a quick text—one of dozens she had desperately sent over the last few days.

> NICOLE
>
> I got the scarf. It's beautiful.
>
> Please call me so I can explain. Just five minutes, that's all I'm asking.
>
> Please, Atticus.

She stared at the screen. Nicole watched the notification blink that the messages had been received and read, but no response came back. The vampire didn't even start to type. The message sat ignored, just like every other desperate missive she had already sent.

Nicole turned the phone off and laid it on the counter, her heart breaking into even smaller pieces. She couldn't take it anymore. Never in her life had she felt as alone as she did now in her own home.

Her monsters were gone, and they had taken the important bits of her with them.

Clutching the scarf tight, Nicole slipped into the laundry room and fished through the baskets until she found a familiar t-shirt. Dragging Drake's work shirt over her head, she folded herself into the soothing scent of the werecougar.

She couldn't bring them back—their silence was promise enough of that—but for just a little while longer, Nicole could pretend. Until their scent faded from her home, she could lie to herself.

Drifting up the stairs, Nicole crawled into Hawthorne's empty bed. She pressed her face into the cold sheets, the scent of dirt and fragrant flower petals teasing her nose. If she closed her eyes, she could almost feel his strong arms wrapped around her, his soft kiss on her cheek, that hot flush burning his pointy ears.

Wrapped in memories of her monsters, Nicole sobbed into the mattress and let sleep take her.

33

NICOLE

Nicole stared into the darkness, curled into a ball as the abyss swirled around her.

"*Get up,*" a familiar voice whispered.

She spun, her head swiveling in every direction. There was no one with her but the darkness smothering her every breath.

"*Get up!*" The voice hissed again.

Rising to her feet, Nicole started to run. Fear lapped at her heels with every step. Why was she running? What was chasing her? What would happen if she stopped?

Terror hammered her heart, but she forced herself to skid to a stop. She turned in a slow circle, studying the blackness of the void freezing her from the inside out.

Nicole frowned. That wasn't quite right.

She was cold, but not inside. A bright heat ignited in her stomach, burning and licking at her with white flames. She blinked, her hand stroking over her abdomen.

"*It's too late,*" Jasper's voice hissed.

"*Too late for her,*" Atticus agreed.

Flames burst from her belly, spilling over her skin.

Nicole tried to back away, but the fire climbed up her body and ignited her clothes. The silk scarf around her neck tightened.

"The perfect fate for a liar," Wes' voice added to the darkness.

A ball of fire consumed her, burning away her flesh. Nicole screamed as laughter surrounded her, the faces of her monsters jeering at her through the flames. Thick smoke filled her lungs and choked the air from her throat.

"See you in hell—"

Nicole bolted upright, her heart pounding like a jackhammer. What the hell kind of nightmare was that? Her hand, still wrapped in the silk scarf, was clutched her chest. She took a deep breath and paused as the scent of smoke tickled her nose.

Patting down her body, she checked her body for burns. A sigh of relief split the silent night. It was *just* a dream. A cursed dream that would haunt her for days to come, but still, just a dream.

Scrubbing her hands over her face, Nicole forced herself to breathe. The smell of smoke teased her nostrils, and her head shot up.

That definitely wasn't a dream.

Climbing out of bed, she flipped on the light and gasped. The bedroom was filled with smoke. Dark plumes of choking haze poured through the gap under the door.

Nicole stared dumbly at the crushing smoke. "What—?"

It was just a dream. As disturbing as it had been, it couldn't follow her to reality... right? Drake and Jasper, and all her other monsters weren't waiting in the shadows to jump out and set her on fire. That was just ridiculous.

Fire. The logical part of her brain slapped at her like a splash of cold water, and Nicole finally caught up to the panicky animal half of her mind.

Her house was on fire. Her *house* was on *fire*!

"Oh, fuck me!"

Whirling around, she fumbled for her phone on the nightstand. She dialed 911 and crawled across the bed to open the window. Her muscles strained as she pulled as hard as she could, but the pane stayed stuck in place. Her hand slapped against the glass.

"Fuck you, you piece of shit wreck of a house!" Nicole shouted.

"Hello? What's your emergency?" a tiny voice called from the speaker on her cellphone.

Nicole raised the phone to her ear. "My house is on fire."

Smoke filled her lungs, and she coughed hard. Slipping off the bed, she crouched low to the floor and turned in desperate circles. There were only two ways out of the room: the window and door, and the window wasn't exactly cooperating.

"Where are you in your house? What's your address?" the operator urgently asked.

"301 Pine Street," Nicole coughed. "I'm on the second floor in a bedroom."

"Is the room on fire?"

"Not yet, but there's smoke coming from the hall... and I am *not* dreaming this."

The emergency operator probably didn't need to know that, but Nicole needed to hear herself say it out loud to be sure. This wasn't a nightmare. The nightmare had passed, and this was reality. Hot, smoky reality.

"Is there a window? Can you get it open?"

"No."

The last time anyone had managed to open it, it had been Hawthorne, and she didn't have his preternatural strength. Drake had been making noises about replacing all the windows, but that had been put on the back burner. The plumbing had taken priority after he and Wes had kept clogging the old pipes with loose fur.

Clearly, that had been a bad idea.

Nicole eyed the sheet of glass. She could always break it, a little voice in her head reminded her. Replacing it would be expensive, but then again, so was a coffin.

"I might be able to break it... but I'm on the second floor."

What were two broken legs in the grand scheme of things? Better than being burnt alive. A flash of Atticus and Jasper's burnt flesh teased her stressed mind. No fucking thank you.

"I think if I can get out the door, I can make a run for it straight down the stairs and out the front door," she coughed into the phone.

"I'm not sure that's a good idea—"

No offense to the operator, but she wasn't choking on billowing plumes of smoke. Nicole was.

Fuck it. She didn't have another choice.

Nicole crawled to the door and fumbled for the handle; it was surprisingly cool in her hand. When she twisted it, she jerked the door open and braced herself for flames. She blinked at the empty hallway. Besides the thick smoke rising from downstairs, the hall was clear of fire.

She crawled into the hallway, the old carpet scraping her knees. Nicole squinted into the dark as clouds of smoke filled the house in hazy swirls, blurring her already dim view.

Inching down the hall, she clutched her scarf and phone to her chest and moved toward the stairs. At least, she hoped it was toward the stairs. In her panic, Nicole might have gone the wrong way...

No. She had turned left. Definitely left.

Patting her hands on the floor, she felt for the lip of the

stairs. It had to be there somewhere. Her fingertips found empty air.

"There!" Nicole's gasp morphed into a hacking cough.

She hurried over the top step, crouching low with each step down. Nicole's mind whirled as she moved through her burning house.

Had she left the stove on? No, she hadn't cooked in days. She'd been surviving off microwaved ramen and peanut butter and jelly sandwiches because she couldn't bring herself to make anything resembling a meal since her heart had been shattered.

Nicole quickly slid down the stairs and stumbled into the front hall. Blistering heat washed over her as she passed the kitchen door. The cabinets and kitchen table were engulfed in flames, spreading from the back door in her direction. The sight nearly stopped her in her tracks.

How? Where the hell had the fire started?

Flames crackled, sending a fresh wave of scorching heat in her direction. Nicole quickly unlocked the front door and threw herself off the porch steps.

Cold, crisp air enveloped her lungs. Sprawled on the gravel, Nicole breathed.

"Are you out of the house?" a tiny voice called. "Are you okay?"

Right. The operator.

She pressed the phone to her ear. "I'm outside now. The fire is in my kitchen."

"The fire department is two minutes out. I need you to get as far back from the house as possible."

Nicole scrambled to her feet and hurried down the driveway. Rocks bit her feet with each step, and the cold air nipped at her bare legs as she waited for the fire truck in nothing but a dirty t-shirt and her panties.

She stared at the flames lighting her kitchen window.

How many times had she joked about setting her house on fire? How many times had Nicole teased about collecting the insurance money and starting her life over debt-free?

Pain twisted in her chest like a dagger. Suddenly, she was desperate for the flames to die. Because that's where they had been—them. If she lost her house, they were gone for good, and nothing she could ever do could get them back.

Without the house, it was like her monsters had never been in her life at all.

The sharp siren of the fire engine cut through the night, and the vehicle rolled up her driveway, an ambulance close behind. Firemen poured out of the truck and started snapping directions at one another.

Nicole stood there, watching them crawl all over her house and drag hoses up her driveway. There was nothing she could do but watch as her home burned. A warm hand gently touched her arm and turned her slowly to meet a familiar face.

"Wes?"

"Cole." The EMT smiled a familiar brilliant smile. "Wes is my little brother."

Little was clearly subjective. The werewolf in front of her was just as tall as her Wes, every bit the muscled physique. The same golden eyes gleamed back at her.

Her heart sank. "Oh, great. There are two hot werewolves to look disappointed in me."

Ushering her back toward the ambulance, he raised his eyebrows and eyed her bare legs up and down.

"I don't know about disappointed, but all I heard was that you think I'm hot."

Nicole snorted. "Yeah, you're definitely Wes' brother. Is he okay?"

She couldn't stop herself from asking. Desperation

clawed at her. Even bad information was better than none when Nicole felt as empty as she did.

"He's okay," Cole promised. His golden eyes looked her over curiously. "Sleeping on my couch and drinking all my beer in some kind of depressed state... but overall, he'll be okay."

Nicole nodded, ignoring the tears welling in her eyes and turning to stare at her house. She was wrong—it was better not to know at all.

Grabbing a blanket from the ambulance, Cole wrapped it around her shoulders. The werewolf was all business as he looked her over and peppered her with questions.

Nicole ignored him. He didn't have a cure for heartbreak in the back of his ambulance, so unless it had to do with saving her house, she really didn't care. Her nightmare—as terrifying as it had been—had woken her in time to get out in one piece. She was fine.

Well, as fine as she could be when her heart and soul had been scooped out.

For the first time, she was glad her monsters had left her. She was glad that Hawthorne had left without a backward glance, that Drake and Wes had leaned on each other on the way out the door. She was relieved that Atticus and Jasper had drifted out the door in silence.

They hadn't been there to burn. Watching Jasper and Atticus burn in the sunlight had been horrifying enough. As much as it killed her, their leaving her might have saved their lives.

She watched the firemen extinguish the inferno in her kitchen as Cole checked her for burns. Nicole bit back a sigh; it wasn't like she'd liked those countertops anyway.

"We need to get you to the hospital," Cole interrupted her silent musing. "They need to make sure you don't have any lung damage from all that smoke."

Nicole eyed her smoking house. Well, it had to be better than being here.

34

WES

Wes hurried down the sterile hallway, a takeout bag swinging in his hand. Cole had let him in a side door, but his idiot brother had neglected to point out exactly what direction he was supposed to head in.

He skidded to a halt at the nurses' station. Smiling brightly at a frazzled nurse with a pile of paperwork, the werewolf leaned on the counter and pretended like he didn't have a care in the world.

"Would you mind pointing me to Nicole Dunn's room?"

She frowned. "Are you family? I'll need to double-check with the patient that you're allowed in."

He could explain... but neither of them had time for a ten-minute breakdown of polyamorous monster relationship dynamics and the ensuing chaos of a breakup.

"I came in with her. I'm her boyfriend," Wes lied smoothly. He waved at the stark halls and flashed her a cheeky grin. "She asked me to grab her some food, and now I'm all turned around and can't seem to find my way back. These halls all look alike."

"I'm not sure—"

A high-pitched beep screeched from her computer monitor. Ignoring him completely, she picked up the phone and wedged it under her ear.

"Hey, it's Taylor in the ER. Is the cardiologist on his way down yet?"

Wes itched to grab the nurse and shake the answer out of her. If it wouldn't get him dragged out by hospital security, he just might have. Patience was *not* in a wolf's nature.

"Nicole Dunn?" he asked, pointing at the bag of food.

"Uh, over there." She waved absently. "Room 203—well, tell him to move his ass!"

Hurrying off before she could change her mind, Wes hugged the bag to his chest. He stopped outside the hospital room and knocked.

"Come in," a weak voice called.

The werewolf walked through the door, and his heart stopped. Nicole sat in the middle of the bed, her knees hugged to her chest, and her dark hair a tangled nest. She looked so small in the hospital gown, a vulnerable human curled into a ball to protect herself.

Nicole looked up as he closed the door behind him. Teary streaks cut through the soot darkening her gaunt cheeks as they stared awkwardly at each other. What was a person supposed to say after a messy breakup, three days of sulking on their couch, and a house fire?

Wes cleared his throat. "My brother called about the fire."

Nicole nodded and hugged her knees tighter against her chest. Looking down at her feet, tears welled in her eyes.

Pity stabbed at his heart. As hurt as the wolf had been when they'd received the footage of her lies, it still broke him to see his sweet human looking so sad and desolate. Need clawed at his chest.

Wes sat down on the edge of the bed and tossed the bag

aside. He gripped her wrists and dragged her into his lap; folding his arms around her, he hugged her tight.

As frustrated as he still was... Nicole could have died. The last time he'd seen her, he'd turned his back on her tears and her explanations, and walked away. If the fire had been worse, that would have been Wes' last memory of her.

Nicole pressed her face into his chest. Her arms clutched him tight, hands fisting in his shirt. She held him desperately, as if terrified that she would open her eyes and find that he'd vanished.

"Are you okay?" Wes whispered against her hair.

"My house was on fire... and I smell like camping," she sniffled.

He rubbed her back, tracing soothing circles between her shoulders. "I like camping."

Raising her head, Nicole swiped away her tears. "Camping is only fun if there are s'mores."

That was doable. There was a grocery right down the street from the hospital.

"We can get s'mores if you want," he promised. "I even know of a fire we can toast the marshmallows over."

"Too soon."

"Yep. I knew it as soon as I said it."

Her watery giggle was like music to his ears. Anything was better than sobbing into his shirt. Wes wasn't sure if tears could stain fabric, but he didn't want to find out.

"Why do you smell like you bathed in fried chicken?" Nicole asked.

Laughing, the werewolf picked up the discarded takeout bag and dropped it in her lap. She ripped it open and looked up at him with wide eyes.

"You brought me chicken strips?"

Tears dripped down her cheeks. Wes winced and wiped at the wet spots with the edge of his sleeve. Lip trembling,

Nicole stared at the chicken strips and fries he had brought for her.

He winced at her welling eyes. Maybe food had been a bad idea.

Shifters fed the people they cared about—it was just what they did. When Cole had called and told him Nicole was okay, Wes had calmed his hammering heart and made a pitstop at her favorite diner on the way to the hospital.

If she could eat, then she was really okay, and if Nicole was okay, then he could breathe again.

Something clattered outside the door. Raised voices echoed from the sterile hallway, drawing both of their attention.

"I'm her boyfriend!" a familiar voice argued.

"I thought the other guy was her boyfriend?"

"We all are," Drake's growling voice cut in.

Nicole looked back and forth between Wes' face and the door. "How—?"

"Cole called me... and I texted the group chat."

"You guys have a group chat?"

Yes. And Hawthorne kept sending them all funny cat videos. Wes and Jasper had a bet going to see how long he could keep it up before Drake threatened to twist his head off his shoulders by that silvery-y man bun.

The door flew open and the rest of the monsters piled in. Wes wasn't quite sure who looked more shocked; the pitiful human being swallowed up by an oversized hospital gown, or her pack of fanged boyfriends.

Nicole took one look at them and burst into tears. So much for stopping her from crying.

"What's wrong?" Jasper looked at the shellshocked nurse lingering in the doorway. "Is she hurt?"

"No." Wes shook his head. "She's okay... just crying... again."

Atticus looked deeply alarmed. For once, the cool, bossy vampire was anything but calm and collected.

"Fix it," he demanded.

"I'm s—sorry!" Nicole sobbed. "So, so s-so-sorry!"

Wes petted her hair awkwardly. Every stuttered apology slipping between her sobs was like a blade in his heart. He gritted his teeth and clenched his fists to contain his claws.

He glared at the others. All of them looked as alarmed as he felt.

Jasper nudged the fae. "Do something!"

"Me?"

"You're the sensitive one!" the vampire hissed.

"How am I—?"

"You're a vegetarian!" Wes growled.

Hawthorne rolled his eyes. "Suddenly being a vegetarian makes me 'sensitive'?"

"I'm surrounded by idiots," Drake grumbled as he shoved his way to the front of the group. "She's crying, not spitting venom."

Wes jumped out of the were-cat's way. If Drake thought he could fix her broken heart, then by all means.

Sitting down on the bed, the cougar pulled their sobbing human into his lap. He folded his muscled arms around her and hugged her tight. His fingertips stroked her jaw in gentle pets.

Nicole cried harder, curling up in his lap and turning back into a pitiful ball as she sobbed.

"You're making it worse!" Atticus hissed.

"No, I'm not," the cat insisted. "She needs to cry it out."

Wes winced as the heart-wrenching sounds continued. He'd better be sure, or the rest of them were going to murder him for letting this go on.

"He's definitely making it worse," Hawthorne agreed.

"If you can't shut up, then get out," Drake snapped. He

smoothed his heavy hand over Nicole's tangled hair and gentled his tone. "I have five sisters. Go ahead and cry it out, kitten."

By the time her tears subsided, every last one of them looked like they would promise her the moon if she would just stop. Nicole opened her mouth—probably to apologize again.

"Don't," Wes interrupted her. The tears were bad enough; he couldn't take any more shaky apologies.

The door swung open, banging against the wall, and the monsters spun, already on edge.

"Oh, good. You're all here," Ashley sighed. "She was being such a bummer."

Miri smacked her arm. "Ashley!"

"What? She was!" The blonde turned to glare at them. "Does this mean you're all done being drama queens?"

"Leave them alone. It's my fault—" Nicole started.

"It is not! If they'd let you explain for more than two seconds, they would know that the whole debt thing was *my* idea and I bullied you into it."

Ashley took a step forward, and every monster eased away from her. She might be a skinny, weak human, but Wes had no doubt that she could throw a mean punch.

"She's barely gotten out of bed all week because you dicks all dumped her and bailed without a backward glance!"

Wes blinked. He'd laid on his brother's couch and knocked back bottles of scotch. It had never occurred to the wolf that Nicole was taking it just as hard. He'd thought she didn't care.

The men exchanged awkward looks. Hawthorne stared down at his shoes, cringing as Ashley took a deep breath.

"*Do you even realize—*"

Miri's elbow drove into her stomach, and the air whooshed out of the blonde in a surprised gap.

"Well, now that we see she's alive and okay—" Miri threaded her arm through her friend's and started to drag her toward the door—"we'll leave her in your capable hands... claws... whatever."

"No! I'm not done!" Ashley argued.

Miri closed the door behind them, their argument carrying through the door as she dragged her away.

"Be quiet! They need to make up!"

"If they hurt her again, I'll kill them."

"Yeah, I'd love to see that. What are you going to do, Pilates them to death?"

The room fell into an awkward silence as the two women disappeared down the hall. They turned back to the sweet human covered in soot and tears, none of them daring to speak a word.

Nicole opened her mouth and closed it again. Looking at each of their forlorn faces, she sighed.

"Can we just go home now?"

35

NICOLE

Nicole stood in the driveway, staring at her house. From the outside, it didn't look too bad, but she knew that once she stepped through the door... well, the inside was going to be a burnt, smoky mess.

It had taken all her energy to convince her monsters to bring her home. They had peppered her with excuse after excuse to keep her in the hospital overnight. Atticus had even tried argue that she needed to stay in the hospital for a week, but the nurse he had dragged into the room had threatened to stab him in the eye with a syringe if he touched her again—Nicole needed to take lessons.

"But what if you're dying from smoke inhalation?"

"What if the house collapses on top of you?"

"You could have brain damage!"

And on and on. Nicole had finally shut down their excuses by telling them she was going home with or without them. She had never seen the vampires move as fast as they did then. They had demanded discharge paperwork, doctor recommendations, and to have the car pulled around within minutes.

Apparently, the way to get monster boyfriends to do

what you wanted was just to threaten to do things independently. Go figure.

The six of them piled into one car, Nicole in the back seat resting in Drake's lap. His thick arms wrapped around her, stronger than any seat belt that had been invented, and she was fairly certain it would take an act of god to pry her out of his hands.

It had been a quiet ride. Only the sound of Jasper and Atticus passing a cell phone back and forth in the front seat broke the silence. She had no idea how they did it, but the lawyers had already spoken to the fire marshal, the police, and the mayor. Somehow, they had gotten approval for them to return to the house in record time.

They were awfully good at getting people out of bed in the middle of the night when they wanted. Too bad they didn't use their superpowers for good. They just had to be bloodsucking lawyers... literally.

From what they had learned, the house was mostly fine. The firefighters had managed to put the flames out fairly quickly, and most of the damage was from smoke. Specifically, in Hawthorne's and her bedrooms right above the kitchen.

And the kitchen itself... well, that was kaput. From what they had relayed to Nicole, it was a burnt-out husk. The rest of the house would be completely fine once it was done airing out, so that was at least some small boon of comfort.

The vampires assured her it was completely safe to stay in for the night... so why was she lingering outside in the dark? Steeling her spine, Nicole trudged up the steps and shoved open the front door. Ignoring the unnerving scent of ash and smoke, she moved to the kitchen doorway and stared inside.

Cold ash covered the room. Her kitchen cabinets were completely unidentifiable now, her stove a scorched mess, and even her dining room table was nothing but charred remains.

On one hand, Drake had been planning on gutting the kitchen anyway. Maybe this would move things along... or have them eating off paper plates for the next year.

Closing her eyes, Nicole pinched the bridge of her nose and started calculating how much it was going to cost to fix. There was going to be a lot of zeroes on the back of that number. How much did a new refrigerator cost? She didn't even know.

Tears welled in her eyes, and Nicole scrubbed them aside with the cuff of her sweater. The scent of green things and dirt tickled her nose from the sweatshirt Hawthorne had tucked around her back at the hospital. The green scent soothed her anxiety.

She was not going to cry again. She had done her crying at the hospital, and she was done now.

Hawthorne leaned past her, his chest flush against her back. He winced.

"I can fix some of it," he murmured in her ear.

He raised his hand and placed it on a charred beam, the glyphs on his arms flaring to life. Nicole could feel the heat radiating from the ones marking his chest through the thin fabric of his T-shirt.

He stepped back, the light dying. "That should take care of the framing."

"What did you do?"

"I encouraged the wood to grow back." He shrugged like it was nothing. "You're probably going to have quite a few dead spots on the lawn from the siphoned energy, but I can fix that the old-fashioned way, with grass seed and fertilizer."

Nicole turned on the spot, her eyes round as coins. "You're growing the house back?"

It was satisfying to see she wasn't the only one staring at him. Even the shifters and vampires were looking at the quiet fae like he'd grown a second head. If her brain was going to break, Nicole was fairly sure this would be the monster fact that pushed her over the edge.

He blushed to the tips of his precious pointy ears. "Just the organic bits. Whiskers over there will have to do his handyman thing on the rest."

Drake cocked his head to the side and eyed the damaged kitchen. Nicole knew he was thinking about the measurements he had already taken when he first surveyed her kitchen and doing some quick calculations in his head.

"Some drywall, electrical, upgrade the cabinets..." He trailed off, muttering a to-do list under his breath. "New appliances... maybe an island..."

Nicole turned back to Hawthorne, shock still coursing through her system. How was nobody else freaking out about this?

"You're *growing* the house back? Like... actually growing?"

Her brain still couldn't quite wrap itself around that little tidbit. Something to think through tomorrow... in the daylight... after she had managed to get a couple of hours of sleep and ventured out into the world to find coffee. Since her coffee maker was essentially a scorched lump of metal, she was going to be a regular at the nearest coffee shop.

If they ran out of cinnamon syrup, Nicole was going to have a nervous breakdown right there at the coffee counter. She just needed one thing to go right this week.

She glanced back at the gathered monsters, and some of her panic eased. Then again, she really didn't need cinnamon syrup in her coffee. Nicole could live without it, just so long as Drake was taking the first sip of her coffee every morning.

Atticus gripped her elbow in his cool hand and led her to the smoky couch while Drake and Wes took off to take a walk around the house. They didn't say why, but Nicole assumed they were checking out the extent of the damage so that Drake could start an assessment.

More zeroes for her to cringe about.

Atticus crouched in front of her with a damp cloth and swiped at the streaks of ash still lingering on her face. He scrubbed as gently as he could, but by the time he was finished, Nicole was fairly certain she wouldn't need to exfoliate for the next month.

At least her complexion would be dewy in the morning.

"Let's get you to bed," Jasper said gently. "You need sleep, pet."

"I don't know where to sleep."

Her bedroom was right above the kitchen. Even if she pried the window open, it was going to be a smoky mess for at least a week. That left her with the sagging couch.

She would rather take a nap inside of a wood stove.

Nicole scrubbed a hand over her raw face. Maybe she shouldn't have insisted they bring her back home. It could have waited until the morning. She just wanted to crawl into a bed, any bed, with every one of her monsters in it. Was that too much to ask?

"I want all of you," Nicole sighed.

She wanted comfort, and to be wrapped in the arms of all of her monsters. Actually, forget comfort—Nicole was suddenly wide awake. Sleep was the last thing she wanted as she stared at the men surrounding her.

"I want all of you. Right now."

Jasper raised his eyebrows, and Hawthorne looked at her like she was crazy. Atticus seemed to be the only one who looked unfazed as they stared back at her.

"I don't think that's a good idea..." Hawthorne started.

"What isn't a good idea?" Wes asked as he and Drake came strolling back into the house.

"The monster orgy Nicole wants to have in her burnt wreck of a house," Jasper said dryly.

Why were they saying that like she was insane? Hadn't they all been trying to get into her pants from the very beginning?

Clearly, they didn't understand the scorched kitchen. That could have been her. It almost *had* been her. They could have lost this chance forever and now they wanted to stall?

Drake looked her over. "I think we need to take her back to the hospital. She might have a concussion."

"My head is fine," Nicole argued. "I could have burned to death—"

Wes growled, his whole body bristling as she casually reminded them how close she'd come to burning to death. She shushed him; he could be annoyed with her tomorrow.

"I nearly died," Nicole said again. What were they not getting about this? "I don't want to pretend anymore. I want to live it."

"Pretend what, love?" Atticus asked gently.

"That I'm not madly in love with all of you." Nicole looked at each one of their worried faces. "I'm tired of pretending I don't want every single one of you. I want this. I want *us*."

The monsters just stared at her. Hawthorne's mouth was actually gaping. Why was nobody saying anything? Her confidence wavered as the silence dragged on and on.

"Unless... you don't want to?"

36

NICOLE

"You think we don't want to?" Drake raised his eyebrows.

The big were-cougar stalked toward Nicole, and she leaned back, her heart fluttering in her chest. His calloused hand wrapped around her throat and dragged her up onto her toes. Gray eyes glaring down into her face, she looked up at him.

"There is no universe where that could ever be true, kitten," he said fiercely.

Nicole met his bruising kiss with one of her own. Drake fumbled with the sweatshirt Hawthorne had wrapped her in, peeling it down her arms and tossing it aside.

Cool hands gripped her elbows and turned her around. Atticus caught her mouth, teasing her lips with his fangs. Someone gripped the back of her t-shirt and tugged it away. The fabric cleared her head and landed on the floor.

Nicole stood, surrounded by monsters in nothing but her panties. Hawthorne stepped forward, his tattooed arms wrapping around her waist as he dragged her against his chest. His hand rubbed down her back to squeeze her ass, and she had a second to breathe before her underwear was dragged down her legs.

Someone lifted her up and carried her in their strong grip. Nicole couldn't even tell who it was, there were so many hands touching her at once. Lips pressed against her, devouring her mouth. She was vaguely aware of stairs passing underfoot before she landed in the next set of arms.

Claws nipped at her naked ass cheeks. A tongue teased her jaw. Strong fingers threaded through her hair and tipped her face back.

This. This was exactly what she had wanted all along; the desperate touch of their hands on her body, the need to feel them all at once.

When Nicole opened her eyes, they stood in the vampires' attic suite. Jasper held her tight against his chest, his tongue painting wet kisses up her throat as the shifters pushed the two beds together to make one.

Four sets of gleaming eyes watched as the vampire set her on the bed and arranged her on her knees. Jasper turned her around, her shoulders pressing into his chest. Hands stroking down her sides, Nicole tilted her head to the side and readied herself for what was coming next.

His fangs sank into her throat, and pleasure melted through her, curling like liquid gold under her flesh. Nicole moaned, the orgasm building before anyone had even touched her.

Jasper palmed her breasts. His hands slid lower, stroking over her soft belly to reach between her thighs. Nicole floated on a cloud of bliss as his fingers reached between her folds and teased her clit.

The orgasm hit her too soon. The vampire had barely touched her, and her legs were already shaking. Jasper released his fangs and let her fall forward onto the bed.

She was gasping into the pillows when warm hands gripped her hips. Dragged up onto her hands and knees, she didn't have to look to know who was touching her as a cock teased her pussy before driving deep.

Such an impatient wolf.

"Yes!" she moaned.

"Don't worry, baby," Wes growled. "I'm going to breed this tight little pussy just the way you like."

He slammed his hips forward, fucking her hard and fast. Nicole bounced on his cock as moans and whimpers poured non-stop from her lips, the lingering effects of Jasper's bite turning the pleasure blasting through her into a typhoon.

"That's it, babe. Keep coming," the werewolf ordered. "Show them what a cum-hungry slut you are."

Her hands fisted the bedsheets. "Please, please, please!"

Drake dropped onto the bed in front of her, his gray gaze catching her dizzy eyes. One hand stroking his cock, he caught her chin and kissed her. The were-cougar grinned at her as every sharp thrust forced her to meet his lips again and again.

He stayed like that, his thick cock tight in his grip as Wes slammed her pussy. Her cat had always loved a show.

His lips were still devouring hers as her hardest orgasm yet slammed through her. Nicole's thighs trembled beneath her, threatening to spill her on the bed if Wes let go of her hips for even a moment.

The werewolf slapped her ass and spilled his own release deep inside her cunt. He pulled out, and she braced herself for the next cock to drive in, but none came. Instead, Wes pressed a gentle kiss to her lower back. She glanced over her shoulder and watched his mouth fill with sharp, wolfish fangs. He bent low and bit her ass.

"Fuck!" Nicole bucked against the sharp pain.

"You wanted to be claimed, baby?" His golden eyes laughed as his thumb spread the blood across her ass cheek.

Nicole was pretty sure the word "claimed" had never left her mouth, but sure, slap a scar on her ass. Jasper had already had his fangs in her, so why not a werewolf too?

Drake gripped her forearms and flipped her onto her back, the ceiling spinning as she tried to orient herself. It was Hawthorne's sweet, lingering kisses trailing up her body that brought the world to a gentle halt.

Soft lips teased her breasts, a tongue flicking over her nipples before heading north to her lips. The fae kissed her, tender and gentle, everything the wolf wasn't. Hawthorne moved over her, his chest brushing her aching breasts.

Nicole wrapped her legs around his slim waist, other hands stroking her flesh as his cock stretched her pussy. Hawthorne thrust slowly. His pale eyes caught hers and refused to let go as he fucked her decadently slow.

Smooth, easy kisses teased her lips, and each thrust of his hips teased the flames in her belly higher. The gentle fae took his time, dragging her orgasm out with agonizing patience. Hawthorne wasn't a wildfire or an inferno—he was the steady warmth of a hearth, embers burning and waiting to scorch you from the inside out.

"I'm so close!" Nicole moaned.

The orgasm was building bigger and bigger, always teasing, just out of her grasp. His light fingers reached between them and rolled her clit, hurtling Nicole over the edge.

She gasped, bliss burning through her like a starburst. Hawthorne raised his head and nodded at the cougar, and Drake's calloused fingers teased her nipples.

The fae's cock still rocked inside her as he pulled back. Resting his hand flat on her sternum, he caught her confused, pleasure-drunk gaze.

"This might sting a bit."

"What—?"

Nicole barely had time to wonder what he meant before Drake was pinching her nipples, and a vampire was sinking his fangs into her thigh. Pleasure exploded through her like a grenade detonating in her belly. Wave after wave drowned her, dragging her under until she wasn't even sure she was breathing anymore.

She was vaguely aware of Hawthorne coming deep inside of her before a flash of pain burned her chest. His arms flashed blue, the glyphs glowing like Christmas lights on his skin as his fingers smoothed over the ache in her sternum.

Nicole raised her head as he lifted his hand away. A bright blue glyph was inked between her breasts, the faint glow matching his. What in the actual fuck?

Hawthorne bent down and pressed a kiss to the small symbol before backing away from her. Atticus replaced him, her blood still staining his lips. So he was the thigh biter.

They really need to have a chat about what Wes had meant by "claiming." Nicole had a feeling the others were taking his lead, and she was very much left in the dark.

The vampire licked the bloody spot on her thigh and a spike of pleasure speared through her. Later. They could definitely talk about it later.

Atticus rolled back on the bed. Gripping her thighs, he dragged her over his body.

"Ride me, love," Atticus ordered.

Nicole could barely move after what felt like a dozen back-to-back orgasms, and he wanted her to *ride him*? Clearly, they had different expectations about how this was supposed to go.

His ringed fingers slapped her ass. "Ride, Nicole."

"So bossy," she grumbled.

He reached between them and notched his cock into her waiting pussy. She slid down the length, burying him to the hilt as she gyrated on top of him. Admiring her with his blood-red eyes, Atticus watched her curves jiggle.

Ah, she understood what he wanted now.

Nicole bounced gently, her thighs already burning as his eyes locked onto her breasts and the vampire licked his lips.

"Faster, love."

He didn't wait for her to pick up the pace. No, Atticus gripped her hips and did it himself. Hands dropping to his stomach, Nicole gasped as he bucked his hips up into her, and she bit her lip to keep from screaming as his cock stroked every hidden spot inside of her.

"Good girl," he praised. "Just like that, love."

Nicole panted, the air sawing in and out of her lungs as she was thoroughly fucked... again. Maybe she hadn't known exactly what was in store for her when she'd demanded all her monsters fuck her tonight—not that she was going to ask them to stop.

She was human, not stupid.

Atticus curved a hand around her ass and teased her second hole. A groan ripped through her—she knew what was coming, but not who.

"I'm warming you up, love." Atticus bounced her harder on his cock, and a second finger slipped into her tight opening. "Good girl, just a little more."

A muscled chest pressed against her back as stubble teased against her jaw. Atticus dragged her down to his chest, trapping her wrists as strong hands spread her ass cheeks and the head of a thick cock inched into her ass.

"A couple more inches, kitten," Drake growled in her ear. "You can take it."

She didn't know if she could, but Nicole was damn well going to try. Rocking her hips back, she took them both balls deep, and a wanton moan spilled from her lips.

"That's it, love." Atticus ground his cock even deeper. "Take it nice and deep."

Sandwiching her between them, the vampire and the were-cougar fucked her together. Stuffed full of hard cock, inky blackness inched into her vision. This time, Nicole was sure: she was actually going to die from pleasure. Her obituary would read "dead and full of monster cum", and she was happy with that.

Very, very happy.

Sharp claws dug into her hips, and Nicole didn't have to look know Drake had drawn blood—she could feel a tongue lapping it up.

Jasper lifted his head and moved to kneel beside Atticus. She knew what was coming and opened her mouth before he could demand it.

The vampires laughed. Apparently, her need for dick was humorous to them now. It wasn't her fault the monsters in the house had turned her into a cock-hungry hussy.

Jasper threaded his fingers in her tangled hair and lowered her face. Her tongue swiped at the tip of his cock before sucking the head between her lips. Each drive of the cocks filling her holes pushed her mouth further down his length.

"Fuck, pet." Cool fingers petted her jaw. "You have such perfect pink lips."

Nicole sucked harder, silently celebrating as she heard him hiss.

Atticus and Drake must have taken it as a sign that she wasn't appreciating their efforts enough, because they doubled their speed. She came hard, her pussy dripping over them both. There was nothing to do but hold on as Jasper fucked her face and waited for the other two to finish.

She was fairly certain that by the time the night was over, either her body would be broken, or her mind. There were only so many orgasms she could take before the universe would punish her for her hubris, and Nicole had lost count long before the first rush of Wes' cum had spilled inside of her.

Jasper slipped his dick from her mouth and bent to kiss her, his mischievous grin was practically glowing as he watched her come again and again.

Atticus and Drake came at the same time, a flood spilling into her. Their cocks slid out, and they eased her gently onto the mattress. Nicole lay limp, every muscle in her body spent, but she knew she wasn't done.

There was still one vampire left to stake his claim.

Jasper's hands smoothed down her back. Fingers hooking under her knee, he dragged it up to her side and thrust inside her. Nicole didn't even have the energy to moan anymore.

"Tired so soon, pet?" the vampire teased. "We can't have that."

His face nuzzled her neck. She felt the first prick of his fangs and braced herself for the rush of pleasure as they sank deeper than ever before. Bliss slammed through her, arching her back against him.

Jasper released his fangs and licked the wound. Hips slapping her ass, he pounded her pussy.

"Is that better, pet? Or do you need more?"

"Pl-please," Nicole stuttered under the teeth-chattering force of her orgasm. "I can't—"

"You can tell me to stop, pet." The vampire's tongue swirled over her throat. "Say the word, and I'll stop."

Nicole opened and closed her mouth. She couldn't.

Jasper chuckled. "I didn't think so. You might be our precious human, but you're also a greedy cum slut."

The vampire fucked her harder, the only sounds filling the silent room were her gasping breaths and the sucking sound of her cunt. Nicole could feel every set of eyes eagerly watching her as she floated on a cloud of bliss.

"Look at how well you were made for us," he growled in her ear. "Taking every one of us monsters, one after another, and still wanting more. So perfect, pet."

His fangs drove into her neck and everything went black. Nicole was vaguely aware of her entire body shaking and her pussy squirting helplessly, but she couldn't move. She couldn't even blink as the dirty-mouthed vampire gripped her hips and hammered his own release. She lay there boneless as she came again and again and again, no end in sight.

When Jasper finally released his fangs, she was fairly certain she was dead. Nicole wasn't quite sure what she had done in her lifetime to earn a place in heaven, but she wasn't going to argue and risk getting thrown out.

Jasper pet his hand over her hair, easing the tangles back from her tired face. His lips gently kissed her cheek before whispering in her ear. "I meant what I said, Nicole. You were made for us, and we were made for you."

He was right. The six of them fit perfectly together, all flawed in their own way, but like puzzle pieces that could only form a picture when they made a whole. They were her monsters, just as much as she was theirs. They had claimed her, and that night, she had claimed them too.

Until Nicole lay on their sex-covered sheets, she hadn't known the meaning of "bone tired", but she did now, and it was worth it. So fucking worth it.

Even if she had actually died mid-orgasm, it would have been worth every second of letting her monsters claim her.

"Get some sleep, love." Atticus kissed the top of her head. "We'll take care of you."

Nicole was vaguely aware of vampire mouths healing her bleeding wounds and a gentle hand easing a damp towel over her body. She drifted off to sleep with five pairs of inhuman eyes smugly watching her.

37

DRAKE

Drake glared at the empty courtroom, his thick arms folded over his chest. He stood beside Wes, hovering behind Nicole like a wall of muscle. It had been a long week since the fire had nearly taken her from them, a week since they had claimed every part of her as thoroughly as she had claimed them—and it had been one very long week since any of them had slept through the night.

Without letting Nicole know, they had been taking turns staying up through the night; someone was always watching, just in case the saboteur returned. The monsters weren't taking any risks with her. Not again.

They had nearly lost her once already—twice if he counted that awful video.

Every one of them was walking on eggshells, watching her like she was going to vanish right in front of them. It was all they could do to let her leave the house. At some point, Nicole was going to snap and browbeat them into giving her some space, but until then, she would stay tucked in their cocoon of safety.

Somehow, Jasper and Atticus had gotten Nicole's court date moved forward. Ready to end the worry, they had all agreed. Drake didn't even want to know what kind of bribes they'd had to pay to get the lawsuit over with.

And to get the case overseen by a shifter judge? The dent in their back accounts had better be worth it. They needed to end this... or Drake would.

Nicole shifted nervously in her seat as Jasper and Atticus rose and prepared to do their lawyer thing. Drake rested his hand on her shoulder, so soft and delicate underneath his rough touch. Nicole reached up and twisted her fingers with his, and he squeezed her hand, offering up any strength she might need.

Her cousin, Tyler, sat on the other side of the courtroom, looking over at them with a grimace of disgust and more than a little bit of smug pride. Hawthorne shifted in his seat to block Nicole from his view.

It was awfully bold of the human prick when the only thing stopping the monsters in the room from tearing him limb from limb was the assurances of two vampires. They wanted to handle it, and Nicole wanted this done legally, so they were stepping back to let the bloodsuckers take charge.

Of course, if they failed... well, Drake had always thought he would do rather well in prison.

The judge ambled into the room and flopped down into his seat. He was a short, pudgy man, his white hair earned from decades of ruling over evening trials run by vampires. If Drake couldn't smell him, he would never have guessed the man was a shifter.

"Alright, this is my last case of the night, and I want to go home. If we can get this wrapped up today, I might actually make it home to see my husbands before daybreak." Judge Crest tapped his little gavel and waved them forward. "Let's get on with this."

Atticus greeted the judge. "Your honor, we also would like to end this quickly, and if you give us a few minutes, I think we can be out of here in less than half an hour."

"You have my attention." The old judge nodded. "What's your reasoning for the motion to dismiss?"

"Fraud," Jasper said smoothly.

"Now you really have my attention. Make it quick, counselor; there's a breakfast burrito and a king-sized bed calling my name."

Pulling out enormous stacks of documents, Jasper and Atticus placed them one by one along the judge's stand, and Drake smiled. Maybe the leeches had their uses after all. They would never be best friends, but the cougar could appreciate two predators circling their prey so neatly.

Drake glanced at the other side of the courtroom. Nicole's cousin looked furious, but his lawyer was pale and sweaty. He almost laughed. Dear cousin Tyler must not have told him he was about to tangle with two vampire lawyers with a vengeful streak.

"As you can see here, this is the will that Mr. Harrington provided." Atticus handed over two documents. "And this is a copy of the will that Ms. Dunn provided. The two signatures of Ms. Harriet Dunn do not match, nor are they even remotely similar."

The judge looked down at the two signatures and nodded. "Yes, I see that. Keep going."

Jasper handed him yet another document. "This is a copy of the original mortgage agreement for the house in question. You'll note the signature for Ms. Harriet Dunn. It is nearly identical to the documents provided by our client."

Judge Crest nodded, his white hair gleaming under the court room lights as he glanced in her cousin's direction. Drake wondered what was stewing in the old were-badger's mind. "Okay, what else have you got?"

Atticus handed over a small, leather-bound book. "This is a journal found in the residence in question, 301 Pine Street, in a box in the attic. Please note the name and date written on the inside cover."

The judge read the scrawled handwriting. "Harriet Dunn. 1963."

"This is another journal taken from the same box. Please note the matching leather binding and handwriting."

The badger raised his eyebrows at the scored-up leather and shredded pages. "It looks like it was chewed up by a dog?"

He raised it between two pudgy fingers. "A very small dog."

"Squirrels, actually," Jasper said cheerfully.

Nicole scrubbed a hand over her face, her skin paling as she stared at the massacred journal. "I knew I should have evicted those beasts," she muttered under her breath.

Drake tried not to laugh. At least she wasn't crying. If he never had to hold her in his arms while she sobbed again, it would be too soon.

Atticus flipped through the pages of the ruined journal to a section at the back.

"The date at the top of this passage here reads October 3rd of last year, mere weeks before Ms. Dunn succumbed to her late-stage renal cancer. As you can read for yourself, your honor, the passage reads—and this is a direct quote—'Tyler is a detestable pig. The little jerk finally showed up to sniff around about an inheritance. The joke's on him; he'll set foot in my house over my dead body.'"

Grinning gleefully at the fuming little weasel across the courtroom, Jasper dropped an enormous stack of paper on the judge's stand.

"Here you will find Mr. Harrington's tax returns for the

last six years." He flipped the top page over and waved at the bottom of the paper. "Please note the highlighted sections in which he attempted to claim his great aunt as a dependent and declared that her residence was his home... which, according to Ms. Dunn's tax statements, is fraudulent."

His eyebrows soared. As if reading his mind, Nicole looked up at him with a frown.

"How the hell did they get Auntie Harriet's tax returns?"

Drake shrugged. When the vampires had said they were going to bury the prick, he assumed they were being metaphorical. Now, the cougar wondered if they were going to actually bury him in stacks of paperwork.

Document after document landed in front of the judge. By the time Jasper placed a copy of Tyler Harrington's thick criminal record on the pile, even the bailiff was glaring at the hateful man.

Atticus produced a final sheet of paper and laid it on top of the pile.

"Ms. Nicole Dunn's criminal record for comparison. A singular traffic ticket." The vampire turned to narrow his eyes at the human. "In which our client skipped a curb and took out a 'no parking' sign because she was trying not to drop a powdered donut in her lap."

Nicole shrank under his judging red eye, and Drake coughed to hide his laugh. Oh, she was definitely getting shit for that later.

Judge Crest sat back in his seat and waved at the stacks of paperwork surrounding him. "Anything else?"

"We also have the name of the notary who sealed the will, and she is willing to testify," Atticus sighed. "However, Mrs. Claire Turner is now retired in Hawaii, so unless the court wants to call and bother her at this early hour..."

He trailed off with a shrug. They watched the judge with

interest, waiting for a decision as Judge Crest tapped his fingertips along the edge of his pulpit.

"Alright, I'm ready to rule. No need to drag the dear old Mrs. Turner out of bed."

The badger waved for Atticus and Jasper to get their mountains of evidence off his stand.

"Don't you need to make a case?" Nicole's cousin hissed, but his lawyer shushed him.

Drake rolled his eyes. Couldn't the idiot see he had already lost?

"I think it's pretty clear I cannot rule in Mr. Harrington's favor. His claims appear to be completely false." He nodded at Nicole. "Ms. Dunn has more than provided the proof that this lawsuit is completely fraudulent."

He raised his gavel. "I rule in favor of the defendant, Ms. Dunn. This lawsuit is dismissed with prejudice. Court is adjourned." The gavel slammed down.

"Are you fucking kidding me?" Tyler Harrington shouted. He turned and glared at his lawyer. "Do something!"

"There's nothing I can do, you moron! They proved it was bullshit in the first minute. The rest of it was just making you look like an asshole!"

Throwing his chair back, Tyler stomped up to Nicole, pausing to glower at all of them. Atticus and Jasper walked up behind him, the disdain clear on their pales faces.

Did he even realize what kind of danger he was in? Between the vampires and the shifters in the room, there was a good chance he would be dead before his body hit the floor—and that wasn't even including the bear-shifter bailiff watching them all with interest.

"I'm surprised your lawyers were so willing to represent a gold-digging whore," Tyler spit in her direction. "I guess they don't mind slumming it."

Wes took a step toward him, ready to snap his neck, but Nicole raised a hand and pressed the werewolf back a step.

"Don't bother. He's not worth the air in his lungs."

Drake elbowed the wolf. "Focus."

They had a job to do. The vampires were supposed to handle the bastard legally and the shifters were there to confirm the rest. Hawthorne... well, the fae was just there for moral support.

Leaning forward, Drake and Wes sniffed the rat of a man as he stormed away. They locked eyes and nodded; Drake would know that scent anywhere. He'd certainly smelled it often enough around Nicole's house.

"It was definitely him," Wes growled.

Nicole looked up at him, frowning. "What?"

"He was the one who sabotaged your house, kitten," Drake hissed, his hands clenching into fists. "He set the fire."

Nicole's serene face twisted in fury as she whirled to face her two vampire lawyers.

"Can we press criminal charges? Destruction of property or arson? Literally anything?" she growled. "Can he just be charged for being an asshole?"

"Unfortunately, no." Atticus shook his head and reached out to squeeze her hand. "I'm sorry, love."

"Why not? He set my house on fire!" Drake squeezed her shoulder as her voice grew louder. "What if all of you had been there? We might not all have made it out alive!"

"We don't have any evidence to make it stick, pet. Only the word of two shifters that they smelled him there," Jasper waved at Wes and Drake, an apologetic smile on his face.

No offense taken. He was right—they had all heard of cases thrown out for the very same thing. A shifter's nose wasn't evidence in a court of law.

Hawthorne stepped forward to wrap an arm around her slim shoulders.

"Don't worry, honey." He pressed a kiss against her cheek. "Karma has a way of taking care of people like him."

He looked up, his pale eyes locking with Drake's. Yes, yes it did.

38

NICOLE

Nicole bounced on the squishy lounge chair. It had appeared with three others in the backyard at some point, and she had no clue where it came from. One day, there was a patch of dirt, and the next, there was a deck. A week later, lounge chairs.

Her fingers were still crossed for a pool next summer. She was planning on making it into an experiment—if she said nothing, how long would Atticus make it before he started to worry it was too hot outside for her and bought one just in case? Nicole was pretty sure she'd be splashing in her backyard by June.

"Where did you get these?" Miri bounced on the soft cushions.

"I honestly have no idea." Nicole shrugged. "Either Atticus finally figured out how to order furniture online, or Drake built them."

Her friend clinked her beer bottle against hers. "You chose your monsters well, Nic."

Nicole settled back into the cushions and glanced around the bustling barbecue. The guys had wanted to celebrate kicking her cousin's ass in court last month, and she hadn't argued. It was well deserved; plus, Drake had a knack for grilling ribs just right.

"Where is Ashley with the drinks?" Miri shook her empty bottle.

"Over there." Nicole pointed over her shoulder. "I think she's putting the moves on Wes' brother."

Miri craned her neck for a look. The blonde stood laughing in the center of a group of hot monsters, half of them were staring at her like they wanted to eat the leggy woman while the other half looked like they wanted to do a lot more than eat her.

Cole, Wes' hot firefighter brother, looked awestruck as Ashley swished her long blond hair over her shoulders. Someone could have screamed "fire" right behind the werewolf, and he wouldn't have blinked.

"She totally forgot about us, didn't she?" Miri laughed.

"Oh, definitely."

It was the "Ashley Effect"; the second men realized the beauty was available, they flocked to her like moths to a flame until she couldn't take a step without trodding on some lovesick sap's toes.

"It must be hard being a gorgeous blonde," she said dryly.

"I can't even imagine her daily struggle," Miri scoffed. "We're going to die of dehydration, aren't we?"

Ignoring the dramatics, Nicole watched Hawthorne skirt the edge of the group. He might be a monster, but he was giving any guest with a hint of fur a wide berth. His eyes were red and irritated—the poor fae had been popping allergy meds like breath mints since he'd accidentally sneezed on Cole when he shook his hand.

She made a mental note to order him some disposable masks. It wouldn't matter when it was her and her five monsters, but if these get togethers were going to be a regular thing, he was going to need something to get him through.

Nicole studied the strange assortment of monsters in her yard. She had never met most of them. The guys had insisted on inviting some of their friends, and since her friends pretty much consisted exclusively of Miri, Ashley, and Marta from work, Nicole hadn't been opposed.

The more people to celebrate the downfall of her shitty cousin, the better.

"There are more monsters playing croquet over there than I've ever seen in one place," Miri whispered.

"I didn't even know I owned a croquet set!" she whispered back.

They burst into a fresh round of giggles. Choking on their laughter, they studied the monsters eating chips and knocking back beers. Demons, werewolves, vampires—there was even one scruffy looking guy that looked like he'd just wandered out of the woods and stuck a baseball hat on his head.

"Any idea what that guy is?" Miri muttered. "He looks awfully furry."

Nicole's gaze had slipped right past him as she looked for the most important monsters; hers. Hawthorne's silver hair shined next to a tiki torch as he hovered around the grill, arguing with Drake. The were-cougar waved an eggplant in his hand, gesturing wildly.

Nicole had no idea what they were arguing about, but she couldn't help but laugh. Knowing Drake, he'd already prepped some vegetables for the fae at the party. She was pretty sure Hawthorne just enjoyed riling him up.

The empty beer bottle slipped from her fingers, and she grasped at air before a fresh one landed in her hand. She tilted her head back and looked up at the vampire looming over her. Atticus bent down and pressed a kiss to her forehead.

She grinned up at him. Nicole was convinced he was some kind of vampiric mind reader—it was the only explanation for the way he anticipated her needs.

And maybe she was counting on it just a tiny bit for that pool.

His thumb stroked her cheek, one of his rings flashing in the light. A tiny tingle shocked her neck where his fangs had been only that morning. He winked, silently promising more later.

Straightening up, Atticus passed a fresh beer to Miri and walked back to his conversation with Jasper and a short satyr in a blazer. Nicole had caught a snippet of their conversation earlier—something boring about tax law and dependent credits. How they managed to look so excited over something so dry, she would never understand.

And she was a computer analyst, for fuck's sake. Boring was her bread and butter.

Marta sat down in the empty lounge chair to her left. She balanced a full plate on her thigh, her eyes wide as saucers as she took everything in. Shoving her dark hair away from her face, she picked up a meaty rib.

"This is the weirdest barbecue I've ever been to... but these ribs are so worth it."

"And to think, Hawthorne's yeti friend couldn't make it."

She shook her head. "I can't tell if you're joking or not."

"Neither can I anymore," Nicole laughed.

She hadn't even told her that the yeti had missed the barbecue for a hot yoga class, something she was still wrapping her own head around. She'd been sure Hawthorne was fucking with her when he crossed his friend's name off the guest list.

Ashley flopped down on the end of Miri's chair and

sighed dreamily.

"That's it," she announced. "I'm downloading the MOSNTR app tomorrow. Work be damned, I need some of... all that."

Her manicured hand gestured at the group of monsters still shooting her interested looks. If Ashley so much as crooked her finger, Nicole had no doubt every one of them would come running.

"What about you, Miri?" Nicole asked. "Are you ready for a horde of monsters to take over your house and eat all your food?"

"Maybe when the school year ends... or my dry spell finally drives me insane," she grumbled.

Her money was on insanity. Kindergarteners were one thing, but Miri's libido was the far more pressing problem. After the loser history teacher had ended things, her friend hadn't been particularly interested in anyone else.

Maybe it was her turn to play matchmaker.

"I could see you with a couple fae." Ashley beat her to the punch and looked one of Hawthorne's cousins up and down. "Hawthorne seems like a sweetie pie, just like you. And that silver hair? Yum."

She gripped a handful of her long blond hair and studied it in the light of the lanterns lighting up the party, probably considering whether she could rock a silver-blond dye job.

"Maybe..." Miri didn't look at the fae. Her eyes skidded right past him to a tall demon with dark red skin, horns, and neck tattoos poking out of his collar.

Or maybe not.

Nicole raised her eyebrows. The demon looked like he would rather rip out the heart of the first person who asked than sit through coffee date... then possibly eat it.

His dark eyes flicked up. He glanced in their direction, as

if he had sensed them watching. The demon's black gaze landed on Miri and studied her curvy body before he flashed her a fanged grin and turned back to his conversation.

Ashley leaned over Miri's legs to catch her eye.

"*Oh my God!*" she mouthed.

Swallowing her laughter, Nicole turned to Marta. "What about you? Is there a monster out there who could tempt you?"

She shrugged. "Maybe after my divorce is finalized... or an existential crisis... or I need to bribe that cougar for more ribs."

Marta had never talked about what had gone down with her ex-husband, but Nicole got the impression it hadn't ended well. Maybe what she needed wasn't a crisis, but a hot monster boyfriend.

What was it Ashley had said? The best way to get over a man was to get under a new one?

Maybe she could nudge the guys into setting sweet Marta up when the time came. If Ashley didn't jump on Wes' brother, maybe Marta would like him.

He certainly had the same werewolf charm that got Wes in trouble so often... and into her pants.

Clearing her throat, Ashley interrupted Nicole's scheming. She raised her bottle. "To Nicole—"

"Not this again," Nicole groaned. "Last time you played 'to Nicole', I ended up with five boyfriends and a lawsuit."

"Hush," Ashley shushed her. "To Nicole and her fine ass monster boyfriends!"

"May we all be so lucky!" Miri raised her bottle in salute.

Marta raised a barbecued rib. "I'll toast to that!"

Nicole raised her own bottle with a sigh. Clinking it against theirs, she couldn't help but smile.

At least it wasn't tequila.

EPILOGUE - HAWTHORNE

Hawthorne winced as Drake's meaty elbow drove into his ribcage for the umpteenth time. Would it have killed the vampires to have sprung for a car with a third row? If they were going to keep going on these group excursions, someone was going to have to bite the bullet and buy a van.

The SUV pulled to a stop in the shadow of a thick copse of trees. One by one, the monsters spilled out into the night. The fae stretched his back as he took his first step from the vehicle.

Any more impromptu adventures, and he was going to have to make an appointment with a chiropractor.

"Did you pick out a good spot?" Atticus' deep voice cut through the dark.

Hawthorne pointed into the trees. He had scouted the area earlier that week and found the perfect place to get the job done. Leaving this kind of thing to chance wasn't his style.

"Start walking," Drake grunted. "We'll handle the trash."

Leading the group into the woods, Hawthorne winced at every cracking branch and crunching leaf under their feet.

It's a good thing vampires could order their food from a blood bank now. If Atticus and Jasper had to rely on stealth, they would die of starvation.

The shifters brought up the rear, dragging a tarp-wrapped bundle between them. At least they walked with some respect for nature. The only sound coming from the back of the group was the occasional crinkle of the tarp as they shifted it between them.

Stopping in a small clearing, Hawthorne waved at the ground. "Here."

He had chosen the place carefully: not too far from the road, but deep enough in the trees that no one but the birds would be able to see them. The ground was in need of a little nourishment, perfect for the gift they were giving back to the Earth, and forgiving enough not to mind their toting a wad of plastic into its presence.

Drake and Wes dropped their wrapped bundle on the hard ground, and a muffled yelp sounded from under layers of thick, plastic tarp. Wiggling his fingers, sharp claws extended from the werewolf's hands. One quick swipe, and the quivering coward rolled out of his cocoon.

Shivering and weak, the pathetic human curled into ball before he looked up at the grinning monsters circled around him and paled.

"Hello, Mr. Harrington." Atticus flashed his fangs. "We didn't have a chance to introduce ourselves at the courthouse."

"What—?"

"Shhh," the vampire hushed. "Now would be a very good time for you to be silent."

"But I—"

Drake flashed forward, his claws gleaming and dripping in the moonlight. Crisp red lines formed across the whimpering face of their new friend.

"Be quiet."

"Thank you, Drake." Atticus crouched in front of the sobbing mess. "You made a very large mistake, Tyler. You threatened our mate—worse than that, you endangered her with your petty little schemes. You went too far with the arson."

Hawthorne's stomach rolled. Just the thought of Nicole in danger made him want to throw up. The house fire was utterly unforgivable. She could have died, and she was *theirs*.

"Please," her cousin begged. "I didn't mean—"

"Pray we don't meet again in the next life, or the one after, human. It's already too late for you in this one." Straightening up, Atticus brushed a fleck of dirt off the cuff of his jacket and gave them a small nod.

Hawthorne rolled his shoulders as claws and fangs unfurled around him. He might not grow fur and fangs like the rest of them, but there was a reason humans learned to tread carefully in the woods and not to make deals with shadows.

Glyphs glowing across his flesh, his face lost all its soft edges, and darkness pooled in his eyes as he made his ancestors proud.

"What are you?" Tyler whispered, sweat beading on his pale, horrified face.

The nightmares around him grinned. Hawthorne cocked his head to the side and caught his teary gaze.

"Karma."

The vampires moved as one. Sharp fangs tore through his exposed throat, offering his blood to the earth as the pathetic human gagged. Choking on his screams, his lungs filled slowly.

The shifters circled him next, and shining eyes studied the quivering waste of humanity as they chose their targets.

The cougar's claws flashed and his belly split open. The werewolf drove his claws into the blood-soaked chest, lifting the fool clear off the ground. They dropped him in a heap and moved away.

They stared down at the whimpering carnage. Right... it was his turn.

Hawthorne crouched down beside him and drove his fingertips into the grass. The ground rumbled, dirt crumpling beneath Nicole's cousin. The fae reached into his pocket and pulled out an acorn, tossing it into the hole and letting the earth close over him.

A swell of satisfaction washed over Hawthorne as he caught one last glimpse of the human's terrified eyes—eyes that would never look at their mate and wish her harm again.

He pumped magic into the ground, and the grass parted as a sapling burst through the dirt, consuming Tyler Harrington alive with its roots.

Hawthorne rose to his feet and studied his work. His magic and the decaying corpse would feed the tree well. By the end of the month, it would blend in with the rest of the forest and the foolish, forgotten cousin would fade into nothingness.

He turned away without a second glance and headed back to the car. One by one, the rest of the monsters followed after him. They rode home in silence, creeping back into the house like shadows and pausing outside Nicole's bedroom.

"Whose turn is it?" Jasper whispered.

Hawthorne pushed past the hulking shifters. "Mine."

He slipped into the room to the tune of their quiet grumbling. Nicole was curled on her oversized bed, a blanket-wrapped lump waiting for his company. The corner of his mouth curled up into a smile.

Shrugging out of his clothes, the fae crawled into bed beside his favorite human and cuddled her close. Nicole rolled to face him and yawned sleepily as her face settled into the crook of his neck. Small butterflies fluttered deep in his stomach at the soft press of her lips.

"You're home late," she mumbled. "I'm glad you guys are getting along so well."

Hawthorne kissed the top of her head and hugged her close. "We're definitely starting to bond."

"Good."

He listened to her breathing soften as she slipped back to sleep. The fae closed his eyes and let his thoughts of Tyler Harrington drift away for the final time. It's not like any of them were going to lose any sleep over their late-night errand.

They were monsters, after all.

If you want bonus epilogues and deleted scenes, you're gonna want to click here!

WHAT'S NEXT?

I only have three things to say about this one.

1. Swipe Right For Monsters is the book that dragged me kicking and screaming out of depression. It was happy and light and required like 2% brain power (pretty much all I could manage at the time).

Nicole is the embodiment of every girlie I know who is just trying to survive to the end of the day so that she can crawl back into bed—so, like, all of them lol—and for that, I will adore her until the day I die. Also, she's straight up living my dream of being worshipped by a bunch of hot monsters. Get it girl! :)

2. Yes, the werewolf and the cougar should've fucked. I KNOW. Trust me, I tried to fit it into the book. The chapter ended up getting cut because it was messing up the timeline and the focus of the story (our babe, Nicole).

I'm reworking that chapter into a bonus scene instead. If you picked this up on release day, give me a bit to recharge my brain and then I will send it out. You will get your MMF moment, I promise you... and maybe someday a future MMF scene with Jasper too.

3. Yes, this will be a series. Technically, this will be a RH

trilogy with a bunch of connected standalones. Miri is up next with *Download For Demons* and then Ashley will finish off the trilogy. As for the standalones, I have a LOT of ideas. And Marta will be first.

After I tie up Raven Falls and the Galactic Fairy Tales this year, I'm going to be living in this happy monster world for a while.

Now... what's the next release? Scorching Moon. It just needs one last quick spell check and it's done. Finally. Seriously, FINALLY. I don't know who will be more relieved to have it done; me or all of you. I'm not even going to bother with a pre-order. Some random day soon, I'll probably just upload it and surprise everyone!

Thanks for sticking with me through a really tough year. I appreciate you all!

- R. O'Leary

ALSO BY R. O'LEARY

Monster Mates:

Swipe Right For Monsters

Raven Falls Cursed Romances:

Furbidden Attraction

Unbearable Temptation

Howling Devotion

Deathly Desire

Bewitching Allure

Siren Craving

Screaming Sins

Novellas:

Frosted Kiss (Christmas Novella)

Winter Caress (Christmas Novella)

Prequels:

Deerly Beloved

Hexed Heart

Galactic Fairy Tales:

Vermilion Stars

Crystal Nebula

Bound Nova

Novellas:

Gilded Moon

ABOUT THE AUTHOR

R. O'Leary lives in North Pole, Alaska (no, really). When she's not spending half the year freezing to death, she's writing about shifters and aliens and anything else that strolls through her head. Most of her day is spent in pajama pants, chasing the pack of corgis that have claimed her living room as their own.

For bonus content, cover reveals, giveaways, and other fun stuff, sign up for my **newsletter** or check out my **website**! If merch is more your thing, check out my **store**!

Made in United States
Orlando, FL
11 July 2024